I AM NUMBER FOUR

A DCI DANNY FLINT BOOK

TREVOR NEGUS

INKUBATOR
BOOKS

Published by Inkubator Books
www.inkubatorbooks.com

ISBN (eBook): 978-1-83756-063-9
ISBN (Paperback): 978-1-83756-064-6

PROLOGUE

10.00am, 6 March 1986
Sunnybank Cottage, White Gate Farm, Misterton, Nottinghamshire

The antique bed dominated the tiny room in the cottage. Its size made the woman's wasted frame seem even smaller. The stage four cervical cancer she had been diagnosed with, three months earlier, had ravaged her once-strong body. The weight loss had been dramatic, and the pain had intensified steadily.

As soon as doctors had told her there was nothing more that could be done, she had taken the decision to return to the two-bedroom cottage on the family farm. She had lived here with her son ever since her parents had died and her brother had taken over the main farmhouse. His new wife hadn't wanted to share the big house with them. There was something about the hulking, brooding figure of her son that her sister-in-law seemed to find disturbing. He was a twenty-five-year-old giant of a man, but his mind was still that of a child.

Because of this sense of ill feeling, the dying woman had never visited the main farmhouse. She had been content to stay in the cottage with her son. They had been happy at Sunnybank. She doted on her boy, met his every need, and had raised a weak, sickly child into a strong young man. She had home-schooled him, aware that a childhood dominated by relentless bullying would have been her son's fate had she opted to send him into mainstream education. The boy's generally slow demeanour, hulking shape and disfiguring harelip would have seen to that. She felt she was quite capable of teaching the boy everything he needed to know to live a good life.

As a result, the man he had become felt challenged whenever he was around people. He had no personal skills and found it extremely uncomfortable talking to strangers. He was far more at ease around the farmyard animals.

The dying woman knew the end of her life was close and she worried about her son's future.

Ignoring the pain that racked her abdomen, she shouted, 'Boy! Come in here!'

The door to the bedroom opened and her son walked in. He sat down at his mother's bedside and held her hand.

He lisped softly, 'Can I get you something?'

Her breath came in short gasps, and she wheezed, 'No. Just listen. I'll be gone soon, son. I need you to promise me that when I've gone, you'll go out and find a good woman to take care of you. Will you do that for me?'

He nodded. The tears were starting to fill his eyes and he blinked furiously, not wanting to appear weak in front of her. He put his head on her bed and said, 'What's going to happen to me when you've gone? Where will I live? You know my uncle hates me.'

She stroked his hair and tried to reassure him. 'Your uncle doesn't hate you. I want you to go down to the farmhouse and fetch him back here. I need to talk to him before it's too late.'

'I don't want to leave you alone.'

'Just go. I'll be fine. Hurry, now.'

Twenty minutes later, and her now-breathless son opened the bedroom door and said, 'Uncle's here, he's downstairs.'

'Good. Go back down and tell him I want to speak to him – on his own. You wait downstairs, son.'

She heard the heavy boots on the wooden stairs as her brother climbed them. The door opened and he walked in. He remained standing, at the foot of the bed.

In a voice little more than a croaky whisper, she said, 'Sit down, brother. We need to talk before I die.'

Her older brother sat down and said, 'What do we need to talk about?'

'I haven't got long left, and I need to know that my boy will be alright. You must let him stay here, living in this cottage and working on the farm. It's all he's ever known. He wouldn't be able to survive anywhere else.'

'I don't think that's possible. You know what my wife thinks of him. She worries about him being around our two girls.'

The dying woman rallied all her remaining strength and said angrily, 'My boy's harmless! He would never hurt your girls. I know he's slow and looks intimidating, but he's a child in a man's body. It's not his fault he's the way he is.'

Her brother shook his head. 'I'm sorry. I just can't take that risk.'

The woman could feel the anger continuing to rise inside her. 'You owe me this much, brother. I never breathed a word to our father about how you forced yourself upon me when I was just fourteen years old. I never let on once who the father of my bastard child was. Do you think you'd be living in that big farmhouse, with your lovely wife and your two beautiful daughters, if I'd told him how you raped me in the barn? You were my brother, a grown man, and I was still a child.'

'That's all in the past. It was one stupid mistake. I was drunk.'

'Yes. And the result of that drunken mistake is now sitting downstairs, terrified about what's going to happen to him when I'm not here to look after him. We both know why he's so slow. Brothers and sisters aren't allowed to have kids for a reason The way he is now is that reason. Now, I'm not asking you; I'm telling you. You're going to allow him to remain in this cottage and work on the farm. Do you understand?'

'And when you're dead? Who's going to care if I kick him out?'

'My solicitor has a sealed letter from me that explains everything that happened to me when I was fourteen. What you did to me. How you raped me. Who my son's father really is. I have left instructions with him that he is to open that letter if anything ever happens to the boy. If he is ever forced to leave Sunnybank Cottage for any reason, my solicitor will read the letter and, on my instruction, take it to the police, who will investigate the allegation I've made. If you don't look after the boy and let him stay here, I'll reach out and punish you from my grave. He's your son, for Christ's sake.'

The brother stared up at the ceiling, weighing up his options.

Finally, he growled, 'Very well. He can carry on working at the farm, and living here, but if there's any trouble like before, he'll be out. It won't be me evicting him; it will be the police arresting him. We both know what he did to that foreign farm labourer when he was still a teenager. He was lucky I managed to pay her off, and the police weren't involved back then.'

'We both know that Agnetha was an old slag who teased the boy into being with her in the barn. She thought she was being clever, undressing and tormenting him. She had led him on. She had started fondling him first. He was never going to stop once she got him aroused. What did she expect?'

'He raped her.'

'Don't you dare lecture me about rape. Unlike the way you attacked me, that grown woman brought what happened on herself. Her disgusting behaviour towards a child in a man's body, my son, caused the problem. Do you think you would have been able to buy her off so easily if she hadn't started it?'

Her brother shook his head. 'Any other trouble like that and he's out, letter or no letter. I'll call the police myself.'

'I've talked to the boy, and he knows that what he did back then was wrong. He hasn't done anything since, has he? He's no interest in women. I've also told him about the letter. He knows if anything ever happens to him and he's scared, he's to call Mr Carruthers.'

The pain in her abdomen was increasing; this time she could feel her heart racing. It was pounding in her chest and she could hardly breathe.

She grabbed her brother's big, calloused hand and gasped, 'Promise me you'll do this one thing for me, brother.'

He knew she was dying and said through gritted teeth, 'I promise.'

A deathly rattle escaped her throat as she took her last breath.

He shoved his thick index finger into the side of his sister's neck, seeking a pulse. There was none.

He stood up, leaned over his dead sister and closed her eyelids.

He walked slowly back down the stairs and opened the door to the living room. The hulking figure of the woman's son was standing in front of the fireplace.

He said quietly, 'She's gone, boy. I'm going back to the big house, to call for the doctor. Are you going to be okay here, on your own, until I come back?'

As his uncle reached the door, in an almost childlike voice the boy shouted after him, 'Can I stay here, uncle?'

The farmer turned and said, 'Yes. You can stay. You have a strong back and you know how everything on the farm works. You can live here and look after Sunnybank Cottage for me. But I don't want you turning up at the farmhouse all the time. This is your home; you'll live here. I don't want you bothering my wife or the girls. Is that clear?'

'Yes. I won't be any trouble. Thanks, uncle.'

His uncle stepped outside the cottage and was about to walk off, but then stopped and turned around. He jabbed an accusing finger into the giant's chest and growled, 'One other thing, lad. Any more trouble like Agnetha and I'll hand you over to the police myself. Understood?'

With a nervous grin, the man nodded and said, 'There won't be any more trouble, uncle. I don't like girls.'

As his uncle stomped back to his Land Rover, the boy closed the front door, walked back into the living room and sat down on the threadbare sofa. The words of his dying mother were ringing in his head: 'Promise me that when I've gone you'll go out and find a good woman to take care of you.'

He closed his eyes and whispered, 'I will, Mum. I will.'

1

11.00am, 2 September 1988
Clipstone Drive, Clipstone, Nottinghamshire

PC Chris Walker could see a woman waiting on the pavement outside the detached bungalow at the end of Clipstone Drive. He hated these calls. One of the residents had telephoned the police to say they hadn't seen their elderly neighbour for a few days. With over twenty years' service as a street cop, Chris Walker was experienced enough to know that usually meant only one thing. The neighbour would be dead inside the property, and it would be down to him to force entry and find the deceased.

He glanced at his colleague in the passenger seat. PC Jason Roe had only been at the station in Mansfield for two weeks. He was fresh out of police training college, and Chris knew the youngster had never seen a dead body before. The nervous demeanour and pale face of the young constable betrayed how he was feeling.

Chris spoke quietly: 'Try not to let this woman see how you're feeling, Jason. All the public ever see is the uniform. She will be relying on us to sort out this problem for her. Okay?'

The youngster swallowed hard and nodded.

Chris gently brought the police patrol car to a halt and both officers got out. The woman immediately approached the older constable and said, 'I'm Mrs Gathercole. I called you. I'm worried about my neighbour, Mrs White. I usually see her pottering about, but I haven't seen her for four days now.'

Chris said, 'Is it possible she's away on holiday?'

The neighbour shook her head. 'She always tells me when she's going away, so I can keep an eye on the place for her.'

'Have you had a look around the property?'

'As much as I can. The gate to the back garden is bolted, so I haven't been able to go around the back. I have a spare key for the front door that she gave me, but I didn't like to go inside, in case something isn't right.'

'Why don't you unlock the door, so me and my colleague can go inside and make sure Mrs White's okay? What's her first name?'

'Margaret, but everyone knows her as Maggie.'

The neighbour used the Yale key to unlock the front door and then stepped back, handing the key to the officer. The two men stepped inside the spacious hallway of the bungalow and pushed the door closed behind them.

Chris turned to Jason and said, 'Put your gloves on and try not to touch anything.'

Jason wrinkled his nose and said, 'What's that smell?'

Chris knew exactly what the smell was. 'I think Mrs White is dead. What we need to do now is go through the bungalow and find her. Are you alright?'

Jason nodded.

Chris could see the young policeman was increasingly anxious. 'Just stay behind me. We'll check the rooms together. This is something you're going to have to get used to. Come on, let's go.'

The two officers made their way methodically through the property. Every interior door had been wedged open with folded cardboard. The first room they entered was the lounge. It was empty. Double doors led into the dining room. As the officers walked through, Chris saw that a small transom window had been smashed. Whoever had broken it had then reached in and opened one of the larger windows before climbing through. There were dirty footmarks on the windowsill and the carpet below the open window.

From the dining room, they walked back into the hallway. The doors leading off the hallway were also wedged open, so Chris could now see bare legs on the bed inside the main bedroom at the rear of the property.

He stepped forwards and was shocked by the sight that confronted him. He had been expecting to find a dead body, but in his twenty years' experience he had never seen anything like this.

The body of an elderly woman was lying face up on the bed. She was naked and had a clear plastic bag over her head. The bag had been secured by a plastic tie wrap and was clinging to her black and swollen face. He could see her open mouth and sightless eyes through the clear plastic. Her wrists had been tied to the bedposts, using tights that had been taken from the top drawer of the nearby chest of drawers. The contents of the drawers had been removed and scattered all over the floor of the bedroom.

Jason stepped inside the bedroom and gasped at the enormity of what he was seeing. He immediately backed out, retching.

Chris turned after him, grabbed him and hissed, 'Don't be sick in here!'

Jason swallowed hard and nodded.

In a gentler tone, Chris said, 'We need to get out of here and call the CID. You need to compose yourself before we go back outside. That woman is going to bombard us with questions. Say nothing. Let me talk to her. Do you understand?'

'I'm okay now. I understand. Has she been murdered?'

'Yes, she's been murdered. That's why we need to get some assistance. Come on.'

The two officers stepped outside and were immediately confronted by Mrs Gathercole. 'Is Maggie alright?'

PC Walker put his arm around the neighbour, ushering her back up the path and said, 'I'm afraid she's passed away. I need you to have a quick word with me in my car, okay.'

'I knew something was wrong, I just knew it.'

Chris turned to Jason and said, 'Stay here by the front door. Nobody goes inside the property. Get out your notebook and start a log. The first entry is the time we first went in and the time we came out. You must make a note of every person from the CID or scenes of crime who enters the property from now on, got it?'

Pleased to have something physical to do that could take his mind off what he had just witnessed, the young officer took out his notebook and began writing.

As Chris walked up the garden path towards the patrol car with Mrs Gathercole, he turned and said, 'Nobody goes inside the bungalow, understood?'

'Understood.'

2

11.45am, 2 September 1988
Clipstone Drive, Clipstone, Nottinghamshire

Detective Chief Inspector Danny Flint parked his car behind the two scenes of crime vans. From the boot, he retrieved a forensic suit, gloves and overshoes, before walking towards the small gathering of officers on the pavement outside the detached bungalow.

He recognised the experienced PC Walker and said, 'What have we got, Chris?'

'I've never seen anything like it, boss. I know there are some sick fuckers out there, and I thought I'd seen everything in this job, but to do that to an old lady is just evil.'

'Who's that doing the log?'

'PC Jason Roe. He's a brand new probationer. He's with me for the next six weeks. He only arrived from Dishforth Police Training College two weeks ago.'

'Was he okay inside?'

'He did okay. I thought he was going to throw up at one point, but he held it together, thankfully.'

'Thank God for that. Do you know who the dead woman is?'

'There's been no formal identification – you'll see why when you go in – but according to the neighbour who called us, the woman who lived here was Margaret White. She looks to be in her late sixties.'

'Have you got the neighbour's details?'

'Yes, boss. One of your detectives is getting a statement from Mrs Gathercole now. I've also got the spare front door key she had for the deceased's property. She let us in using that, so we didn't have to break the door down.'

'Thanks, Chris. Make sure you exhibit the key and hand it to Tim Donnelly. I'll get PC Roe relieved from the scene log duties as soon as I can.'

'Will do, boss. Tim Donnelly is already inside.'

Danny walked down the path to the front door and put on the forensic suit, gloves and overshoes.

Danny took out his identification and said, 'PC Roe, I'm DCI Flint from the Major Crime Investigation Unit. Would you sign me into the scene, please?'

The officer wrote the details and said, 'Done, sir.'

'Are you okay?'

'Yes, thank you, sir. It was a bit of a shock seeing the old lady like that, but I'm okay now.'

'The day it doesn't shock you, is the day to pack this job in. PC Walker tells me you held yourself together in there, so well done. I'll get you off the scene log as soon as I can.'

'Thank you, sir.'

Danny walked into the hallway and saw Tim Donnelly talking to Detective Sergeant Andy Wills. The scenes of crime supervisor approached Danny and said, 'You're not going to like this one, boss.'

'That's a strange comment, Tim. I don't like any of them.'

'Sorry. What I mean is, it's all very worrying.'

'You'd better show me the body, then I might understand what you're talking about.'

Tim turned and walked back into the main bedroom. 'She's in here.'

Danny walked into the bedroom and saw the dead woman on the bed. Staring at the scene before him, Danny whispered, 'Now I know exactly what you mean.'

'Does it look familiar to you?'

'Too bloody familiar. What about you, Andy? Do you recall seeing a scene identical to this one?'

DS Wills said, 'Looks exactly like the murder of Florence King at Warsop, around four or five years ago.'

Danny immediately looked at the bedroom door and saw the folded cardboard that had been used to wedge it at the bottom.

Tim saw him looking and said, 'Every door's the same. Folded cardboard taken from the rubbish bin has been used to wedge open every interior door.'

'Phone line?'

'Has been severed outside.'

'Entry?'

'The dining room transom window has been smashed, and then a larger window opened to gain access.'

'So, pretty much the same as Florence King, then. Food and drink had been consumed on the premises at Warsop.'

Andy Wills said, 'It's the same here. Food has been taken from the fridge and partially eaten.'

Tim said, 'Was anybody ever charged for that murder?'

'There were never any arrests, never mind charges. The inquiry ground to a halt quickly. I was a newly promoted detective inspector at the time and came into the inquiry towards the end.'

Andy said, 'I worked on it for a while, but as it ground to a halt I was moved to another inquiry. The investigation was led by DCI Les Swift; he's been retired a few years now.'

'If I recall correctly, Les was always bitter about how quickly the inquiry was wound down. Any idea when the pathologist will be getting here?'

'Seamus Carter's on call. He was informed thirty minutes ago and was travelling from home, so he shouldn't be much longer.'

'Show me the rest of the bungalow while we're waiting. Start with the point of entry.'

'That's through here, boss.'

Andy led the way into the dining room and pointed out the smashed window.

'What's that on the windowsill and carpet? Mud?'

Tim said, 'I thought it was mud at first, but now I've had a closer look I don't think it is. We've taken samples, anyway. We've also recovered a fragment of cloth from one of the jagged pieces of glass in the smashed window. I think it's been torn from whatever the offender was wearing, as they reached through the window.'

'How big?'

'It's an inch-long strip of cloth, looks like some sort of heavy cotton material, possibly overalls or similar.'

'Well, that's a start. Any prints?'

'It's early days yet. My team still has plenty of work to do. The actual murder scene in the bedroom has been photographed. I didn't want to start lifting samples from the body, or the bedroom, until the pathologist has examined the deceased.'

Danny heard a raised voice coming from the front door of the bungalow and instantly recognised it. 'I've told you who I am young man. I need to get inside.'

Danny smiled and walked through the bungalow. At the

front door, he found an exasperated Seamus Carter being held up on the doorstep by PC Roe.

He heard the young officer say, 'And I need to see some identification before I can let you inside.'

Danny placed his hand on the officer's shoulder and said, 'PC Roe, this is Seamus Carter, the Home Office pathologist. He's okay to come inside.'

The officer immediately stepped aside and said, 'Sorry, sir.'

'Sign him into the scene.'

'Done.'

Seamus stepped inside and blustered, 'It's years since I've been asked for any identification. I don't even know if I've got any. I suppose I must have, somewhere. I thought the forensic suit and the bag would have given away who I was.'

Danny said, 'PC Roe is very young in service and has no idea who you are, or what you do. Don't worry about it. No Brigitte today?'

'No, my wonderful trainee is visiting her folks back home in Dublin. It's just me today. What have we got?'

'The body is through here, in the main bedroom. Follow me.'

The two men found Tim Donnelly and Andy Wills waiting. Seamus stepped forward and examined the seal around the bottom of the transparent plastic bag. He could see where the black plastic cable tie had bitten into the flesh of the dead woman. The seal was airtight.

He said, 'Whoever tightened this cable tie meant business. Even if this poor woman could have reached it with her hands, there's no way she could ever have released it.'

Danny said, 'Do you think suffocation is the cause of death?'

'It certainly looks that way, on face value. I'll know for

certain at the post-mortem. Have you taken photographs in here?'

Tim Donnelly said, 'Yes, we have.'

'Can we cut the tights that are securing her wrists, please? I want to be able to turn her over.'

'No problem.'

Tim stepped forward and used a craft knife to cut the tights, leaving the knots intact. He immediately placed the two pairs of tights into exhibit bags.

Seamus rolled the body of the dead woman over so he could examine her back, returning her to the original position afterwards. He said, 'Rigor mortis has been and gone, so she could have been here anything between twenty-four and forty-eight hours. Sorry, I can't be any more specific. The central heating is on quite high, so obtaining the temperature of the body isn't going to assist me much. Do you know when she was last seen alive?'

Danny said, 'Four days ago, by a neighbour.'

The big pathologist stroked his beard and said, 'Hmm, that doesn't help me much either. Are the undertakers on their way?'

Andy Wills said, 'They'll be here in the next twenty minutes.'

Seamus continued his preliminary examination and said, 'There appears to be dried semen on the inside of the right thigh. Get a swab of that please, Tim.'

As the scenes of crime supervisor dealt with the pathologist's request, Danny said, 'Do you think she's been sexually assaulted?'

'If that turns out to be semen, it's more than likely she was. I'll know for sure at the post-mortem.'

'Where will you be doing the examination?'

'Kings Mill Hospital mortuary is the nearest; shall we say three o'clock this afternoon?'

'I'll see you there.'

Danny looked at Andy and gestured for him to step outside the bedroom. He said quietly, 'Florence King was raped and then suffocated in exactly this way, so it looks like we could have a repeat offender. What other staff do we have here?'

'I've got DC Williams and DC Singh speaking with the immediate neighbours. DC Bailey is getting a statement from Mrs Gathercole, the neighbour who called it in. DC Pope and DC Lorimar are conducting a search of the rear garden of the property.'

'DI Cartwright is also travelling here. She was in the city earlier, so it's taking her a while to get over here. When she arrives, I want the two of you to work the scene with Tim and Seamus. Ask Tina to join me at Kings Mill hospital for the post-mortem at three o'clock. As soon as the search of the garden has been completed, I want you to task Glen Lorimar with mastering the streets for the house-to-house inquiries we'll need to do. There will be a full briefing for everyone at five o'clock. I'm going back to the office now to try and get hold of all the paperwork I can from the previous murder at Warsop.'

'They certainly look identical, but where's this killer been hiding for four years?'

'Good question. I'll see you at the debrief at five.'

3

3.00pm, 2 September 1988
Kings Mill Hospital Mortuary, Mansfield, Nottinghamshire

Danny and Tina stood together at one side of the mortuary. DC Nigel Singleton was at the end of the room, waiting to carry out the role of exhibits officer.

There were two scenes of crime technicians in attendance, ready to take photographs and assist the pathologist when required.

Seamus Carter said, 'Let's make a start.'

The big pathologist spoke into a Dictaphone as he made a cursory examination of the deceased: 'The body is that of a well-nourished white female, aged between sixty and seventy. There is bruising evident on both thighs and the pelvic area. There are marks on both wrists where the deceased had been secured using nylon tights. The cause of death appears to be asphyxiation. There is a plastic bag secured on the head that is airtight. I'm going to start the examination by removing the bag and the cable tie securing it.'

Seamus Carter passed the items to Nigel Singleton, who placed the articles in evidence bags. Carter then began to gather samples from the deceased, taking hair from the head and pubic area, as well as scrapings from the fingernails.

When all external samples had been taken, he turned to Danny and said, 'I'm going to start the examination proper now. I'll start with the head and neck, and then determine if she was sexually assaulted.'

Danny nodded and said nothing.

Almost an hour later, Seamus turned away from the stainless steel examination table and stepped over to where Danny and Tina were observing.

'It's as I suspected at the scene: this poor woman was raped vaginally either just before, or at the time she was killed. I know Tim took samples from the woman's thigh at the scene, but I found further semen inside the vagina. The bruising on the thighs and pelvic area indicate that the rape was violent and forceful.'

Tina shook her head and whispered, 'The poor love. What a way to end your life.'

Seamus continued, 'The cause of death is asphyxia. The bag was sealed airtight around the neck, preventing oxygen getting to the lungs. She would have succumbed quickly.'

Danny asked, 'Did you do the post-mortem examination of a woman called Florence King from Warsop four or five years ago?'

'That name doesn't immediately ring any bells with me. I'd have to check my records.'

'I need to establish who the pathologist was who examined King. I have gathered all the documentation I can find from that investigation, but I can't put my hands on the post-mortem findings. Would you be able to help me with that?'

'If you let me have the full details – name, address, date, etc. I should be able to find that for you.'

'Thanks, Seamus. How long before you can let me have your report?'

'I'll have the full report, including toxicology, on your desk in the next two days. Let me have those details and I'll find out what I can about the other post-mortem examination.'

'Any other observations you want to share?'

'Only that whoever did this must be physically strong. He has overpowered this woman without resorting to blows. There was no underlying bruising to the face and head. The bloating and discoloration of the face, caused by the suffocation, can mask injuries to the naked eye, but when I've examined the underlying tissue, there were no marks of violence found. You're looking for a very dangerous individual.'

'Thanks. I'll get those details to you this evening.'

Danny and Tina made their way through the long hospital corridors back to the car park. As they walked, Tina said, 'At the scene, Andy told me there had been a similar murder four or five years ago.'

'It was identical. It happened just before the miners' strike in 1984. The investigation was going nowhere, but as the strike loomed, the bosses closed the inquiry down. That decision incensed the senior investigating officer, DCI Swift. He handed his papers in the same day.'

'He resigned?'

Tina unlocked the car and the two detectives got inside.

Danny said, 'Yes. He was raging. He always said the killer would strike again, and now it appears he was right.'

4

5.30pm, 2 September 1988
MCIU Offices, Mansfield, Nottinghamshire

'Okay everyone, quiet down.'

The gathered detectives immediately responded to Danny's instruction and the briefing room fell silent.

'The first thing you all need to know is that this will be a murder inquiry. The post-mortem revealed that the victim was suffocated. The cause of death was asphyxia. There will be a full album of photographs available from tomorrow morning and I want you all to make yourselves familiar with the method used. Basically, the killer has placed a clear plastic bag over the victim's head and then secured it using a plastic cable tie.'

Danny paused to let the information sink in and then continued: 'The post-mortem has also revealed that the victim was raped vaginally, either just before or at the time of her death. The pathologist believes the offender is physically strong, as he managed to subdue the victim without the need for blows to the head and face. I would temper that opinion by noting that the deceased is an elderly female, well into her sixties. How much physical force would it take to subdue such a victim?'

Again, he paused before saying, 'Andy, what can you tell us about the victim?'

DS Wills addressed the gathered detectives. 'The victim has now been identified as Margaret White. She was sixty-five years of age and lived alone at the bungalow on Clipstone Drive. She has been identified by her son, Richard. He turned up at the scene just before the undertakers removed the deceased. Richard White is a county councillor who sits on the police authority. He did inform me that he would be contacting the chief constable as soon as he got back to his office. I think there will be calls about an early resolution heading your way, boss.'

'Let me worry about that. What else do we know about Margaret White?'

'The son has helped me draw up a comprehensive list of all her family, friends and associates. She had lived alone at the bungalow for the past three years, following the death of her husband, George. There appears to be nobody who holds any grudges against this woman. The neighbours all liked her. She was always friendly and approachable. According to both the son and her immediate neighbour, Margaret was conscious of crime. She always kept her doors locked and would never answer the door after dark.'

Danny sought out DC Helen Bailey. When he saw her, he said, 'Helen, I would like you to concentrate on this part of the investigation. I want you to trace and interview all the people on the son's list. Start with family and then move on to friends and associates. I want a full picture of Margaret White established. I want you to contact Richard White again today and assure him that you will keep him informed as to how our inquiries are progressing. Come and see me after the briefing. I have paperwork from a previous case I want you to refer to. I need to establish if Margaret had any associates who were also associates of Florence King.'

Helen nodded and said, 'Will do, boss.'

Danny said, 'DI Cartwright will now describe the murder scene.'

Tina said, 'The property on Clipstone Drive is a detached bungalow situated on the outskirts of Clipstone. It backs onto farmland. There is a low hawthorn hedge that borders the garden at the rear of the property. There are gaps in that hedge and our offender approached the bungalow from this direction. A search of the garden revealed footprints in soft earth in the back garden. Scenes of crime have taken casts of these footmarks. Access was gained by smashing a small transom window that led into the dining room. The offender has reached through, opened one of the larger windows and climbed in. There were boot prints found on the windowsill and carpet that appear identical to those lifted from the rear garden.'

The experienced inspector paused, allowing detectives the time to make notes, before continuing. 'The offender has carried out several unusual behaviours at the scene. Firstly, he has removed cardboard from the waste bin in the kitchen and then folded it to make wedges used to prop open all the interior doors. Secondly, food and drink has been taken from the refrigerator and partially consumed, so the offender was comfortable enough inside the property to take his time after the offence. The telephone line was cut outside the property. Drawers in the bedroom had been emptied, and clothing owned by the deceased was used to bind her to the bed. The knot used to secure the wrists was a double reef knot.'

Danny interjected at this point, saying, 'For those of you who don't know, there was a previous murder four years ago that had all these unusual offender behaviours and remains unsolved. The victim in that case was Florence King, also an elderly female who lived alone. She was also suffocated with a plastic bag and raped. Part of this inquiry will be to revisit the Florence King case in detail.'

Danny turned to Tim Donnelly and said, 'What did you find at the scene?'

Tim said, 'Starting with the exterior of the property, we lifted boot marks from the rear garden that appear to be a size ten work boot. Photographs were taken of the severed telephone line. At the point of entry, we found glove marks and a scrap of cloth that we believe was torn from whatever the offender was wearing as he reached through the smashed transom window.'

'That's great work. What will you be doing with the cloth?'

'It will be sent for a full forensic analysis to the Forensic Science Service.'

'How soon will they get back to you?'

'I spoke with the lead scientist and she assured me she will have a full analysis in seven to fourteen days.'

'Okay. Chase her and let her know we need that evidence. What else did you find in the property?'

'Glove marks throughout. I had hoped that when he ate the food and drank the milk he may have taken his gloves off. No such luck. I have taken swabs from everything that was half-eaten and containers he drank from. There was also a swab taken of dried semen on the thigh of the deceased. All these swabs will also be sent to the Forensic Science Service for analysis. We have taken fibre tapings from the deceased. Those and the bedding will also be sent for analysis.'

'That's good work, Tim. Keep me informed as you get responses from the Forensic Science Service.'

'Will do.'

Danny looked for DC Lorimar. When he saw him, he said, 'Glen, come and see me afterwards so we can go over the house-to-house inquiries. I need to know what staff I'm going to need to carry them out.'

Glen nodded.

Danny said, 'Does anybody have any questions?'

DC Simon Paine asked, 'Are you one hundred percent linking this murder to the unsolved murder of Florence King?'

'The similarities are so great, we must look at both crimes. I'm not able to categorically state right now that we're looking for a repeat offender.'

Danny waited to see if there were any further questions, then said, 'That's it for tonight. I want everyone back on duty at seven o'clock tomorrow morning. We've got a lot to do.'

As he made his way through the briefing room, Danny spoke to DC Jefferies. 'Fran, did you manage to get those details I need from personnel?'

'Yes, boss. DCI Les Swift currently resides at an address in Caythorpe. I've put the details on your desk. There are also three messages from Detective Chief Superintendent Potter. He wants to see you at headquarters at nine o'clock tomorrow morning.'

'Marvellous. Thanks, Fran.'

5

9.00am, 3 September 1988
Nottinghamshire Police Headquarters

Danny knew exactly why he had been called in to see Detective Chief Superintendent Potter so early. It had nothing to do with concern over the state of current inquiries being carried out by the Major Crime Investigation Unit, and everything to do with politics.

Within one minute of him walking into Potter's office, the diminutive head of CID had confirmed this, informing Danny that the chief constable was under pressure to find the killer of Margaret White. It was still less than twenty-four hours since her body had been discovered.

It appeared that Councillor Richard White had carried out his promise, made at the scene, to pile pressure on the chief constable to find his mother's killer.

Danny stared at Potter. 'The MCIU will treat this horrific crime in the same way we investigate every murder. My team always give one hundred percent in everything they do. We will work with the evidence we have, and I will utilise staff in the best way possible to generate new lines of inquiry. I don't need you, or anybody else, telling me how to run a murder investigation just because of who the victim is related to.'

'That's a very simplistic way to look at life, Chief Inspector. It's one that bears no resemblance to the real world. Of course, Richard White is going to apply whatever pressure he can to try and bring his mother's killer to justice, wouldn't you?'

Danny was thoughtful for a moment. 'I suppose I would, but you and the chief both know by now how effective the MCIU can be when we're allowed to get on with our work without interference.'

'Nobody is trying to interfere, Danny, but you must understand that shit always rolls downhill. If the chief's being pressured, he pressures me, and I invariably will then pass some of that onto you. I will endeavour to shield you from most of it, but I need to be kept totally in the loop to do that. I know it's very early in the investigation, but what have you organised so far?'

'I intend commencing the house-to-house inquiries this morning. The streets immediately surrounding Clipstone Drive were mastered yesterday, so we're in position to start this morning. I have already prepared the parameters and questions to be asked by the detectives tasked.'

'Good, good. There will be two sections of the Special Operations Unit joining you at ten o'clock, ready to start any house-to-house inquiries. The chief constable organised that last night.'

Richard White really does have the chief constable's ear, thought Danny.

'That will be a huge help, sir. It means I'll be able to use my staff to track and trace any potential witnesses, as well as speak with family and friends of the deceased.'

'The chief wants it made clear that staffing levels and overtime are not issues in this investigation. What else are you doing?'

'The potential forensic evidence found at the scene and at the post-mortem will be sent to the Forensic Science Service for full analysis. Obviously, I'll keep you informed if we get any breaks in the investigation from that. Are you aware of the previous identical murder?'

'An identical murder?'

'It was before you joined this force, sir. It happened a month or so prior to the start of the 1984 miners' strike. A woman named Florence King was murdered in her home at Warsop. There are too many similarities in the two crimes to ignore the possibility that the same offender has committed both.'

'Did you work on the Florence King murder?'

'Only for a couple of weeks. When I was promoted to DI, I spent two weeks working alongside the senior investigating officer before the previous chief constable decided to close the investigation.'

'Were there ever any suspects?'

'None. And no new lines of inquiry were being found. The SIO was so enraged by the decision to wind it down he resigned. He was due to retire anyway, but he was so incensed he quit immediately.'

'Who ran that inquiry?'

'DCI Les Swift.'

'I understand he was angry, but did he really resign over that?'

'Les Swift was a hardworking, conscientious detective. He was convinced the Florence King murder could be solved if they kept working, and he always believed if the killer wasn't found he would strike again.'

'Are you looking at the King murder again?'

'I've already arranged for all the paperwork and previous evidence to be brought to the incident room at our offices. I had intended to go and see Les Swift at his home address today, but he's away for a few days. I've arranged to see him on the seventh.'

'Good. Anything else I can tell the chief?'

'Part of the possible forensic evidence is semen found inside and on the deceased. That will be analysed to hopefully provide us with a full DNA profile of the offender. I'll keep you informed how that goes.'

'Excellent. Keep in mind that anything you need will be given on this investigation. The DNA evidence might be the breakthrough DCI Swift didn't have on the Florence King murder. How is the MCIU fixed in relation to other inquiries?'

'We only have this murder to investigate right now, but we both know that can change with a telephone call.'

'I do know that, but this investigation must take priority, understood?'

'Yes, sir.'

'Use the special operations unit, use the overtime and keep me informed of all developments. That will be all, Chief Inspector.'

6

6.00am, 5 September 1988
Beckett Wood, near Misterton, Nottinghamshire

The man drove the battered Land Rover along the rutted woodland track. The ground was soft after recent rain and the wheels were sliding around in the glutinous mud. He scanned the woods on either side of the track, looking for the familiar clearing in the trees.

It was starting to get light and he knew he didn't have long to carry out his macabre task. He needed to get the job done and drive back, ready to start work at the farm.

Finally, he saw the break in the trees he had been searching for and stopped the Land Rover. He got out, walked to the back of the vehicle and opened the door.

He grabbed the spade from inside, leaned it against the side of the Land Rover, then stared for a moment at the shape beneath the cream-coloured blanket. His eyes were drawn to the dark staining beneath which he knew lay the woman's battered head.

He was about to grab the blanket covering the body when he heard barking. He turned and saw a golden retriever bounding towards him, coming closer and closer.

In the far distance, he could hear the dog's owners shouting for their dog to return to them. At first, he tried to shoo the animal away by waving the spade at it. The dog was not deterred and barked even more. The shouts of 'Pippin!' from the owner were getting ever closer.

He grabbed the animal by the collar.

He couldn't risk the owner finding him here. They would see the vehicle; they might even discover its grisly contents, then what would he do?

He started to panic. His mind was in a turmoil, wondering what to do next.

He hadn't expected anything like this and was struggling to process what was happening and how to deal with it.

Without really understanding why, he started walking towards the shouting owner, dragging the reluctant dog behind him. In his haste to return the dog, he left the back door of the Land Rover unlocked, walking through the soft mud, down the track towards the commotion.

As he walked away from the vehicle, dragging the boisterous young dog along with him, there was a slight movement beneath the blood-stained blanket.

7

6.10am, 5 September 1988
Beckett Wood, near Misterton, Nottinghamshire

The woman in the back of the Land Rover had been roused from her unconscious state by the incessant barking of the dog. Her head was throbbing and there was an intense pain behind her eyes. As her senses returned, she shivered against the cold. She realised that she was naked, covered only by an itchy woollen blanket.

She moved the blanket away from her face and looked around her, seeing that she was now in the back of a vehicle. She reached behind her and pushed against the back door; she was surprised when it opened a little.

Moving gingerly, she sat up and looked outside. All she could see in the half light, on either side of the muddy track, were trees. In the distance, she could still hear the dog barking and people shouting. There was no sign of anybody around the vehicle. She pushed hard against the back door, swinging it wide open. She climbed out and stood up. Immediately, she felt her head spinning and was forced to sit back down on the tailgate of the vehicle. After a few seconds, her head stopped spinning and she stood up again, slower this time.

Wrapping the blanket around her naked body, she began to stagger towards the trees. She knew she had to get away from the vehicle. It didn't really matter in which direction. She knew if she stayed there, she would die. The soft, black mud felt freezing cold against her bare feet and they soon became numb.

She was desperate to put distance between herself and the vehicle before the man came back. She had no idea how much time had passed since she had been snatched off the street and imprisoned by that hulking monster. She knew it was months, not weeks.

As she staggered through the trees and the undergrowth, she started to feel nauseous again. The throbbing in her head increased. She reached up and touched the back of her head and could feel warm, sticky blood on her fingers. A flashbulb memory burst into her brain. It was an image of the man walking towards her, gripping a hammer in his right hand.

She was just about to give up, as the effort needed to place one foot in front of the other became too much, when the terrain suddenly started to slope downhill.

It was easier going and after a few minutes she staggered out of the woods and onto a railway track.

She looked both ways along the track. In the distance to her right, she could see lights on the track. There were too many lights for it to be an oncoming train, so she started to walk towards them.

She was now pleased she had no feeling in her bare feet. She tried her hardest to place her feet on the wooden sleepers but every now and then she would step on the jagged stones in between them. She stumbled and fell several times. Each time, she ignored the pain and managed to get to her feet and continue walking.

She was now close enough to make out the men working on the track. They were wearing white safety helmets and high visibility jackets. She called out, but her voice was weak and her throat dry.

She shouted again, and this time she saw the nearest man turn and look in her direction. As she started to collapse, she heard the man's voice as he shouted over to his workmates. She fell sideways onto the track and could see the man now running towards her.

As she drifted into unconsciousness, she felt him grab her and heard him say, 'Who are you? What's your name?'

She managed to splutter, 'I'm number four,' before everything went black.

8

8.30am, 5 September 1988
Soss Lane, near Misterton, Nottinghamshire

Danny Flint parked his car behind the other CID vehicles on the narrow lane. The telephone call he had received at home, from the control room inspector, had been short on detail. All he knew was that a badly injured and naked woman had been found on the railway tracks by a maintenance team and that the first officers called to the scene had suspected foul play. They had been convinced somebody had tried to kill the woman.

The first member of the Major Crime Investigation Unit to arrive at the scene had been Detective Sergeant Andy Wills. He still lived in nearby Retford, so was the closest to the scene.

He had arrived a good hour before his colleagues. He had preserved the scene and set everything in motion for a full investigation.

Danny got out of his car and walked towards a group of detectives standing on the stone bridge that ran above the railway line where the woman had been found. The railway maintenance crews were all in their vehicles, which were parked on the other side of the bridge.

As he approached, Danny could see the tall, slim figure of Andy Wills in the middle of the group.

He walked over to Andy and said, 'Morning, Andy. What have we got?'

'Morning, boss. Just over two hours ago, workers saw a woman stumbling along the track. She collapsed just as she reached them and became unconscious. They called an ambulance and she's been taken to Bassetlaw Hospital at Worksop.'

'Injuries?'

'Obviously, she had already been taken to hospital before I arrived, but the workmen who found her have told me that she had serious head wounds and had cuts and bruises all over her. When they found her, she was naked, except for an old blanket. DI Cartwright has gone straight to the hospital to see what the prognosis is for our victim. That prognosis doesn't sound good. This could easily become a murder inquiry within the next few hours.'

'Where's the blanket she was wrapped in? Has it gone to the hospital with her?'

'No, boss. The ambulance crew wrapped her in thick, dry blankets to try and warm her up. She was also suffering from hypothermia when she was found. I've taken possession of the woollen blanket she was wrapped in. It's now in an exhibit bag in the boot of my car. The railway workers had left it on the track and pointed it out to me when I arrived.'

'Do we have any idea who the woman is?'

'No. One of the railway workers said the woman did speak to him before she blacked out, though.'

'What did she say?'

'He asked her who she was, and he's pretty sure she said, "I'm number four."'

'What do you make of that?'

Andy shrugged his shoulders. 'I don't know. Other victims, maybe?'

Danny was quiet for a few seconds, as that comment registered. Then he said, 'What else have you organised since you got here?'

'I requested a dog handler attend, to try and track where she may have come from.'

'Good. Has the dog handler arrived yet?'

'Yes, sir. PC Stark and his dog are still tracking. The last update I had, ten minutes ago, was that they had now moved off the railway track and were heading into woodland.'

'What about the railway workers who found her?'

'As our staff arrived here at the rendezvous point, I've tasked them with getting statements from the maintenance crew. Their supervisor is obviously keen to get his men working on the tracks again.'

'That's good. I'll try and arrange for a section of the Special Operations Unit to attend later this morning, so they can carry out a search along the tracks and wherever the dog handler takes us. Do we know what trains use this line?'

'We've been lucky there. This track is only used by goods trains shifting coal to the power stations along the River Trent. Because the maintenance work has been scheduled for weeks, there are no trains running today or tomorrow.'

'Right, well, let's use that to our advantage. As soon as scenes of crime arrive, I want them to photograph everything. Their top priority must be the blanket. I want it submitted for a full forensic analysis as soon as possible.'

There was the rumble of a diesel engine on the lane and Danny turned to see the scenes of crime van arriving.

He said, 'You know what still needs to be done here, Andy. Get things organised with scenes of crime and brief the special ops lads when they arrive. DI Buxton's working on the Margaret White murder, so can I leave you to manage the scene? I want to drive over to the hospital and talk to Tina. I need to know what the likely outcome's going to be for our victim.'

Andy said flatly, 'No problem, boss. I've got everything in hand here.'

As Danny started to walk away, he heard Andy's radio crackle into life: 'PC Stark to DS Wills, over.'

'From DS Wills. Go ahead, over.'

'The track has ended at a muddy lane, in the middle of Beckett Wood. I think there's probably a vehicle involved. There are numerous tyre tracks and footprints here that could be relevant. Over.'

Danny walked back the few steps and said, 'Tell him to wait there. He will be joined by scenes of crime officers shortly. I want those tyre tracks and footprints photographed and impressions made, if possible.'

Andy said on the radio, 'DS Willis to PC Stark. Remain at your current location. Scenes of crime will be joining you shortly. I want you to identify the tyre tracks and footprints to them. Over.'

'Will do, Sarge. Over.'

Danny said to Andy, 'You've got a lot to organise here. I'll get Rachel to join you, so she can organise the searches with the SOU. I'll be in touch about a debrief time later. Good work this morning.'

9

10.00am, 5 September 1988
Bassetlaw Hospital, Worksop, Nottinghamshire

Danny found Tina Cartwright in the corridor outside the intensive care unit at the hospital. She was sitting on one of the three hard chairs, located outside the main entrance door of the high dependency ward. Her head was resting against the wall.

As he got nearer, Danny could see she was clearly upset.

'What's happened, Tina?'

'They've taken the woman to theatre, about an hour ago. They suspect she has a small bleed on the brain and they need to operate.'

'Is that why you're upset?'

'Not the fact she's going for an operation, no. It was when I saw the woman as they were taking her for scans. I couldn't believe what I was seeing. She was filthy dirty. There were ulcers all over her body. Her hair was matted and greasy. I don't think she's had a wash in a very long time. She absolutely reeked and was painfully thin, emaciated almost. Imagine those black-and-white photos of concentration camp victims – that's what she looked like.'

She stopped speaking, as her voice cracked with emotion.

Danny said nothing and waited for the detective inspector to continue. After a minute, she said, 'I've seen plenty of horrible sights doing this job, but I think what's got to me here is the fact that this hasn't happened over a short period of time. This woman has obviously suffered prolonged abuse for weeks, maybe even months. As well as the two horrendous head injuries, she has cuts and bruises all over her body.'

'Do you think she was being held captive and escaped?'

'Possibly. I think more likely she's been injured while she was being held captive and her captor has then dumped her, believing she was already dead.'

'Have the doctors given you any sort of prognosis?'

'I spoke to an ICU nurse shortly after I arrived. She told me the woman was already critical because of the blood loss and hypothermia. That was before they discovered the bleed on the brain. I just spoke to the neurosurgeon who's going to perform the operation. He was worried that she wouldn't survive the anaesthetic needed for the procedure. He told me that even with those concerns, he intended to proceed with the op, because to do nothing would also mean a death sentence.'

'Why does he think the anaesthetic will be so dangerous?'

'Because of her malnourished and dehydrated state. He told me that he believes the woman has been systematically starved over a long period of time.'

Danny shook his head and muttered, 'This is horrendous.'

The two detectives sat in silence for a few moments

before Danny said, 'Is there anything the medical staff can tell us that may assist with her identification?'

'I asked one of the nurses that very question and she told me that the woman had what looked like an appendectomy scar on her stomach, and a bigger scar from a caesarean section.'

'So she's a mother?'

Tina nodded. 'And physically, she's a white female, early thirties, dark, shoulder-length hair, brown eyes.'

'Any other identifiable features?'

'One. She has a small tattoo at the top of her right thigh. A blue dolphin.'

'If she survives the operation, will the doctors allow us to obtain dental impressions?'

'Very doubtful. The same nurse told me that if she survives the operation and comes back to the ICU ward, she will probably be in an induced coma and will therefore be intubated, so any sort of oral examination would be out of the question.'

'Let's try and remain positive. When the woman returns to the unit after her operation, I want you to get a full set of fingerprints. It's vital we find out who this woman is. I also want her photographed, as soon as the doctors say it's okay.'

Tina nodded. 'I'll get in touch with the local CID. They can bring me a polaroid camera, fingerprint ink and an elimination print form, so I've got them with me.'

'I want to know as soon as there's any update about the operation. I'm going back to the office now, to establish our priority inquiries. As soon as I get back, I'll send DC Bailey here to relieve you. I'm scheduling a full briefing for three o'clock this afternoon and I want you there. I know I said let's stay positive, but I think we should treat this as a murder inquiry from the outset.'

'I agree. From the way the neurosurgeon spoke to me

earlier, I think there's every chance this woman could die on the operating table.'

Danny started to walk back down the corridor, then suddenly stopped and walked back.

'One thing I didn't ask you. Apart from the malnourished state of the victim, are there any particular injuries that make you think this woman has been held against her will?'

'Yes. There are deep bruises around both wrists and both ankles. This woman has been physically restrained over a long time. My guess is metal manacles as opposed to rope. The marks are deep bruises, not rope burns.'

'Christ.'

He paused before walking off, saying over his shoulder, 'I'll get Helen up here to relieve you as soon as I can. Keep me informed of any updates.'

10

2.00pm, 5 September 1988
Sunnybank Cottage, White Gate Farm, Misterton, Nottinghamshire

Sam Morgan sat outside the stone cottage eating a cheese sandwich. He had spent all morning working in the fields, tending a crop of late leeks that were almost ready for picking. He always took a break and came home to the cottage for his lunch. It used to be a proper cooked meal. Fried eggs and bacon, or ham and chips, prepared by his mother. Now she was gone, it was a cold sandwich, always either ham or cheese, washed down with a large mug of sweet tea.

He missed his mother.

He had been in a foul mood all morning after the disaster earlier. He couldn't believe his eyes when he returned to the Land Rover and found no trace of the woman. He had been convinced she was dead. He'd checked for a pulse and held a mirror over her mouth. There had been no signs of life at all. After he lashed out in temper and gave her the two cracks with the hammer, he wasn't surprised when she lay there unmoving. He hadn't meant to hit her so hard, but she had shouted at him and he panicked.

The woman was always so argumentative. She had pushed him too far, for the last time.

From the moment he grabbed her, number four had been nothing but trouble. She always had far too much to say for herself and refused to do anything he told her to. It had confused him when she had turned out be a horrible, moaning, whining cow. After the joy of number three, four had been a disaster. He had thought an older woman would be better when it came to looking after his needs. He couldn't have been more wrong, and he couldn't have picked anyone worse to be number four.

Number three would always be the best.

Whenever he thought of what had happened to his favourite, his mood worsened.

He threw the remnants of his half-eaten sandwich across the yard and cursed out loud: 'That fucking dog!'

He considered going back to Beckett Wood now, to resume the search for number four, but he knew his uncle would be angry if he wasn't working on the field of ripening leeks again this afternoon.

He would have to make an early start and go and find her first thing tomorrow morning. She couldn't have got far, not with those injuries. He had been amazed at all the blood coming from her head. How could the woman not be dead?

She would be lying in the woods somewhere; he would find her in the morning, finish her properly, then bury her with the others.

11

3.00pm, 5 September 1988
MCIU Offices, Mansfield, Nottinghamshire

Danny stepped out of his office and into the main briefing area, where the MCIU detectives had gathered, waiting for the full briefing on the unit's latest inquiry.

A few had returned from the scene of the woman's discovery. They had been engaged in interviewing and obtaining witness statements from the railway maintenance crew who had found the woman.

DS Andy Wills and DS Rachel Moore were still at the scene, directing the search operation being undertaken by officers from the Special Operations Unit. The only other absentees were DC Lorimar, who was overseeing the house-to-house inquiries for the Margaret White case, and DC Helen Bailey, who was now at Bassetlaw Hospital waiting for any further medical updates on the mystery woman.

DI Tina Cartwright had returned to the MCIU office thirty minutes prior to the start of the briefing. She had updated Danny as to the woman's post-operation condition.

He started the briefing by saying, 'Most of you already know what this job entails. I want to start by giving you the latest news from Bassetlaw Hospital. The woman has come through the neurosurgery, but is still critically ill. She will remain that way for the foreseeable future. The small bleed discovered on her brain has now been repaired. That bleed was as a direct consequence of one of the two catastrophic head injuries this woman had suffered. The surgeon found two depression fractures of the skull, directly below the wounds. He has stated that he believes those wounds were caused by blunt force trauma. Since I received that information from the hospital, I've spoken to a pathologist and described the injuries to him. Seamus Carter is of the opinion that the most likely cause of such an injury to the skull is a carpenter's hammer.'

He paused, allowing that information to be noted by his detectives, before continuing. 'The other news from the hospital is grim. Doctors are not expecting this woman to survive her ordeal. The next twenty-four hours will be critical. They have placed her in an induced coma to try and assist her recovery. They have no time scale for when they will be able to bring her out of this coma. Basically, there's every chance this woman will die in the next few hours, or days. If that happens, her death will be as a direct result of the injuries she received. Therefore, we will treat this as a murder inquiry from the outset. Understood?'

The room was filled with murmured responses.

He allowed another pause for the room to fall quiet again, before saying, 'DI Cartwright saw the victim at the hospital. She will now describe her physically. I want you all to pay particular attention to the catalogue of injuries suffered by this unfortunate woman.'

Danny looked at the faces of the hardened detectives as Tina described the parlous state the woman was in when she was found. He could see the same mixture of shock and disbelief on their faces as he had felt himself. Her detailed description left the investigation team in no doubt as to the cruel nature of the depraved individual they were now seeking.

Danny resumed his briefing. 'We have now obtained statements from all the railway maintenance crew working near the Soss Lane bridge this morning. The two most pertinent things to come from those statements are the direction of travel this woman appeared from, and the comment she passed to the witness, Tony Cotham, just before she passed out. She was asked by Mr Cotham who she was, and her response was a mumbled, "I'm number four."'

He paused and then said, 'We all need to keep an open mind on what that comment could mean, but one distinct possibility is that there could be other victims out there.'

Danny scanned the room, looking for Tim Donnelly, the scenes of crime supervisor. When he saw him standing at the back of the room, he said, 'Tim, what updates do you have from the scene?'

Tim coughed once and said, 'Obviously, the searches are still ongoing up there, but to date nothing of interest has been found by SOU. We've photographed the actual point where she collapsed on the railway tracks and have taken photographs of the track followed by the police dog. The relevant locations on that track were pointed out to us by PC Stark. He also pointed out where the track had been lost and identified all relevant tyre tracks and boot prints. We have photographed these and attempted to take casts. Unfortunately, the mud was a little too wet, so I don't think the detail of the casts taken will be good enough for any positive identification tests later. What they *will* show is a general size of the tyres, and size of the boots.'

'Any news on the blanket the woman was wrapped in?'

'There are obvious blood stains on the blanket, but it needs to be dried properly. We're in the process of slowly drying it, before we submit it to the Forensic Science Service for a full forensic examination.'

'How long before you can make that submission?'

'Within the next twenty-four hours. The good news is that because the fabric of the blanket is quite coarse, there's a high probability of fibre transmission. I'd be amazed if the blanket isn't a forensic goldmine. I'll keep you posted, boss.'

'Good. I want you to chase the FSS on this. That blanket is pretty much all we've got right now, until we can identify who our victim is.'

Tim nodded, 'Will do.'

Danny continued, 'On the subject of identification, this has got to be the main thrust of our inquiries. DC Jefferies and DC Pope, I want you to start trawling all missing person files that fit the description given by DI Cartwright. DS Moore will lead this part of the inquiry as soon as she returns from the scene. I want you three to check Nottinghamshire, Lincolnshire and South Yorkshire. It's going to be a huge task, but it will be a vital one. Are you both okay to work overtime and make a start this evening?'

The detectives nodded.

Danny continued, 'This is unlike most of our usual inquiries. At this point, I'd normally be talking to you about mastering local streets, to start house-to-house inquiries, and trawling for any CCTV opportunities. Because of the remote location involved here, we're going to need to think a little out of the box. This woman's injuries were so severe it's doubtful she would have been able to survive in the open for long. One of the doctors, who first assessed her when she was brought into the hospital, has informed DI Cartwright that the woman would only have been able to survive her injuries for approximately one hour because of the huge blood loss, hypothermia and her appalling physical condition. We know where the track ended and have estimated it would have taken her at least twenty-five minutes to have staggered from that point to where she was found. That means there's a window of around thirty-five minutes for her to have sustained her injuries, been bundled into a vehicle and then dumped.'

He paused and then said, 'DC Singh and DC Baxter, I want you to drive from the point where the dog lost the track for a duration of thirty-five minutes. Take as many different routes as you can find. Once you've established every route possible, I want you to draw a line at the end of each route. Once that's done, I want you to start listing every building within that area. Again, this is going to be a huge undertaking, so when DS Wills returns from the scene he will be running that part of the inquiry. Depending on the size of the area you identify, he will decide whether he needs more staff. Like I said, I need you both to utilise some lateral thinking. Don't be afraid to approach other agencies to help you. Aerial photographs could be a massive help. Education providers, such as geography professors or tutors, may also help. Do you understand what I'm saying?'

DC Singh nodded. 'Yes, boss.'

'Are you both okay to stay on overtime this evening and make a start with the route planning?'

They both nodded, so Danny said, 'Good. Work until it's too dark, then get off home.'

He then addressed everyone in the room. 'I anticipate that as the geographical work and the missing person inquiries start revealing information, there will be numerous inquiries generated, more than enough to keep you all busy. I'm conscious of the hard work you're putting in regarding the Margaret White inquiry, and I know some of you had an early start this morning, so I want you to finish up what you're doing, then go home. I want you back on duty tomorrow morning, at eight o'clock.'

Danny walked back into his office, followed by Tina. She closed the door and sat down. 'Do you think we've got any chance of finding this sadistic bastard?'

Danny was as much shocked by her sense of negativity as he was by the bluntness of her question.

'We've got every chance. Personally, I don't think she was dumped and left for dead. I think this woman somehow escaped his clutches. And it's that mistake by him that will give us the tiniest edge. That error will allow us to catch him. It could be a fibre or stain on that blanket, it could be from the missing person files, or something else completely. I want you to lose that sense of negativity, especially in front of the staff. We will find him. Got it?'

Tina stood wearily and said, 'I'm sorry, boss. For some reason, seeing that woman in such a state really got to me. I'll be fine tomorrow.'

'I know you will. Go home and get some rest. Our search starts again tomorrow morning, and it will start again every morning until we find this monster.'

12

10.30pm, 10 May 1986
Manton Estate, Worksop, Nottinghamshire

Susan Claymore cursed under her breath as she rounded the corner just in time to see the last bus trundling down the road, away from the stop.

She always caught the bus after the youth club, even though her house was only four streets away. The vast Manton housing estate in Worksop was no place for a young girl to be walking alone at this time of night. Her parents would be livid if they found out. They would be even angrier if they discovered the reason she had missed the bus was because she had been snogging Billy Ayers behind the club.

It was rare for Susan to be shown any sort of affection. Especially so, from the gorgeous Billy Ayers, a boy she had fancied for ages. She had completely lost track of time as she kissed the object of her crush, and by the time Billy had said goodnight and run off into the night, she was left to hurry alone to the bus stop.

Running wasn't really Susan's thing. She had walked as quickly as she could, but all to no avail. As she watched the bus disappear in the distance, she pulled her thin jacket around her as best she could and started the long walk home. The cold wind whipped around her bare legs and she soon began to shiver, now bitterly regretting wearing the mini skirt that had proved so effective in luring Billy at the youth club.

She had negotiated the first two long streets and was only five minutes from home when she heard a diesel engine rumbling along the road behind her. She glanced over her shoulder and was surprised to see that the scruffy Land Rover in the distance had no lights on. She moved away from the kerb edge and tried to walk a little quicker. She wasn't worried about the vehicle on the road behind her. It would be passing her soon, as she had to turn left into the next road.

She walked around the corner and again glanced behind. She was dismayed to see the vehicle had also turned left and was now much closer.

This road on the estate was poorly lit and had large trees either side. The houses had large front gardens and were set well back from the road.

Suddenly, Susan felt very alone and vulnerable. The goosebumps were now more to do with the gnawing fear growing inside her than the cold. The engine was louder, and when she looked back she was startled to see the vehicle being driven straight towards her.

She pushed herself into a privet hedge, as the vehicle mounted the pavement and came to a stop beside her. The driver's door opened and a huge man jumped out, ran around the front of the Land Rover and grabbed hold of her arms.

A terrified Susan tried to scream, but no sound escaped her mouth. As the man began dragging her towards the rear of the vehicle, she struggled gamely, trying to pull away from his grip. He was far too strong and his huge hands gripped her tightly.

She tried to scream again and this time a shrill sound did escape her lips. The man drew back his huge fist and punched her hard in the face.

The blow dazed her and she felt her legs turn to jelly. The scream turned into a whimper and she could taste blood in her mouth. As the man opened the back door, she spluttered, 'Why are you doing this? Please let me go. My mum and dad will be worried.'

The man said nothing as he lifted her off the floor and bundled her into the vehicle. He used some sort of plastic tie to bind her wrists and ankles, then stuffed an old, foul-tasting rag into her mouth before tying a gag around her head.

Her eyes were wide open with fear, but then a rough hessian sack was placed over her head and everything went dark. She heard the back door close and the engine change, as the vehicle was driven away.

She sobbed as a blind panic overwhelmed her and questions filled her mind. Who was this headcase? What was going to happen to her now? Would she ever see Billy Ayers again? Would she ever see her mum and dad again?

The thrill and pleasure Susan had experienced after her first-ever kiss with Billy Ayers now felt an awful long time ago.

13

9.00am, 7 September 1988
Main Road, Caythorpe, Nottinghamshire

As Danny got out of the CID car, he turned to his colleague and said, 'How's the leg this morning, Fran?'

DC Jefferies stretched as she got out of the car, reached back inside for the walking stick she used permanently and said, 'Most days it's okay. When the weather's cold and damp it plays up a little, that's all.'

'I know you worked on the Florence King murder and I thought you might like to escape from the office for a morning,'

'It's great to get out, even though you are breaking the rules.' Fran smiled before continuing, 'As my supervisor, you must know that because I'm on restricted duties, I shouldn't interact with members of the public.'

Danny laughed. 'Les Swift is ex-job. He doesn't count as a member of the public.'

'I remember him vaguely. He could be a surly bugger when he was on the job. I hope retirement has mellowed him.'

Danny started to walk down the path to the detached cottage and said, 'We'll soon find out.'

The front door was opened immediately after Danny had rapped on the ornate knocker.

Les Swift was a small, wiry man with a full head of steel grey hair. He was dressed casually, in brown corduroy trousers and a check shirt with the sleeves rolled up.

He smiled and said, 'Danny Flint, it's good to see you. Excuse the tatty clothes; I'm intending to do a little gardening later. Come in, come in. I'll get Nettie to put the kettle on.'

The two detectives followed the older man into the lounge.

He turned and said, 'Tea or coffee?'

Danny said, 'Tea will be fine, thanks. How are you and Nettie keeping?'

'We're okay. Best thing I ever did, resigning. I didn't like the way policing was going, all about money. That's not how it should ever be.'

'I couldn't agree more, Les.'

Les smiled and said, 'It was making me a grumpy old man before my time.'

Without waiting for Danny to respond, Les looked at Fran and said, 'I remember you, DC Jefferies. Always knew you'd make a cracking detective. Is tea alright for you as well, love?'

'Tea would be great, thanks.'

'Right. I'll get the drinks organised, and then we can have a chat. Nettie said you wanted to talk to me about the Florence King case.'

As the retired detective left the room, Danny said, 'I think he's mellowed a lot. Seems totally at ease with retirement. There's none of the bitterness that you often see with retired cops.'

'That could change when you start talking about the murder case that effectively ended his career.'

Danny nodded just as Les Swift walked back into the room. He was carrying an A4-size notebook with a blue-coloured hardback cover.

He sat down opposite Danny and said, 'Nettie will bring the drinks through in a minute. This is my notebook from the Florence King murder. Are you reopening the case?'

Danny chose his words carefully. 'We're looking at the inquiries you and your team carried out back then, but it will form part of a current investigation.'

Still sharp as a tack, Les Swift replied, 'The bastard's killed again, hasn't he?'

Danny nodded. 'There's been another murder, this time at Clipstone. There were a lot of similarities to the scene at Florence King's house.'

The old man put his head in his hands and muttered, 'I bloody knew it. I told the chief he would kill again, but he wouldn't listen.'

Danny paused for a second, then said, 'I remember you saying at the time you always thought he would kill again. If it is the same killer, why do you think there's been such a long delay between offences?'

'Could be any number of reasons: work, illness, prison. That's something for you to work out. It's not going to be easy, though.'

'I've retrieved all the paperwork from your inquiry, but what I can't locate is any of the physical evidence. You must have taken samples from the scene at the time?'

'We did. All the bedding was seized and stored correctly. There were samples taken from the post-mortem as well.

They would have all been stored correctly. They'll be somewhere. It's only four years ago.'

Fran asked, 'Did you find any semen at the scene in Warsop?'

'There was semen found on the sheets and on the victim during the post-mortem. Florence King was brutally raped before she was suffocated. Why is semen so important?'

Danny said, 'Have you heard of DNA?'

'Only snippets on the news.'

'We've found semen at the new murder. I'm hopeful that a DNA profile will be obtained from that. If we can find the exhibits you raised on your inquiry, I may be able to obtain a DNA profile from that, too. If the profiles are identical, it will definitively prove the same man is responsible for both rapes and murders.'

'It's that certain, is it?'

'Yes, that's why it's important I find your physical exhibits.'

Les flicked open his blue book and turned the pages quickly. 'Here it is. The exhibits officer on the King inquiry was DC Fred Armitage. He was always extremely thorough. If anybody can locate your exhibits, it will be Fred.'

'I didn't know Fred. Was he a good detective?'

'As I said, very thorough. Meticulous even.'

The door to the lounge opened and a ruddy-faced woman bustled into the room carrying a tray with three cups, a sugar bowl and a plate of biscuits.

She placed the tray on the coffee table and said, 'I didn't know who took sugar, so I've brought a bowl in so you can help yourselves.'

Les looked up and said, 'Thanks, love.'

Danny stood and said, 'Thanks, Nettie. I hope you're keeping well and looking after Les.'

She smiled. 'It's Les who looks after me these days, Danny. We're doing okay. Enjoy your tea.'

Nettie closed the door behind her.

Les whispered, 'She's developed diabetes since I retired, so we have to be really careful what we eat and drink.'

Fran said, 'She looked well enough. You must be doing something right, sir.'

'It's not sir anymore, lass. Just plain old Les is fine by me. Now let's go through this book of mine and see if there's something that will help you.'

An hour later, and Danny and Fran got back into the car after going through all the inquiries noted by Les Swift. Danny felt disappointed at the lack of any breakthrough, and said, 'Let's hope DC Armitage will be able to help us.'

'That will be difficult, boss. Fred Armitage lived just down the road from me when he retired. He died in 1986; heart attack.'

'Bloody hell. I don't remember seeing that.'

'You won't. He had nothing to do with the police after he retired. His funeral was family only.'

Danny started the car and drove slowly away. He was deep in thought. There had been nothing startling from the original notes made by Les Swift, and from what he had read in the paperwork so far, there was nothing that warranted further investigation.

He said, 'Fran, I'm going to take you off all other duties. I want you to spend your time finding the exhibits from the Florence King murder. I don't care if you have to visit every police property store in the county. I need to have those exhibits. Seamus Carter has told us who the pathologist was who carried out the Florence King post-mortem and where it was done. That's all useful information that will help you track these exhibits down.'

'No problem, boss. I'll start as soon as we get back to the office.'

Danny knew that he needed something to give to Potter. Now there was another potential murder inquiry, resources were going to be at a premium. All his instincts were telling him he needed to push on with the woman found near Retford. He also knew that if the woman didn't die, he would come under serious pressure, from Potter, to drop that inquiry.

He felt the pulse in his temples start to throb.

14

10.00am, 8 September 1988
MCIU Offices, Mansfield, Nottinghamshire

It had been three days since the woman had been found collapsed on the railway lines near Misterton. Danny was worried that they were still no closer to identifying her than they had been on that first day.

He had called in Tina and Rob to discuss their options and to assess the progress in the Margaret White murder.

He handed them both a copy of the photograph DC Bailey had taken of the unconscious woman. 'What do you think?'

Rob said, 'Are you seriously thinking about circulating this photo to the press?'

'I don't see any other option. The fingerprints we took at the hospital have come up negative, so she obviously has no criminal record. The missing person inquiries carried out so far have also drawn a blank.'

'It's not through want of trying, boss. Rachel and Jane have been working nonstop, trawling misper files.'

'I know that. The problem we have is that the woman we're seeing now is probably unrecognisable to how she looked prior to this horrendous ordeal.'

'What about the previous press appeal?'

'There's been very little response. We just put out a general description last time. I think publishing this photograph will make more of an impact.'

Tina had remained silent, but interjected, 'Do you think the public will be able to see past the life support tubes, the bruising and the swelling well enough to be able to identify her?'

'I hear what you're saying, but I want to try a fresh press appeal using the photograph as well as the physical description this time. The scars found on her body would indicate that she's a mother. There could be a husband and family out there going frantic with worry, wondering where the hell their wife and mother has disappeared to. The other factor I need to consider is that until we do identify her, we can't move the inquiry forward.'

'I understand your motives, boss. Don't you think the hospital will also have a say on releasing a photo like that?'

'They might not like it, but, as I said before, I don't really see any other options. Dental records are never going to be available while she's intubated. I'm going to see Potter later today and run it past him. If he has no strong objections, I'm going to arrange for another press appeal this evening.'

Rob said, 'As you say, needs must, boss. Do you want me to arrange some staff to be available this evening to answer the telephones, just in case we do get lucky?'

'Give them the heads up now. I'll confirm their hours after I've spoken to Potter. We need to start to generate our own luck or this inquiry is going nowhere fast. How are things progressing on the Clipstone murder?'

'The house-to-house inquiries are almost complete. Another day, two at the most, and they'll be finished. Nothing from them so far; do you want to extend the parameters?'

Danny glanced at the map of Clipstone spread out over his desk.

'We could extend the house-to-house while we've still got the special ops officers.'

He was thoughtful for a second, then said, 'Extend it to cover the houses on Clipstone Road West and New Mill Lane. We think the offender approached the murder scene across the fields at the rear of Clipstone Drive, so we may locate a witness from those two areas.'

'I'll speak to the sergeant in charge of the two special ops serials and get that arranged.'

'Thanks, Rob. Did the press appeal we put out reveal any new leads?'

Rob shook his head. 'Nothing. What we need are some positive results from the Forensic Science Service.'

'Speak to Tim Donnelly today and see if he can push them.'

'Will do, boss.'

15

7.00pm, 3 July 1986
Sunnybank Cottage, White Gate Farm, Misterton, Nottinghamshire

Sam Morgan was desperately trying to keep his temper in check. He had spent a backbreaking day working in the fields. He'd been up since first light and had only stopped for thirty minutes at midday to grab a quick sandwich. He was starving hungry and already in a bad mood.

He had left everything out for the girl to cook an evening meal: chicken breast, potatoes, carrots and onions. She was to prepare them, put them in the casserole dish and place them in the oven.

He had taken the time once again to move her from the cellar to the kitchen to carry out her duties. And once again, she had done fuck all and was still sat at the table, where he had left her, chained up, at midday.

There were no excuses. The chain was easily long enough for her to move around the kitchen to get things ready for him. She could have prepared an evening meal and they could have both been eating it right now – but no, she had spent the day sat on her fat, lazy arse.

What was the point of having her here, if she wasn't going to look after him?

With simmering rage in his voice, he asked, 'What have you been doing all day?'

The young woman did what she always did and ignored the hulking brute who had snatched her off the street.

Fighting to control his rising temper, he said again, 'I asked you, what have you been doing? Why isn't the food ready?'

The girl whimpered and whined, 'Because I don't know what to do.'

'For fuck's sake! You fill the casserole pot with water, peel the veg and put that and the chicken in the water. Then you put it all in the oven for a couple of hours. It's not rocket science.'

'Don't shout at me. I don't know how to do it.'

Feeling his anger rising, he unlocked the chain and dragged her from the chair. 'Come on, you lazy bitch. Back downstairs.'

'Please don't. I'm starving.'

'Yeah, me too. Perhaps tomorrow you'll do as you're told.'

He pushed her backwards through the basement door, switched on the light and followed her down the stone steps.

As he descended after her, he was consumed with his own thoughts. He could see no way out of this useless situation. It had seemed so obvious when he had grabbed her off the street. She would stay locked in the basement of the cottage until he needed her to do something. When he needed her to cook, do the dishes or the laundry, he would bring her upstairs and secure her on a long enough chain to carry out her task and stop her running off.

It was a simple plan, and would have worked if she hadn't been so bloody thick and so bone idle. Whatever he asked her to do, never got done. He had starved her, beaten her, left her in the basement for days on end in the dark, and still, she did nothing.

Number one needed to go. He didn't know what he was going to do yet, but once she was gone, he could go out again and grab another one.

Maybe number two would be less of a problem and do as she was told.

At the foot of the stairs, he grabbed the young woman and pushed her towards the single bed on the other side of the dimly lit basement.

Distracted by his own thoughts, he had failed to notice the kitchen knife she now held in her right hand. It should have been used by her to peel the vegetables, but she had hidden it up her sleeve when she heard the Land Rover returning to the cottage.

He pushed her down onto the bed and started to place the first metal manacle around her already bruised ankle. As he secured the first lock, she suddenly sat bolt upright and lunged forward. He caught a glimpse of the shiny blade just before it pierced his right forearm. He pulled his arm back before the blade could penetrate too deep. His swift movement yanked the slippery bone-handled knife from the woman's grasp and it clattered onto the stone floor.

The pain tipped his anger over the edge and he lashed out at the woman, punching her hard in the face. The force of the heavy punch knocked her backwards onto the bed. The back of her head made a loud crack as it collided with the wrought iron bed frame.

He looked down at the woman. She was unmoving. Her eyes were open and staring at the ceiling. Blood, from a gash above her right eyebrow, started to trickle down the side of her face.

He turned her face away from him and secured her. Once all four manacles were in place, chaining her to the bed, he muttered under his breath, 'You just won't be bloody told, will you? Now look what you've made me do. You can bloody well stay here and maybe next time I ask you to do something, you'll do it.'

He had spoken to her the way his mother used to scold him when he had failed to do chores around the house and was being punished.

There was no response.

He picked up the bone-handled kitchen knife. He could see his own dark blood glistening on the blade and his arm started to sting again. He shoved the bloody knife in his pocket and stomped back up the steps. He needed to tend to his injured arm and then get something to eat. He switched off the light at the top of the steps and locked the basement door.

He shouted through the door, 'I'll be back in a day or so.'

There was no response. The basement remained silent; the cottage was silent.

Number one was already dead.

16

7.30pm, 5 July 1986
Sunnybank Cottage, White Gate Farm, Misterton, Nottinghamshire

Sam Morgan carried a mug of water in one hand and a plate containing bread and cheese in the other. It had been two days since he left the woman chained and asleep on the bed.

Throughout that time, there had been no sounds emanating from the basement. He knew that she would be starving hungry and need water by now. Hopefully, she would have learned her lesson and would start doing what he told her to do. His patience was running thin, but he didn't really know what to do to change his situation. He just wished he had chosen a better option than he had. Maybe she was just too young and really didn't know how to take care of his needs.

He put the mug on the floor and unlocked the basement door.

He flicked the single light on, picked up the mug and made his way carefully down the slippery stone steps.

There was a strange smell in the claustrophobic room. It always smelt musty and damp down here, but this was different. It was a sickly sweet, cloying smell that reminded him of something.

Apart from the bed in the corner of the stone room, the only other object to be seen was the large black bucket that was his captive's toilet. The chains that secured her to the bed were just long enough for her to sit up and walk the two paces to get there.

'Wake up! I've brought you food and water.'

There was no response, and no movement from the woman on the bed.

As he crossed the basement towards the bed, the smell grew stronger.

He put the food and drink on the floor and grabbed at her shoulder, turning her over roughly.

The sight that greeted him made him gasp and step back from the bed. The woman's face was blackened and bloated. The blood from the cut above her eye had congealed and crusted on her swollen face. The smell, up close, was almost overpowering. He knew it would take a long time for the basement to be rid of it.

He picked up the food and water, walked slowly back up the stairs and closed the door.

He stepped outside into the fresh air and took a couple of deep breaths. His mind was spinning. He couldn't understand how she had died. She had been fine when he left her. His bottom lip started to quiver, and he became upset about what had happened. He didn't know what to do next, how he was going to clean up this mess. His mother would have known what to do.

Eventually, he calmed down and felt less panicky. His thoughts then turned to what he was going to do next.

First, he would need to move the body out of the basement. Then he would have to hide her where nobody would ever find her.

He racked his brains, thinking of all the remote, inaccessible areas around the farm.

A sense of calm descended on him as he remembered Beckett Wood. It was hardly ever used by anybody. It was thick with brambles, with little clearings beneath, oak, ash and birch trees. The only way to get to it was by a single muddy track, which very few people knew existed.

It would be perfect.

He took a bite of the strong cheese and glanced at his watch. It would be getting dark soon. He would wrap the body in the bedding and throw her in the back of the Land Rover. Later, when it was dark, he would drive over to Beckett Wood and bury the woman in one of the many clearings.

Once he had moved the body, he would need to clean up the mess in the basement before the rancid stench crept into the house. If he used the farmyard disinfectant on the stone floor, it would hide the smell until he could air the room properly.

He threw the bread and the water on the ground and swallowed the last lump of cheese before trudging over to one of the outbuildings, where the disinfectant was kept.

Ten minutes later, he returned to the basement. He wrapped the body in the bedding and used twine to secure the blankets. He could now see the huge injury to the back of the woman's head. The pillow underneath her head had been saturated in her blood. He would have to bury everything.

He hauled the now-cocooned body up the stone steps and out to the Land Rover. He opened the back door and hurled the dead woman inside. Grabbing the bucket of hot water, disinfectant, mop and cloths, he went back down. The acrid smell of the strong chemicals soon overpowered the stench of death. He slewed the stone floor with the hot water, before mopping it back up. There was a pool of dried blood immediately below the bed, so he paid particular attention to that area. The last thing he did was wipe down the wrought iron bedposts.

The single lightbulb hanging from the ceiling offered a dim and dingy light, but he could just make out blood splashes on the wall behind the bed. He used the same cloth to wipe down the stone walls, then made his way back outside.

He moved a few steps away from the front door, then threw away the bloodstained water from the bucket. He would leave the door to the basement wedged open for a few days and hopefully the odour would gradually diminish.

He placed a long-handled spade into the back of the Land Rover and closed the back door. He stared through the rear window at the bundle of blankets containing the body.

Glancing again at his watch, he saw that in a few hours' time it would be midnight. The witching hour would be the perfect time to make the drive to Beckett Wood and get rid of the problem.

He had the perfect location in mind.

As soon as he had buried number one, he would start looking for number two. This time he would be patient. Number two would need to be someone who could look after him, like his mother had. He needed help around the cottage, and someone to prepare his food. Somebody older than number one would know how to do that.

17

3.00pm, 9 September 1988
Mansfield Woodhouse Police Station, Nottinghamshire

Fran Jefferies followed the shift sergeant through the small police station. As they walked up the stairs to the first floor, he said, 'After your phone call yesterday, I began thinking about items being stored here by the CID. We used to keep boxes of old exhibits in one of the garages in the back yard here, but that was a couple of years ago. Anyway, it suddenly occurred to me, all that stuff was put into the attic when one of the inspectors working here complained there was no garage space for his new car.'

'Do you think the exhibits I'm missing could have been put in the attic?'

The sergeant shrugged. 'Possibly. I do recall shifting a lot of boxes up there at the time. Daft thing is, that bloody inspector was only here for a couple of months. He had us shifting all that stuff. I don't know – all that work for nowt.'

'I don't want to cause you more work, Sarge, but you know the situation with my injury. There's no way I can climb up into the loft to check out what's up there.'

The old sergeant winked and said, 'I know about your ankle, Fran, and I know how you were injured. I wouldn't expect you to climb up into the loft. That's why I arranged for two police cadets to come over this morning from Mansfield and empty the attic. All the boxes are neatly stacked in here.'

He smiled as he opened the door into an unused office. Fran could see a dozen large boxes with the words 'KING MURDER' written in felt tip on the side.

'You're a star, Sarge. Have you looked in any of the boxes?'

He winked again and said, 'That's CID work, nowt to do with me. I'll leave it with you. I've got work to do.'

'Thanks, Sarge.'

18

8.00am, 10 September 1988
MCIU Offices, Mansfield, Nottinghamshire

Danny had called in Rob, Tina, Andy and Rachel to discuss progress on the different strands of the two inquiries.

He was troubled by the lack of progress in both. He knew that sometime in the future Potter would be insisting that he place more emphasis on one over the other. He had so far resisted all attempts by his immediate supervisor to prioritise the Margaret White murder inquiry.

Both cases needed equal attention. He was walking a tightrope and needed the support of his senior detectives.

Top of the agenda was what developments, if any, had arisen from the fresh press appeal. Staff had been on duty following the appeal to answer the telephones in the incident room.

Danny said, 'Andy, did we get anything from the press appeal using the woman's photograph?'

A crestfallen Andy answered, 'We took quite a few calls, and all that information has been passed to Rachel and Jane to cross-check against any of the missing persons files they're looking at, but I think it's fair to say there haven't been any eureka moments.'

Danny looked to Rachel, who said, 'Checking the outstanding missing-from-home reports is a mammoth task. Obviously, we can rule out quite a few on description alone. Sex, age and build are all good thinners. What makes it so tricky is the state the woman's in now. It's quite possible that she looked nothing like she does now before her ordeal, so I'm having to err on the side of caution and check all white females around her age. Over the three counties you asked us to check, that's an awful lot of files.'

'Do you need more staff?'

'I've raised checks on all missing persons reported over the last six months, and we have almost drawn up the full list of possibles. I do think the next phase will require extra staff. We will then have to start visiting the people who made these reports, to try and get a definitive yes or no on our mystery woman.'

'Okay. I want to know as soon as that list of possibles is completed. We need to start getting staff on this as soon as possible. We need to establish who this woman is. Once we've done that, we can start examining the circumstances of her disappearance.'

He paused and then said, 'Tina, what's the latest from the hospital?'

'I called Helen just before this briefing. There's no change, which the doctor has assured her is a good thing. He is now far more hopeful that the woman will make some sort of recovery. How good that recovery is will depend on the extent of any brain damage suffered as a result of the head injuries.'

'Okay, thanks. I want to know of any updates immediately.'

He turned to Rob, 'How are DC Singh and DC Baxter getting on with the geographical survey I tasked them with?'

'Jag and Phil have done well, boss. We now have a complete list of farm buildings and other properties all within that thirty-five minute radius from where the dog lost the track in Beckett Wood.'

'Are we ready to start visiting these properties yet?'

'The lads are trying to establish who owns the properties identified by using the Land Registry and the last census. It's a slow process, but they're working hard and making good headway.'

'Come and see me with a list of the ones you've done all you can with. I'm going to see if I can get a section of the Special Operations Unit to supplement our numbers and start making visits to these properties. The house-to-house inquiries at Clipstone will be concluding soon, and I think we need to be proactive. Just sitting around waiting for a breakthrough isn't going to solve this. We can use the special ops staff from the house-to-house inquiry to supplement our numbers.'

Rob heard the edge in Danny's voice. The two men had worked together over many years and he knew when something was troubling his boss. He said, 'Is there something else bothering you, boss?'

'It's the comment the woman made. This "number four" business. I keep thinking about it, and all I can come up with is that there must be other victims out there.'

'I think we're all thinking the same thing. That's why everyone's grafting so hard, putting in the hours. I'll let you have that list this morning.'

'Thanks. Let's get cracking. There's more than enough work for everybody with the inquiries we've discussed this morning; let's start working our way through these lists. Andy, keep somebody answering the phone. The new press appeal may still turn something up.'

Danny paused and then said, 'I had a phone call from Fran late last night. She has finally located all the physical exhibits from the Florence King murder inquiry. Apparently, they had been stored in the attic at Mansfield Woodhouse police station. The boxes were dry and in good condition. She will be submitting the bedding taken from the crime scene for a full forensic analysis today.'

Rob said, 'Hopefully, there will be semen on there that's still viable, to get a DNA profile from. It will be touch and go after this length of time, but a DNA match to the samples found at Clipstone would be a huge breakthrough. Has she found the samples taken at the post-mortem yet?'

'No. She's going to check storage facilities at Bassetlaw Hospital. Seamus Carter's information was that the post-mortem for King was held there. It's possible samples taken could have been placed in their refrigeration storage units.'

'I'll chase her today and see if she located them.'

'Okay, thanks. Keep up the hard graft, and we'll make progress on both inquiries.'

19

8.00am, 10 September 1988
Sunnybank Cottage, White Gate Farm, Misterton, Nottinghamshire

Sam Morgan grunted as he lifted the heavy wrought-iron bed frame and dragged it from one side of the cellar to the other. He tipped water and disinfectant from the bucket, then used the mop to soak up the pungent-smelling liquid until the stone floor was virtually dry.

Dragging the bed back into position, he tore open the packets of sheets and blankets and made the bed. The last thing he did was stuff a pillow into the fresh pillowcase and place it at the head of the bed.

He took a set of keys from his pocket and tested them in the locks of the steel manacles that were secured to each of the iron legs of the bed. The locks were all fine. He left the manacles in the open position, ready to receive the next captive.

He scooped up the soiled bedlinen from the previous occupant and stuffed it all in the large chest that stood against the far wall. He made a mental note to have a bonfire soon, so he could burn the bloodstained and soiled bedding.

He placed the empty black plastic bucket near to the bed and stood back to admire his handiwork.

The cellar was now ready to receive its fifth occupant.

He picked up the discarded linen packets, stomped heavily up the stone steps, flicked off the single light bulb and closed the cellar door behind him.

He glanced at the clock on the kitchen wall and saw that he still had time to have some breakfast before he needed to start work. He had another full day of back-breaking work ahead of him.

As he fried four eggs in the blackened frying pan that was a permanent fixture on the stove, he thought back to the visit he had made to Beckett Wood to find the woman. He had been surprised to see all the police officers in the wood and felt fortunate they had not spotted him, skulking around the bushes. He had quickly left the wood and given up any hope of finding the woman. He hoped she had collapsed and died somewhere she wouldn't be found.

He shovelled the fried eggs into his mouth and smiled. Even if they had found the woman, there was nothing to connect her with this place. Nothing to connect her to him. He would be fine; there was nothing to worry about.

He wiped egg yolk from his chin and belched loudly, before standing up and stretching. It was time for him to be at field number seven to start lifting the number three carrot crop.

His life revolved around numbers. Each of the fields around the huge farm were numbered, and each of the crops had a number, so they were harvested in the right order. Just like each of the women he had snatched off the street had a number.

As he walked to the Land Rover, he thought of number five. Everything was ready. It was time for him to find her and bring her back here, so she could take care of him.

20

2.00pm, 10 September 1988
MCIU Offices, Mansfield, Nottinghamshire

DC Glen Lorimar was bored rigid. He had been sitting at his desk since nine o'clock that morning. He had been allocated the onerous task of answering the incident room telephone that had been set up to receive incoming calls generated from the previous night's press appeal.

There had only been four calls in five hours, and none of them were of any use. He sighed heavily and stood up. He walked leaden-footed across to the hot water urn and made himself a coffee. He placed the coffee on his desk and was about to nip to the toilet when the phone started to ring.

Typical. Just as I'm about to turn my back, it rings.

He snatched up the telephone and said, 'MCIU incident room. Can I help you?'

A timid, almost frightened voice said, 'I don't know if I've come through to the right place. I'm calling about a photograph I've seen in today's local paper.'

'Are you calling about the injured woman, sir?'

'Yes. I think the woman in the photograph could be my wife.'

'Could be?'

'Well, it's hard to be sure, but it looks a bit like her.'

'Okay. I'll need to get some details from you. What's your name and address?'

'Trevor Wright. I live at 6 St Martins Close, Blyth.'

'Thank you. And what's your wife's name?'

'Fiona Wright. She's been missing for the last six months.'

'I take it you've reported your wife as a missing person?'

'Yes, I did, but that was months ago. We haven't heard anything from her or the police since.'

'You said we?'

'I have two young daughters.'

'Will you be at home for the rest of the day, sir?'

'Yes.'

'I'll arrange for police officers to see you at your home address, just as soon as I can.'

'Thank you. Do you think it's her? What's happened to her?'

'The officers will explain everything when they get there. Thank you for calling, sir.'

Glen put the telephone down, grabbed his notepad and rushed over to Danny's office. He knocked on the door and walked straight in. 'Boss, I think I may have something here.'

Danny was in mid-conversation with Rachel. Slightly annoyed at the interruption, he looked up at Glen and said, 'Well, what is it?'

'A man just called the incident room and said he thinks the picture in his local paper could be his wife, Fiona Wright.

She went missing six months ago, leaving him and their two young daughters behind.'

'Where does he live?'

'St Martins Close in Blyth, which isn't a million miles away from where she was found.'

Danny was on his feet. 'Rachel, have you heard this name before? Is she on your list?'

She quickly scanned the rows of names on her list. 'She's here. Reported missing on the tenth of March by her husband, Trevor.'

'Grab her missing persons file, and let's go and see Trevor Wright.'

Danny smiled at Glen, saying, 'Good work, Glen. Now get back to your desk in case someone else calls.'

'Yeah. Cheers, boss.'

21

3.00pm, 10 September 1988
St Martins Close, Blyth, Nottinghamshire

Danny studied the neat, three-bedroom semi-detached house from the car. It was very ordinary, on an unremarkable street. The front garden was bordered by recently trimmed privet hedging. There were a couple of kids' bikes on the front lawn, still lying where eager young riders had abandoned them.

The two detectives got out of the car. Rachel said, 'This is the house, number 6.'

As they walked along the concrete path, the front door was opened by a slight, bespectacled man, wearing jeans and a sweatshirt.

Danny took out his identification and said, 'Trevor Wright?'

The man glanced quickly at the identification and said, 'Yes.'

'I'm Detective Chief Inspector Flint and this is Detective Sergeant Moore. May we come in?'

Opening the door wider, Trevor Wright placed his index finger to his lips and whispered, 'Of course, but be quiet, please.'

He directed the two detectives into the main living room, where a young girl who looked to be around four years old was fast asleep on the settee.

He whispered, 'Step through into the dining room, so we can talk. She's just this minute dropped off to sleep.'

As they walked quietly into the room, Rachel saw a family portrait on the sideboard. 'Is that your wife, Mr Wright?'

He picked up the photograph and placed it on the dining table next to the newspaper, which was open on the page showing the photograph of the unidentified woman.

He said, 'Yes, that's my Fiona. This was taken a couple of months before she went missing.'

Rachel could instantly see the resemblance and looked at Danny, who nodded.

Mr Wright indicated the dining chairs and said, 'Please, sit down.'

Danny sat down. 'You told my officer on the telephone that you have two daughters?'

'Yes. I've got Tanya, who's asleep in the next room, she's three and a half. And Jenny, who's seven and will be home from school soon.'

'Have you got to collect her?'

'No, my neighbour will bring her home when she picks up her own child. I've tried to keep some sort of routine going, since Fi went missing, but it's been hard.'

'It must be difficult with two little ones. What about your work?'

'I'm the chef at the Red Hart hotel in Blyth. They've been really understanding and have organised somebody else to do the lunches. It just means I'm there every evening. I'm so lucky to have such brilliant neighbours. They all love Fiona and the girls, and have rallied around us so much. They take it in turns to babysit my girls, so I can still work and earn money. I do my best to make sure I'm home by midnight every shift. Do you think the woman in the hospital could be my Fiona?'

'As soon as your neighbour gets here with Jenny, can you come with us to Bassetlaw General to see for yourself?'

'Of course. Can I ask you something, Chief Inspector?'

Danny nodded. There was a brief pause, then Trevor asked, 'Does the woman in hospital have any tattoos? There was no mention in the newspaper about a tattoo.'

'Why?'

'Because Fiona has a small blue dolphin tattoo, at the top of her leg. She had it done on holiday in Spain, when she was still a teenager.'

Rachel said, 'The woman in hospital does have a tattoo like that. Were either of your children born by caesarean section?'

'Yes. There were complications when Tanya was born and the doctors had to perform an emergency C section.'

'Then there's a chance that the woman at the hospital could be your wife. Let's get you over there, so you can see for yourself, and you can speak to the doctors.'

22

4.00pm, 10 September 1988
Bassetlaw General Hospital, Worksop, Nottinghamshire

Danny looked at Trevor Wright as the ICU consultant explained the condition of his wife to him. He saw the hope that had been in the man's eyes slowly fade again, as he was told just how seriously ill his wife was.

Danny put a consoling hand on the chef's shoulder and said, 'She's improving every day, Trevor. Don't give up on her.'

The consultant nodded and said, 'The detective's right. There's every chance your wife will be able to make a full recovery from her injuries. The worst moments are behind her, but it could be a lengthy process before she's fully recovered.'

'Thank you, doctor. Can I visit again?'

'Of course. The sister will advise you of visiting times and protocols.'

'Thanks.'

Rachel said, 'Come on, Trevor, let's get you home to your girls.'

As they made the drive from Worksop back to Blyth, Rachel gently quizzed the husband on the circumstances in which his wife had disappeared.

The story the chef related was bizarre. His wife had popped out to the corner shop at around ten o'clock at night to buy a bottle of milk for the girls' breakfast, as they had run out that evening. Trevor had arrived home from work to find his neighbour sitting in the house, looking after the girls.

The neighbour had explained that Fiona had knocked and asked her to keep an eye on the kids while she nipped out to the shop, but that she hadn't returned and that was almost an hour ago.

The worried husband had contacted the police immediately, as something was obviously very wrong. The police had taken details for a missing person report that night, but no follow-up inquiries had ever been conducted. A poor response from the police that Danny would need to address later.

Having dropped Trevor Wright back at his home address, the two detectives made the drive back to the MCIU office. As they travelled along the main A60 road towards Mansfield, Rachel said, 'Well, at least we finally have a name to put to the face.'

Danny shook his head. 'I can't believe there were no follow-up inquiries made into this missing person report. People don't go missing nipping out to buy milk from the shop.'

'Unfortunately, yes, they do. It happens more often than you'd think.'

'But to leave two young kids behind as well . . . does that happen?'

'I take your point, boss.'

'I want all the circumstances of her disappearance going over in detail. I want you and Jane to switch your attention from missing persons to this. I want to know everything there is to know about Trevor and Fiona Wright. I want full background checks, financial and personal. You know the drill.'

'Understood.'

23

11.15pm, 6 October 1986
Lime Tree Crescent, Bawtry, South Yorkshire

It was a beautiful clear night and there was a full moon that lit up the sky. Emma Bridge wrapped her scarf around her neck and buttoned up her coat against the chill.

The air felt cold after standing behind the bar in the warm pub all evening, and she was pleased she had decided to wear jeans and not a skirt. It was only a short walk from The Crown to her house on Lime Tree Crescent. It was a walk she always enjoyed after a busy shift. The fresh air always felt good compared to the smoky atmosphere of the pub.

'Are you going to be okay walking home on your own, Emma love?'

She stopped at the bottom of the three stone steps that led to the front door of the pub and turned to face the landlord. 'Don't be daft, Jim, I'll be home in ten minutes. You know me. I enjoy the walk.'

'Okay, love. Be careful and I'll see you tomorrow.'

She gave a cheery wave. 'Night. See you tomorrow.'

He waved back and shouted after her, 'Don't be late tomorrow evening. It's the darts match and you'll have sandwiches to make.'

Without looking back, Emma waved in acknowledgement and began to stride out for home. She knew both her parents would be waiting up. Even though she was now almost twenty years of age, they still worried about her. She didn't mind; she knew that worry was born out of love and concern over her serious medical condition. She had suffered from type one diabetes since her childhood and was now reliant on insulin injections to keep her condition stable. She would be due another injection when she arrived home.

Emma was determined not to let her illness define her. She tried to live her life to the full. That was part of the reason she had taken on the job of barmaid at The Crown, much to the dismay of her parents.

She had easily made the transition from taking her insulin injection at seven-thirty every evening to eleven-thirty after work. The change in routine had made her feel sluggish and weary to begin with, but now she felt back to normal.

She turned off the main Tickhill Road and onto her estate. The street lighting here was less, and she was glad of the bright moonlight. As she walked towards the junction of Oak Tree Road and Elm Tree Drive, she could see a dirty-looking Land Rover parked on her side of the road. The lights of the vehicle were off, but the diesel engine was still on. The exhaust fumes were visible in the frigid air.

As she walked alongside the vehicle, she saw that the passenger door was slightly ajar. She paused and looked inside; the vehicle was empty, and she could see the keys still in the ignition.

She was just about to start walking again when she was grabbed roughly from behind. A huge hand clamped over her mouth and a powerful arm snaked around her waist. She was lifted off the ground and carried to the back of the vehicle. She had been shocked at first, but now as the man loosened his grip to open the back door she started to struggle. The man increased his grip on her face and pulled her in close to his huge body. Her struggles were futile; whoever had grabbed her was far too big and strong to have any difficulty overpowering her.

As soon as the door was opened, the man used both hands to throw her body into the rear of the Land Rover. The floor was metal and it knocked the wind out of her when she landed. The man quickly gagged her and wrapped her wrists and ankles in twine, before placing a rough sack over her head.

Her mind reeling, Emma sat up in the back of the vehicle and tried to shout to her abductor, who had now slammed the back door shut and was getting in the front.

She shouted through the gag that she needed her injection, but the man just started to drive away. The abduction of Emma Bridge had taken less than a minute.

24

8.00am, 11 September 1988
MCIU Offices, Mansfield, Nottinghamshire

After the breakthrough the previous day, Danny called a full briefing. He needed to update the team this morning on the progress made.

He called for silence and said, 'As you may know, we had a significant breakthrough yesterday. We have now identified the woman found on the railway lines at Misterton. She is Fiona Wright, a wife and mother of two young daughters. She was reported missing by her husband six months ago.'

He paused before continuing. 'This woman disappeared after going to a local shop at night time to grab a pint of milk. It's almost certain that she was abducted during that trip and has been held captive over a prolonged period of time. You have all seen the photographs of the woman's condition when she was found – suffice to say, that period of captivity was both harsh and extreme.'

There were murmurings from the gathered detectives as the gravity of what Danny was saying registered with them.

He raised his hand for quiet and continued. 'We must look on this woman's identification as the starting point for this inquiry. I've already tasked DS Moore and others to look closely into the background of the victim, as well as her family and friends.'

He looked at Tina Cartwright and said, 'I'm not at all satisfied how the initial report of this woman's disappearance was investigated. I want you to take a team back up to Blyth and reinvestigate everything. I know this event happened six months ago, but somebody may remember something. I want you to establish the route to and from the shop that she would have taken and to start door-to-door inquiries along that route. I want the people living there questioned properly. Somebody in Blyth may have vital information about this, and the reason we don't know about it yet is because they've never been asked the question.'

'Okay, boss.'

He then turned to Rachel and said, 'I want you, Jane and Fran to now concentrate on the other missing-from-home files. I'm still worried about this "number four" comment. My fear is that other women may have been abducted by this maniac and are still being held captive somewhere. Go through the files again. This time, try and find misper reports where the circumstances appear similar to the disappearance of Fiona Wright.'

'Will do, sir.'

'Okay, everyone. See your supervisors for individual tasks. This is going to be a busy day, so let's get cracking.'

25

6.30am, 12 October 1986
Sunnybank Cottage, White Gate Farm, Misterton, Nottinghamshire

Sam Morgan stomped around the basement, cursing his luck. It had been six days since he had snatched number two and she was also proving to be useless. He had spent weeks watching her leave the pub every night and walk home alone. She'd looked ideal.

On the very first morning after he had snatched her off the street, she had laid on the bed in the cellar and rambled on about needing an injection for something. He didn't understand what she was saying and just shouted at her to get up. She had tried to stand up but had collapsed straight away, so he had manacled her to the bed again and stormed out in frustration.

She hadn't moved off the bloody bed ever since.

Every time he had checked on her, she had been the same. She constantly wet the bed and moaned about being thirsty, wanting water all the time.

He had changed the bedding once, but when she wet the bed again, he had scolded her in the same way his mother had scolded him. He told her she had made the mess, she could lie in it.

She had turned out to be even more useless than number one.

He stalked over towards the bed, disgusted by the strong smell of urine, and said to the woman, 'Are you going to get up off that stinking bed today?'

There was no response.

He looked closer and could see there were red, open sores breaking out on her face, neck and hands.

He shook her roughly and growled, 'I'm warning you; you'd better be up by the time I get back, or you'll be in serious trouble. I'm not happy with you at all.'

She still didn't respond. Her eyelids flickered a little, but that was it.

He had tried to use the words he remembered his mother using when she had scolded him for being naughty. It had always made him do as he was told; he hoped it would work on number two.

The woman didn't stir or react to his veiled threats, so he gave up. He stomped back up the stone steps, switched off the light and locked the cellar door.

He had a long day ahead of him. There were Brussel sprouts to harvest in field eight. It was the one job on the farm he hated doing. It was back-breaking work that made his hands so sore, they bled.

As he left the cottage, he had no comprehension that the woman in the cellar had slipped into a diabetic coma. Deprived of her life-saving insulin for so many days, it was only a matter of time before she suffered cardiac arrest and died on that urine-stained bed in the dark cellar.

26

10.00pm, 12 October 1986
Sunnybank Cottage, White Gate Farm, Misterton, Nottinghamshire

He shoved the empty plate roughly across the kitchen table and picked up the pewter tankard. He gulped the remaining beer down and slammed the vessel down on the table. The combination of the gassy beer and the acidic strong onion in his cheese and onion sandwiches caused him to belch loudly.

With his stomach full and his thirst sated, he examined his sore and broken hands. The fingers were red and cracked on the ends, and the backs of his hands were covered in a myriad of cuts and scratches.

He would have at least another two days working in field eight, picking the first crop of sprouts. The weather forecast predicted heavy frosts for the next two nights. The perfect time to harvest the crop was when they were still covered in a white frost.

He cursed under his breath at the prospect and filled a bowl with hot water and disinfectant. He would soak his gnarly hands and then check on number two. The woman in the cellar hadn't made a sound since he had arrived home.

He poured the disinfectant into the hot water and watched as the strong chemicals turned the water milky. He decided to go and check on the woman first, then he could take his time soaking his busted and painful hands.

He filled a plastic beaker with cold water and unlocked the cellar door. Flicking on the light switch at the top of the stone steps, he trudged slowly down into the gloomy room.

The stench was almost unbearable. The smell of urine had now been joined by the smell of faeces. He wrinkled his nose in disgust, both at the smell and the fact that the woman was still lying on the bed.

He placed the mug of water on the stone floor, next to the bucket the woman was supposed to use as a toilet. The bucket was empty.

His frustration got the better of him. He yelled, 'You lazy cow! I left the bucket here close to the bed and you still can't be arsed to get up and use it. Oh no, you'd rather lie in your own shit all day!'

There was no response from the bed.

He stepped closer and shook her shoulders. Still not a sound. Getting angrier, he roughly turned the woman on her back.

Her mouth gaped open; her eyes were staring up at the ceiling.

He had seen his mother, moments after she had died, and number one when she was dead. He now recognised the pale, waxy colour of the woman's skin and the glassy film on her eyes. He knew it was the look of death. Number two was dead.

He stepped away from the bed. He couldn't understand what had happened. He had given her food and water to drink every day. Granted, she hadn't eaten much, but she had drunk what seemed like gallons of water. He had never hit her, and yet now she was dead.

Number two had been a disaster. Only when he was sure she would be perfect had he snatched her, and in less than a week she was dead.

He cursed his bad luck and kicked the plastic beaker of water across the cellar floor.

Any thoughts of soaking his battered hands were forgotten. He began the morbid task of wrapping the woman's body in the soiled bedclothes, ready to carry out of the cellar to the Land Rover.

With another dawn start scheduled for tomorrow, he would need to get rid of her body tonight.

He stomped back up the stairs, his mood worsening by the second. Grabbing the keys for the Land Rover, he trudged outside into the cold night air. It was a clear sky, and the predicted frost was already starting to form on the windows of the vehicle. He started the engine and reversed as close as he could to the front door of the cottage. He went back downstairs and began dragging the dead weight up the steps. He grabbed the woman over the blankets and hauled her feet first. Her head made a muffled thump as it hit every one of the stone steps.

Grunting loudly, he lifted the woman and threw her into the back of the vehicle, before throwing a long-handled shovel on top of her.

Slamming the door of the vehicle, he walked back in the house and grabbed his jacket; the air was already frigid, and his breath came out in white clouds. Climbing into the front seat, he started the engine and began the drive to Beckett Wood.

After twenty minutes, he had found the clearing where he had buried number one. He turned off the vehicle's lights and got out. The moon cast an ethereal white light over the clearing. The woods were silent apart from the scurrying sounds of night creatures as they moved through the fallen leaves.

Satisfied he was alone, he opened the rear door of the Land Rover. He grabbed the shovel and walked into the clearing. To his right, he could see the mound of earth where number one lay. He stepped away from that area, then thrust the shovel deep into the ground. The earth here was still soft, the surrounding trees not allowing the ground frost to form.

He quickly dug a shallow grave. Each thrust of the shovel into the soil pained his battered and sore hands, and he cursed his misfortune.

After ten minutes' toil, the grave was deep enough. He placed the shovel on top of the mound of freshly dug earth and trudged back to the Land Rover.

The smell from the soiled sheets wrapped around the body was disgusting, and he dry-retched as he lifted the woman from the rear of the vehicle. Hurling the body into the shallow grave, he immediately picked up the shovel and began piling the soil back into the hole, covering the dead woman.

When the hole was filled in, he grabbed handfuls of dead leaves and scattered them over the soil, concealing the shallow grave.

Without once looking back, he got into the Land Rover and began the journey back to the cottage. As he negotiated the rutted, winding track, his thoughts turned to what he should do next. He wondered if he would ever get a woman who would do what his mother had wanted and take care of him.

He suddenly felt exhausted. He needed to be up and working in field eight in less than six hours' time, ready for another day's hard graft.

27

10.00am, 11 September 1988
Nottinghamshire Police Headquarters

Adrian Potter gestured for Danny to sit down and said, 'I understand there's been a development in your Retford abduction inquiry.'

'Yes, sir. The woman has now been positively identified by her husband. It would appear she was abducted six months ago and has been missing ever since.'

'I'm sure that's all good news, chief inspector. The development I was referring to is that the woman in question is now likely to make a full recovery from her injuries. It means you can now concentrate solely on finding the person responsible for the murder of Margaret White. I don't understand why you're ploughing all these resources into something that isn't even a murder inquiry. You're spending a fortune on what is, in effect, a missing person case. And now you've identified this woman, I think it's time to move on. Bottom line – no murder, no MCIU involvement.'

Danny wasn't shocked at Potter's cold assessment of the case, but he wasn't about to give in without a fight.

He leaned forward and locked eyes with Potter. 'Sir, there's much more to this case than a straightforward missing-from-home inquiry. Fiona Wright was snatched off the street and held captive for six months in what must have been appalling conditions. Somewhere out there is a maniac abducting and holding women. We need to stop him.'

'Woman, not women,' Potter corrected.

'When Fiona Wright was found, she said something disturbing. She intimated there were other women being held captive. You must allow the MCIU to investigate this properly. I'm convinced there are other victims who are related to this woman's abduction and imprisonment, sir. If I'm right, we could still be dealing with the potential murder, or murders, of other women.'

'That's an enormous *if*, chief inspector. How are things progressing with the White murder?'

Frustrated that Potter had steered the conversation straight back to the Margaret White inquiry, he said, 'We're still working hard, exhausting the house-to-house inquiries. There are several new leads we're pursuing, and we've finally located the "missing" exhibits from the previous murder at Warsop. This could be a huge help to the current investigation. We're still waiting for an update on the samples we submitted to the FSS, so there's still a lot more work to do. Nothing about the Margaret White inquiry is being neglected, or put on hold, to investigate the Retford abduction, sir. We need to keep going on both investigations. I know if it eventually becomes a choice between the two inquiries I'll have to drop the abduction. Right now, that isn't the case. The MCIU can professionally investigate both inquiries, in tandem.'

Potter was thoughtful, sitting back in his chair and folding his arms.

Eventually, he sighed and said, 'Danny, I know you understand the political implications involved with the White inquiry, so let's review the situation one week from now. In the meantime, if you get any breakthroughs from the FSS, I want to know immediately. Understood?'

'Understood.'

Danny left the office. As he strode away from the command corridor, he was quietly seething at his supervisor's callous, unfeeling approach to police work. It didn't matter how many times he had these meetings, he always left feeling appalled at how Potter made everything about the pounds and pence. The man was obsessed by money – to the detriment of everything else.

Still feeling disgruntled at having to go cap-in-hand to Potter to ensure the inquiries into Fiona Wright's abduction could continue alongside the Margaret White murder inquiry, Danny made his way to the scenes of crime department. He sought out Tim Donnelly and found the supervisor in his office, eating a sandwich.

Danny knocked once on the open door and stepped inside the office. Tim hastily put the sandwich back in its wrapper and said, 'You'll have to excuse me, boss. I haven't had chance to eat anything today.'

Danny smiled and said, 'Finish your late lunch. We can talk as you eat. I was at headquarters, so I thought I'd call in and see what progress you've made on the Misterton job.'

'Good timing. I've just received the report from the FSS about the blanket found on the woman.'

'And?'

'The blood stains on the blanket match the control sample provided by the hospital staff.'

'So, the only blood on the blanket is Fiona Wright's?'

'Yes.'

'Anything else?'

'They've lifted numerous fibres that are alien to the fibres that make up the blanket. They may come in handy later, as and when you get a suspect.'

'I always admire your positivity, Tim. Have you made any progress on the tyre tracks found in Beckett Wood?'

'It will be difficult to match the tracks we found to an individual tyre. The casts we took just weren't good enough. The mud was too wet. Better news on the type of vehicle we believe left the tracks. It looks like a wide wheel-base Land Rover. Possibly an old-style Land Rover Defender.'

'How sure are you?'

'Like I said, "possibly". I couldn't sit here and say that's definitely it, but again, it's worth bearing in mind for the future, should your inquiries reveal such a vehicle later.'

'Is it worth me doing a check on all Land Rover Defenders registered to people in that area?'

'You could. But like I say, we couldn't definitively identify the tyre on the vehicle, so it might be a pointless exercise.'

'I'll give it some thought. Sounds like you and your staff have been putting in the hours, but you still haven't found the breakthrough piece of evidence I was hoping for.'

Tim shook his head. 'Afraid not, boss.'

'As I always say, you can only find what's there. Anything back from the FSS on the Margaret White murder?'

'I chased them yesterday afternoon. They are dealing with a huge backlog of cases, but it shouldn't be much longer.'

'Keep chasing them, Tim. Did you get the latest submissions from Fran Jefferies?'

'I did. I passed the bedding from the Florence King murder to the FSS this afternoon and informed them that it's imperative we get a DNA profile from the semen on the bedsheets, if possible. As soon as they get back to me and inform me it's viable to raise a DNA profile, I'll task them with comparing it with the profile obtained from the Margaret White murder.'

'Good work, Tim. Enjoy the rest of your sandwich.'

Danny cut a dejected figure as he made his way back to the car park. Hopefully, the inquiries he had tasked his staff with following the identification of Fiona Wright would yield that much-needed breakthrough. With Potter so keen to close the inquiry down, Danny knew that breakthrough needed to come sooner rather than later.

28

10.00pm, 11 September 1988
Mansfield, Nottinghamshire

Danny readjusted the pillows and sat up in bed. His mind was in a turmoil and he knew that sleep wasn't going to come any time soon.

He stared into the darkness of his bedroom, trying to find some order to his thoughts. He felt Sue stir in bed next to him. She turned to face him and said, 'What's wrong?'

He whispered back, 'Nothing. Everything's fine; go back to sleep.'

'I'm awake now, so start talking. What's the problem?'

'It's just a work thing.'

Sue also rearranged her pillows and sat up. 'So, talk to me. It's obviously troubling you. Maybe talking it through will help.'

He put his arm around his wife and said, 'I'm running two inquiries. The first is the murder of an old lady at Clipstone that may be connected to a previously unsolved murder from four years ago. On top of that, I'm also investigating the abduction of a woman in the north of the county. My problem, and what's troubling me, is that Potter wants me to drop the abduction inquiry and concentrate everything on the murder inquiry.'

'Are the two cases connected in any way? Is the abduction of the woman linked with the two murders?'

'There's no connection that we've found, and I don't expect there to be one.'

'Well, in that case, I think Potter's got a point. Surely the murder is the more important.'

'It's not that simple. I can't explain it, but I know there's something more to this abduction case. I'm convinced there are multiple other victims of the man responsible, and my big fear is that some of them are dead, or at the very least at risk of dying.'

'What are you basing this gut instinct on? Or is it just that – a gut feeling?'

'Part of it is just that, an instinct. It all stems from a comment made by the abduction victim when she was first found. She said, "I'm number four." This woman was abducted and held captive somewhere for months. She was starved and beaten, then left for dead in woodland. If her comment meant there were other victims, I've got to find them, hopefully before it's too late.'

Sue was silent for a while before saying, 'Have you told Potter what you think?'

'I've tried. He's getting pressure from above to solve the murders, and he's passing that on to me, trying to dictate how I run the two inquiries.'

Sue snuggled into Danny's side and whispered, 'Trust your instincts, Danny.'

29

10.30pm, 11 September 1988
Wheatfield Crescent, Mansfield Woodhouse, Nottinghamshire

The man slipped across the dark field towards the bungalows. The field had only just had its crop of barley harvested and the remaining stubble made it treacherous to walk over.

It had been almost two weeks since he had killed the woman at Clipstone. He had spent the last seven nights carefully observing the bungalow.

Prior to that, he had driven around the streets searching for the usual tell-tale signs of an elderly resident: gently sloping paths from the front door to the pavement; metal handrails along those paths and at the side of the front door.

As soon as he had spotted the bungalow on Wheatfield Crescent, he knew the location would be perfect. The property backed onto open farmland and there was only a low fence that separated the farmer's field from the low-maintenance rear garden.

He had spent those nights observing activity at the property. On several occasions, he had seen the elderly woman who lived there. She looked to be in her late sixties or early seventies, and obviously lived alone. There had been no visitors to the property during the entire time he had watched it. He now knew everything about the woman's night-time routine.

The property was perfect.

The woman was perfect.

She bore a striking physical resemblance to the root of all his troubles, and it was time for her to be punished again. Whenever he felt depressed and sick of his existence, he sought relief by seeking to punish the source of all his guilt.

He had thought by killing that source, in the first place, it would end his problems, and he would be able to continue his life without the enormous guilt that weighed him down every day.

When he had first killed five years ago, the sense of relief had been enormous, but it hadn't lasted. He soon became aware that the only way the relief could be sustained was if he repeated the process, so he had killed another elderly woman.

After that second killing at Warsop, the move away from the area had been a welcome one. After four years away, he had returned to the isolated property that had been the family home and was now owned by him. The detached house was located outside the village of Old Clipstone. It was hidden from view and set well back from the lane that led to the small hamlet of Gorsethorpe.

He had returned to the house one month ago, after four years working abroad. The familiar feelings of depression and guilt hadn't taken long to bubble to the surface.

Spending time at the old house had rekindled too many bad memories of the abuse he had suffered as a child. He knew there was only one way he could assuage those feelings, and two weeks ago he had killed again. He would be leaving in the morning, so tonight would be his last chance to bury those guilty feelings.

As he approached the bungalow, he felt for the plastic bag in his overalls' pocket. Both the bag and the cable tie were there. Even though he wore industrial gloves, he could feel the items were safely in place.

He reached the low fence and stared at the bungalow that was in complete darkness.

That wasn't right.

There should be a low light still on, in what was the main bedroom. The old lady always kept the light on when she went to bed. With his anxiety levels rising, he climbed over the low fence and approached the property. He felt for the small pair of cutters in his pocket and snipped the telephone cable.

He had already selected which window to enter the property by. He knew it led into the kitchen and wouldn't cause him a problem. He reached up and tapped the glass of the transom window with the same pair of cutters. There was a barely audible crack as the glass broke. He carefully began removing the shards of glass from the frame, throwing them onto the lawn behind him. As soon as he had cleared enough glass, he reached through and undid the larger window below the transom.

With the window open, he slipped through and made his way inside the bungalow.

There was no sign of the old woman anywhere. The bed hadn't been slept in, there was no food in the fridge and every electrical appliance had been unplugged. He suddenly realised that the woman wasn't there.

There were any number of reasons why she wasn't there. An overnight trip to see friends? A week away at the seaside? A hospital appointment?

He felt a surge of rage sweep over him, as he realised there was no way he would be able to ease his pain tonight. He cursed under his breath and made his way out of the property and back onto the farmer's field.

He stomped moodily across the field to where he had parked his car in a layby on Peafield Lane. By the time he got into his car, he had calmed down. He would be leaving at four o'clock in the morning and wouldn't return until April next year.

He started the car and made a silent promise to revisit the old lady upon his return. Right now, he needed to pack everything he would need, ready for his journey north.

30

10.40pm, 11 September 1988
Manton Estate, Worksop, Nottinghamshire

Sam Morgan had parked the Land Rover at the junction of Edinburgh Road and Spur Crescent, near the centre of the sprawling estate. From his location, he had a clear view of the only shop that was open at this time of night.

This was the third night he had been on the estate. He had spotted the woman leaving the shop as it closed on the first night. Keeping a discreet distance, he had made the decision to follow her.

She had left the shop alone and walked along Spur Crescent before turning left onto Kingston Road. He had watched as she walked slowly along the dimly lit street until she went into one of the houses near the end of Kingston Road.

She had followed the same routine the next night, and he

had made his mind up that if she left the shop alone again tonight, he would make his move on Kingston Road.

Two hours ago, he had gone into the shop and purchased a loaf of bread. He was happy to see the same woman serving behind the counter. She was on her own in the small shop, but there was an open door that led into the rear of the shop. As he paid for the loaf, he heard a man's voice shout, 'It's quiet tonight, Doreen. Why don't I shut the shop at ten thirty and you can get away a bit earlier?'

As she handed the customer his change for the bread, she had shouted over her shoulder, 'Whatever you think, Mr Cole. It's your shop.'

He had accepted his change and was smiling broadly as he left the little corner shop.

The woman looked perfect. She was in her mid-thirties, sturdily built, with short, chestnut brown hair. She had sounded strong and confident. He knew she would be able to look after him, cook his meals and keep house for him. If his mother had been with him, she would have approved of his choice.

He had waited patiently in the darkness. After what seemed an age, he saw the lights of the shop go out, plunging the street into darkness. He watched in his rear-view mirror as the woman stepped outside and waved as the door closed behind her. He glanced at his cheap, battered wristwatch; it was now almost ten forty. The woman crossed the road and walked onto Spur Crescent, passing his Land Rover as she did so. Just before she reached the junction with Kingston Road, he started the engine and began following the woman, but still at a distance.

He steered the Land Rover onto Kingston Road and saw the woman was now about fifteen yards away. He scanned the street ahead. It was empty. He accelerated and then stopped the vehicle sharply, immediately behind the woman. It was obvious she had been startled by the engine noise and the sudden appearance of the scruffy vehicle. She had stopped walking and looked nervously over her shoulder.

Jumping from the vehicle, he grabbed her from behind, pinning her arms and dragging her back towards the vehicle.

Even though he was much bigger and stronger, he had badly underestimated the strength and fight in the woman. She instantly began to scream and struggle violently, trying to tear away from his vice-like grip. She reached backwards and clawed at his face with sharp nails. He cried out in pain and was about to punch her when he heard a man's voice shout, 'What the fuck's going on out there?'

Still gripping the struggling woman, he looked around and saw lights in several of the nearby houses coming on. He could also hear heavy footsteps approaching from a couple of those houses.

In panic, he punched the screaming woman, knocking her down and leaving her spread-eagled on the ground, before running back to the Land Rover. Just as he got in the vehicle, he saw the first man emerge onto the road from one of the nearby gardens. This neighbour stepped out onto the road, about twenty yards in front of him, refusing to move. Feeling backed into a corner, he slammed his foot down on the accelerator. The vehicle sped along Kingston Road.

As he passed the man, who was now standing in the middle of the road, he caught sight of a baseball bat in his hands. There was a loud bang as he sped past the man. He looked in the rear-view mirror and could see the man now sprinting after the vehicle, still waving the makeshift club. He changed gear and accelerated harder, leaving the chasing man in his wake.

As he drove away from the Manton estate, he cursed his bad luck.

31

11.10pm, 11 September 1988
Manton Estate, Worksop, Nottinghamshire

As the first police patrol car arrived at the scene, it was pandemonium. A small crowd had gathered on Kingston Road, and as PC Jack Hales got out of the vehicle he could feel a palpable sense of anger emanating towards him and his colleague PC Vicky Kirk.

An angry man approached the officers, waving his fist. 'You took your bloody time! If this had happened at the posh end of town, you'd have been there in no time.'

Jack Hales was an experienced officer who understood the dynamics of dealing with an angry mob. He raised his hands in a placatory gesture and said firmly, 'The report I got was that a woman had been attacked by a person driving a Land Rover. Now what would you have me do? Drive straight here and talk to you? Or try and find the offender's vehicle first?'

The angry man calmed down a little, but there was still an elevated level of hostility in his voice when he asked, 'And did you find it?'

'Not yet, but our colleagues are still out there searching. We're here now to try and establish exactly what happened.'

A woman approached the officers and said, 'Some bloody maniac tried to drag me into his car, to do God knows what to me, that's what happened. Now what are you going to do about it?'

Vicky Kirk spoke directly to the woman. 'Is there somewhere quiet we can go, where I can talk to you properly and you can tell me exactly what happened? My colleague will stay here and find out what he can from your neighbours. Now, first things first. What's your name?'

'My name's Doreen Smedley. I live about six houses down. We can go there to talk, but I'll have to go in and put the dog out the way first.'

'No problem, Mrs Smedley. Let's go.'

As Vicky Kirk and Doreen Smedley walked away, the crowd on the street immediately started to disperse. Jack Hales smiled to himself at how quickly his colleague had defused what had initially been a tense situation.

The angry man who had confronted him when he first arrived was also starting to walk away. Jack caught up with him and said, 'Just a second. Did you see this Land Rover?'

'Yeah, I saw it and I tagged it, so you lot can find it easier.'

'Tagged it?'

'Tagged. As it drove past me in the road, I smashed the rear near-side light cluster with my persuader.'

'And what, exactly, is your persuader?'

The man allowed a grin to form on his hard face. 'It's just a little something I keep next to my bed at night, to persuade anybody who breaks into my gaff that they've made a mistake.'

Jack laughed aloud and said, 'I see. And are you sure you smashed the rear light?'

The man pointed down at the road and said, 'There's enough bits of red glass down there, so yeah, I tagged it good.'

Jack took an envelope from his uniform pocket and began selecting bits of the glass from the road.

He looked over his shoulder at the man and said, 'Nice work, mate. What's your name?'

'I'm surprised you don't know. Are you new here or something?'

'I spend most of my time in the town centre, so fairly new to the Manton estate, I suppose.'

'I'm Terry Jackson. Your colleagues at the nick will tell you all about me. I've been a bit of a bad lad in the past, but I'm too old for all that brawling and fighting shit now. Mind you, I would have made an exception for that dirty bastard. Grabbing our Doreen like that.'

'Sounds like you and your neighbours coming out certainly put paid to his nonsense. Did you get a look at the driver of the Land Rover?'

'Nah, not really. As you can see, the street lights around here are crap. He was a big fucker, though. I saw him as he jumped in the Land Rover, but I wouldn't recognise him again.'

'Will you make a statement saying what you saw?'

'Not really arsed about doing that, mate. You seem alright, but I make it a rule never to talk to coppers. No offence.'

'None taken. But what if this nutter comes back onto the estate and tries to snatch another woman, only this time there's nobody around to stop him? I need your help to catch the dirty bastard and get him locked up. That way, he won't be able to hurt anyone else.'

There was a long pause as the local hardman thought about what the officer had said. He tutted loudly, then said,

'Okay. But just this once. Come inside and take your bloody statement. I'm not promising I'll go to court, though. Excuse the mess when you come in.' He cracked the same grin, winked and continued, 'It's the maid's day off.'

Jack laughed at the man's joke and said, 'Cheers, Terry.'

32

8.00am, 12 September 1988
MCIU Offices, Mansfield, Nottinghamshire

DC Fran Jefferies knocked politely on Danny's office door. In the past she would have knocked once and walked in. Today, she remained waiting at the door until Danny opened it. She was carrying a large folder in one hand and leaning on her walking stick with the other, so needed help to open the door.

Danny had been talking to DI Buxton about the planned inquiries for the day. He opened the door and took the folder, saying, 'Good morning, Fran. Come in and take a seat. Is this everything for the morning briefing? Anything interesting?'

As permanent office manager now, following her injury on duty, it was one of her daily tasks to collate incidents overnight that might be of interest to the head of the MCIU. It included arrests and crimes of interest, gathered from every division in the county.

'Yes, boss. There was an attempted abduction last night in Worksop that I think you'll be very interested in.'

'Let's start with that, then, shall we?'

Fran took out the details from the folder and said, 'It happened on the Manton estate, in Worksop, just before eleven o'clock. The intended victim was a woman named Doreen Smedley. She had closed the late shop on the estate and was walking to her address on Kingston Road when she was attacked.'

Danny was thoughtful and said, 'You said "attempted" abduction. What happened to stop it?'

'Ms Smedley is in her mid-thirties and sounds like an incredibly strong woman. When she was attacked, she fought back and raised enough of a ruckus to alert some of her neighbours. One of those neighbours heard the commotion, came out onto the street and chased the offender off.'

'Who's the good Samaritan?'

Fran flicked over the page and said, 'He gave his name as Terry Jackson.'

Rob Buxton said, 'Not *the* Terry Jackson?'

Danny said, 'Do you know him?'

'If it's the Terry Jackson I'm thinking of, I'm amazed he spoke to the police long enough to give his name.'

Fran said, 'He did more than that, boss. He made a full statement to PC Hales about what happened. Apparently, he chased the man off and damaged the vehicle the offender was using in the process.'

'What was the vehicle?'

'An old-style Land Rover.'

Hearing the vehicle type, Danny remembered his conversation with Tim Donnelly. The tyre tracks found in Beckett Wood were possibly from a Land Rover. He looked at Rob. 'Tell me about Terry Jackson.'

'Terry was always the local hardman on the estate.

When I worked on the CID in Worksop, I dealt with him a few times for serious assaults. Back then, Terry was very handy with his fists and wasn't slow in using them. He was never dishonest – just trouble with a capital T.'

'How well do you get on with him?'

'We're fine. I don't suppose I'm on his Christmas card list, but we always got on okay. I always treated him fairly and he knows that. Why?'

'I want you to drive up to Manton and speak to him. Take the officer's statement with you and see if you think there's anything else you can get from Mr Jackson.'

Danny turned back to Fran and said, 'Has Doreen Smedley made a statement?'

'Yes. The victim's statement was obtained by PC Kirk. I've read it, it's very comprehensive. There's a good description of the vehicle used by the offender. It's not so good of the offender, though. I don't think she got much of a look at him, as he attacked her from behind.'

'Rob, take Jane Pope with you. She can speak to Ms Smedley again. Do some door-knocking while you're up there, and see if you can locate any other witnesses. Visit the shop where Ms Smedley works and see if they have any security cameras. It could be our offender has been watching his intended target and may have been in the shop. The tyre tracks located where Fiona Wright was found could have been made by a Land Rover, so we need to pay close attention to this report.'

Rob stood up. 'Okay, boss. We'll get straight up there.'

As Rob left, Danny turned to Fran and said, 'I know Rachel has finished her research into the outstanding missing persons reports. I want you to run this attempted abduction by her and ask her to pick out any similar scenarios on those outstanding missing persons reports.

Could be this man has a certain way of working and has done this before.'

'Okay, boss.'

'Have you found the samples from the Florence King post-mortem, yet?'

'Yes, boss. I found them late yesterday afternoon. The samples were stuffed in the bottom of one of the refrigerators at Bassetlaw Hospital mortuary. I've recovered the relevant ones, and I'll forward them on to the FSS later today.'

'How the hell did they get stuffed in there?'

'No idea, boss. One thought occurred to me: they could have been placed in there temporarily and then the inquiry was closed down before they were needed.'

'That's possible, I suppose. Will the samples still be viable?'

'They've been in the fridge, so they should be okay. The FSS will soon tell us if they're not.'

'Good work, Fran.'

33

9.30am, 12 September 1988
Manton Estate, Worksop, Nottinghamshire

The door opened slowly, and Terry Jackson snarled, 'Bloody hell. Detective Sergeant Buxton, I could do without seeing your ugly mug first thing in the morning.'

Rob Buxton grinned and said, 'And a good morning to you too, Terry. Any chance of a quick chat about what happened last night?'

'I said all I've got to say to that copper last night. It was something and nothing.'

'Sounds to me like you saved the day. From what the officer told me, if you hadn't acted so promptly poor Doreen would have been carted off by that nutter.'

Playing to Terry's ego worked. Rob saw him puff out his chest a little before saying, 'Anybody would have done it. It's not right for a bloke to attack a woman, is it?'

Jane Pope said, 'Dead right. It sounds like he was a big sod, as well. Not many men would have stepped up like you did.'

Terry Jackson beamed and said, 'Well, Mr Buxton knows, I've never been one to walk away from trouble, lass.'

Rob said, 'Very true. Come on, Terry. We won't take up much of your time. How about a quick chat over a brew?'

Terry pushed the door wider and said, 'Alright. I'll put the kettle on.'

Five minutes later, and the three were sat at the kitchen table with a mug of strong tea each.

Rob said, 'I've read the statement you made last night. Thanks for doing that, Terry.'

'Well, Doreen's my neighbour. She's a good lass.'

'What was it that made you go outside in the first place?'

'It was lucky, really. I'd just taken the ashes from the fire to the metal bin on the yard when I heard this car engine revving loudly and then the vehicle coming to a sharp stop. I thought something was going down, so I ran inside and grabbed my persuader. I was only gone seconds, but when I came back out I could hear all this screaming and shouting.'

Jane Pope asked, 'Could you tell it was a woman?'

'Definitely.'

'So, what did you do?'

'I ran out onto the street.'

Rob said, 'What did you see when you got there?'

'I saw Doreen on the floor and the big bloke getting into a Land Rover.'

'Did you know it was Doreen straight away?'

'Yeah, course I did.'

'What can you tell me about the man?'

'Not much, really. He was big – well over six feet tall and heavy set. He looked very strong, if you know what I mean.'

'What did you do next?'

'I could see Doreen trying to get to her feet, and then I heard the engine of the Land Rover being revved loudly. I knew he was going to drive off, so I stood in the road to try and stop him.'

'I take it he didn't stop.'

'Did he hell as like! He drove straight at me. The bloke's a fucking nutter.'

'So, what did you do?'

'I stepped out of the way and twatted the motor with my bat.'

Jane Pope asked, 'Your persuader?'

'Yeah. My baseball bat. Everyone on the estate's got one. You know that, Mr Buxton.'

Rob nodded. 'Do you know what part of the vehicle you hit?'

'I took out the nearside rear light cluster. Your copper picked up some of the glass last night. I smashed it good and proper.'

'Have you seen either the bloke, or the vehicle, on the estate before?'

'Never.'

'Anything about either that stands out in your memory?'

'Only that the bloke was a giant and the Land Rover was filthy dirty.'

'Do you know if any of your neighbours saw anything?'

'There were a few out on the street after it happened, but apart from Doreen, I was the only one outside when he drove off. She might have got a better look at that nutter.'

'Yeah, we're going to talk to her now.'

'Didn't you catch him last night, then?'

'No.'

'Bloody hell, so he's still out there then. I'll keep an eye out for the freak.'

'You do that, Terry, but make sure you give us a call if you see him or the vehicle again. I don't want you and your persuader to get busy again.'

Terry laughed aloud. 'As if I would, Mr Buxton. Like I said to that young copper last night, I'm too old for all that shit.'

'Cheers, Terry. Take care of yourself.'

34

10.15am, 12 September 1988
Manton Estate, Worksop, Nottinghamshire

Doreen Smedley looked tired and drawn when she opened the door. There was a livid purple bruise on her cheek and her top lip was swollen. Evidence of the traumatic incident the night before.

DC Pope held out her warrant card and said, 'Doreen Smedley, I'm DC Pope and this is DI Buxton. We're from the Major Crime Investigation Unit and we'd like to talk to you about what happened last night.'

'I've already spoken to the police last night. I'm feeling a bit tired today.'

Jane Pope persisted. 'I promise this won't take long. We'll be the detectives investigating this attack and we'd very much like to hear everything you can remember.'

'Okay, love. You'd better come in.'

Ms Smedley showed the detectives into a neat and tidy

lounge and said, 'Would you like a cuppa? I'm going to make myself one.'

'No, thanks. We've just been speaking to one of your neighbours about what happened, and he made us a brew.'

'Was it Terry? He saved me last night, bless him.'

Jane smiled and said nothing.

A few minutes later, Doreen Smedley returned with her cup of tea.

Jane said, 'Like I said, we want to know everything you can remember from last night.'

'The first thing I remember was the Land Rover coming to a stop right behind me. I'd never seen it on the street before.'

She paused to sip her hot tea, being careful not to spill any because of her bruised and swollen lip.

Jane said, 'Then what happened?'

'Next thing I know, I've been grabbed from behind. He pinned my arms to my side and started to drag me backwards. Whoever got hold of me, he was very strong. He just lifted me off the floor and tried to put me in the back of the Land Rover. I mean, I'm not fat, but I'm no lightweight either. He lifted me up like it was easy.'

'Then what happened?'

'I thought to myself, I'm not having this, so I started to fight back. I managed to free one arm and clawed at his face. I started hollering and shouting as loud as I could. Suddenly, he let go of me and punched me in the face, knocking me over. That's how I got this.' She pointed at her bruised face and shook her head.

'Why do you think he let go?'

'I could hear Terry's voice, shouting. He must have come out because of all the noise.'

'Then what happened?'

'I got to my knees and saw the Land Rover being driven off. I saw Terry jump out of the way and hit the vehicle.'

'Do you remember anything else?'

'Not really. My neighbours comforted me on the street at first. Then that police officer brought me home and wrote down what had happened. She was a lovely girl, very caring.'

Rob Buxton said, 'We're nearly done, Doreen, just a couple more questions. Have you seen the man who attacked you before?'

There was a long pause, then she said, 'I don't think so. He grabbed me from behind, so I never saw his face. There is one thing I remember, though: he smelled awful. He reeked of stale sweat and BO. I don't think he takes a bath very often.'

'Have you ever seen that Land Rover on the estate?'

'Never.'

'Have you noticed anybody hanging around when you leave the shop at night?'

'No. And I always walk home, as it's only a couple of streets to my house.'

'Does your shop have any security cameras?'

'There are cameras up, but they don't work. The owner put the empty camera boxes up hoping to deter a bit of shoplifting. To be honest, I think everyone on the estate knows they're dummy cameras.'

'Have you noticed any strangers in your shop lately?'

There was a long pause, then she said, 'I usually see the same people most nights. I do remember a man buying a single loaf of bread quite late last night. I don't recall ever seeing him in the shop before.'

'Would you recognise him again?'

'Probably not. I'm trying to picture his face now, and I can't. He was big, though, and wearing some sort of dark green overalls that were quite scruffy. Sorry I can't help more.'

'And the cameras in the shop are definitely dummy ones?'

'Yeah. Mr Cole, the owner, says he can't afford to buy proper ones.'

'Okay, Doreen. Thanks for talking to us this morning. I'll leave you our contact details, so if you think of anything else you can call us at the MCIU.'

'Do you think you'll catch him?'

'You've given us some things to go on, so hopefully we'll be able to track him down.'

'Good. The bloke's a flaming nutjob.'

35

10.15am, 12 September 1988
Sunnybank Cottage, White Gate Farm, Misterton, Nottinghamshire

Sam Morgan opened the pantry door and swore under his breath. He plucked the solitary egg from the basket and grabbed the fresh loaf of bread he had bought the night before. The old loaf in the bread bin was stale and starting to show signs of mould. He was ravenously hungry and knew this morsel wasn't going to fill him.

He threw the mouldy bread in the rubbish bin, then cracked the egg into the blackened frying pan. The pan was always on the stove and always had cold fat in it. He lit the gas and turned up the heat under the frying pan. He cut the end off the bread and then cut another two doorstep slices. As the egg quickly fried, he buttered the bread and made himself a mug of tea.

No food in the house meant he would have to go to the

big farmhouse and ask his uncle for money. The chickens were all at the farmhouse, too, and he would need to fetch fresh eggs. He hated shopping and tried to avoid it until the very last minute. Now was the last minute; he needed to go today. It always felt like people were staring at him as he walked round the supermarket.

When he went to the farmhouse, there would be hateful glares from his uncle's wife. It was obvious she loathed his presence so much, and he couldn't understand why. He always tried to be friendly with his young cousins and make them laugh. The last time he'd visited the big house he had taken them a present each. Their mother had got angry and thrown the corn dollies straight in the bin.

Just the thought of seeing that frightful woman filled him with dread. He placed the fried egg in between the two thick slices of bread and wolfed it down. He swallowed the last mouthful, then took a gulp of his hot tea.

Taking what was left of his tea, he stepped outside the cottage and sat on the bench near the front door. The sun was out, and it was already warm, perfect weather for the harvest. It was a busy time on the farm and he knew his uncle wouldn't be happy that he needed to take time away to get food.

As he finished his hot tea, his thoughts turned to the near disaster the night before. He still couldn't believe how hard the woman had fought when he grabbed her. He had thought she would be like the others and give up quickly. She had fought like a wildcat; at the memory, he involuntarily touched his cheek where her nails had raked his skin. Luckily, there were no marks on his face, but his cheekbone still felt tender to the touch.

Then there was that lunatic with the baseball bat standing in the road. He had thought he was going to smash the windscreen as he swung the bat.

When he had seen the police car, going so fast in the other direction, he'd felt sure they had seen him. He'd stared in the mirror of the Land Rover for a long time, convinced the police would be chasing him. He'd thought he was going to be caught. The whole episode had terrified him, and he had decided there and then to wait a few days before trying again.

As he thought about the police, he remembered that he needed to look for something today. When he had got home the night before, he thought about the solicitor his mother had told him about. The one he would need to call if he were ever in trouble with the police, or if there was ever any trouble on the farm, and he was being asked to leave. She had told him the solicitor would be able to help him and that his business card was in her bedside drawer. There was a phone number on the card that he would have to call.

He threw the dregs of his tea away and walked back in the cottage. He trudged upstairs and into his mother's bedroom. It was exactly as it had been on the day she died. He had made the bed and put her clothes back in the wardrobe, but otherwise it remained the same. He never went in the room unless he had to; he could feel his mother's presence and, for some reason, that unnerved him.

He would do what he always did when he was frightened and anxious: he began to count inside his head. Numbers comforted him. They had order. He always knew exactly what was coming next. As he silently counted off in his mind, he opened the bedside drawer and began searching. In his mother's pocket Bible, he found the card being used as a bookmark.

He stared at the fancy business card. It was black, and in gold letters was the name Frank Carruthers. There was a telephone number beneath the name. He slipped the card in his empty wallet and walked out of the bedroom.

As he walked down the stairs he began to count, this time aloud. As he said twelve, he stepped off the bottom step.

He grabbed his coat and walked to the Land Rover. If he went to the farmhouse now, his uncle would be there having his mid-morning snack. He could talk to him and wouldn't have to speak to his wife. The sooner he went to the shop and bought some food, the sooner he could be back at the farm, working.

36

10.45am, 12 September 1988
White Gate Farm, Misterton, Nottinghamshire

The woman's voice was full of spite and anger. 'When are you going to tell him to leave?'

'And I've told you till I'm blue in the face, he's harmless and a bloody good worker. He's also my nephew, and I promised my dying sister he would always have a job here. Let's not get into this again.'

The woman wasn't going to leave it that easily. She slammed the man's food down on the table in front of him and said, 'That stupid bloody promise, it's ridiculous. You don't see what I see. I've seen him skulking around the farmhouse, staring at the girls. I just don't trust him. There's something wrong with him. He's not wired up right.'

The man tried to ignore his wife and concentrated on eating the hot food. He had been surprised when he'd opened the door earlier and his nephew was standing there. He never came to the farmhouse, unless it was an emergency.

He had seen the way his wife had reacted when she saw him, so he had quickly given him a handful of banknotes and told him to help himself to eggs from the chicken coop before he went to the shop in Retford.

As soon as the man had driven away, his wife had started nagging.

He ate the last mouthful of sausage, fried egg and beans, used the cuff of his shirt to wipe his mouth and stood up.

His wife said, 'Are you going to bloody answer me? When are you going to tell him to leave?'

He could feel his own temper rising and he was glad both his daughters were already at school. He rounded on his wife and shouted, 'The boy stays!' He grabbed his jacket and continued, 'He has nowhere else to go. He stays!'

'I'm warning you. If you don't talk to him soon, I'll take the girls and go. I'm not risking them coming to any harm because of some half-arsed promise you made to your dying sister about her halfwit son.'

His temper diminished as he heard the serious tone of his wife's voice. He grabbed her shoulders and faced her. 'I don't want to argue about this. Let's talk about it properly tonight. I've got so much work to do today; you know how busy it is right now.'

He could see the intense anger in her blue eyes, and that tears weren't far away. He softened. 'I'll think about what you've said and see if there's a way I can get him to leave. I might be able to get him work on a neighbouring farm or something. I know you don't understand, but I owe the boy something.'

'Any obligations you have are to your own daughters. You owe them a safe place to live. That boy, as you call him, is a grown man, and as far as I'm concerned he's dangerous. He doesn't realise his own strength, and he doesn't understand what he's doing half the time. I mean it, either he goes, or me and the girls do. I'll take them to my dad's farm in Wales. Don't think I won't.'

'It won't come to that. I'll sort something out. It might take me a few weeks, but I promise I'll get it sorted.'

'Just get it done. I want him gone.'

The man was deep in thought as he walked out of the farmhouse. The shit had really hit the fan now, and he didn't know how he was going to resolve the problem of the boy without causing himself a mountain of trouble.

37

11.00pm, 7 March 1987
Ropery Road, Gainsborough, Lincolnshire

It had been another long day for Jessica Massey. She hated the afternoon shift at the textile factory where she worked. In fact, she hated every shift at the factory, but a job was a job and it paid the bills.

Ever since her useless boyfriend had walked out on her, she had struggled to make the payments on the bills for the small terraced house on Haldane Street. She was determined to keep the house, though, so she worked extra shifts whenever they were offered. She still had little money for nights out, makeup or other treats. She was barely surviving; food was always scarce, and she knew she had lost weight. She chuckled as she walked along the dark road at the thought of her losing weight. She had always been quite plump and curvy. Her lack of height accentuated the fact, but she was happy in her skin and wasn't the type of woman who constantly fretted about her weight.

As she walked along rod-straight Ropery Road, she could hear the river. The Trent ran alongside the road here, and she always enjoyed the fresh smell it made. It reminded her of happier times, when she was a child growing up at Saxilby. She had lived next to the canal there, with her mother and two sisters.

The happy memory didn't last long and was quickly replaced by a darker one. Thoughts of the care home she had been raised in, after the premature death of her mother, came to the surface. After that tragic event, at the age of eleven she had been separated from her two older sisters and lived for five years in the care of the local authority at Green Ridge Children's Home in Gainsborough.

She had moved out as soon as she was old enough and, having lost touch with her sisters, she had lived with several different men, constantly moving from one part of town to another.

Just after her twenty-fourth birthday, she had met the handsome Joe at a mutual friend's party. They had started dating, and when she moved in with Joe, eighteen months ago, it had been wonderful. She really thought she'd finally found her soul mate. Everything had been great at first, but very slowly things changed. He started to spend more and more time at the pub on his way home from work, spending money they couldn't afford. Their lack of cash led to bitter arguments. It had come as no real surprise when she had got home from work one day and found that he had moved out, taking all his stuff with him.

It was probably her background of being in care which made her so determined to keep the roof above her head.

Lost in all these thoughts as she walked along Ropery Road, Jessica didn't notice the Land Rover, parked with the engine running and the lights off, at the junction with Acland Street.

38

5.30am, 8 March 1987
Sunnybank Cottage, White Gate Farm, Misterton, Nottinghamshire

Jessica Massey had been awake for five minutes. She reached up and gingerly touched the back of her head. There was a distinct lump just behind her left ear and it felt very sore. She realised as she tried to touch her head that she was restrained. Her wrists and ankles were constrained by metal manacles, which were attached by lengths of chain to the wrought-iron bed she was now on.

Her eyes became accustomed to the darkness and she sat up, trying to take in her new surroundings. There was no light, natural or otherwise, so it was difficult to make anything out.

Sitting alone in the dark, she tried to make sense of what had happened. All she could remember was hearing a diesel engine behind her. The vehicle had come to a sudden stop and then some-

thing had hit the back of her head. She could remember a feeling of being lifted from the ground, and then nothing.

Suddenly, there was a sound above her head. She tensed up and concentrated on listening for the sound again. The noise she heard was the sound of a key being turned in a lock, and now a door on creaking hinges was slowly being opened.

The room was suddenly illuminated as a dim light was turned on. She could hear footsteps descending what looked like stone steps in the far corner of the room. A single light bulb suspended from the ceiling cast a feeble light. She could see she was in a basement, surrounded by stone walls.

She stared at the bottom of the stairs and saw the man for the first time as he emerged out of the gloom and stood under the light. He was a huge, barrel-chested man with a shock of scruffy, unkempt dark hair and a few days' growth of stubble on his face.

He didn't say a word, just stared at her. She shuddered as she looked at the man's dark eyes and wondered what was going to happen next.

She had been a survivor all her life and, although terrified, she tried to think of the best way to react to this giant's menacing presence.

The silence in the claustrophobic space was becoming unbearable, so she broke it. 'Why have you brought me here?'

The question was calm and her voice quiet.

The man paced up and down and looked agitated. He turned to face her and said in a soft, gentle voice that was at odds with his appearance, 'Are you going to do what I say?'

'Like what?'

'Will you cook for me?'

She was slightly shocked by the man's response. She thought eating would be the last thing on his mind.

Before she could say anything, he continued, 'Can you cook?'

'Yes, I can cook.'

'Good. I need you to cook nice food for me. If you do that, you can have some, too. No food for me, means no food for you.'

She nodded. 'Okay.'

There was a childlike manner about this huge man, which looked and sounded strange when compared to his physical presence.

She was almost scared to ask the question, but plucking up all her courage she asked, 'Is that the reason you've brought me here, to cook for you?'

The pacing stopped and he appeared to relax, becoming noticeably less agitated. He said, 'There will be other jobs for you to do. Washing, cleaning, stuff like that. I've brought you here so you can look after me.'

'Isn't there anybody else here to help you?'

'Not now. It's just me. Are you hungry?'

'I'm very thirsty.'

'I'll get you water. There's a bucket over there. If you need the toilet, use that.'

There was a silence, and then he said, 'Are you going to be trouble, number three?'

She shook her head and instantly regretted it, as she felt the throbbing pain at the back of her head again.

She said, 'I'll do as I'm told. You won't have to hit me again.'

'Yeah, sorry about that. Someone was coming, so I had to get you in the jeep quickly. Do as you're told and I won't hit you again. I don't like hitting.'

'Okay.'

'I'll get you a drink of water.'

She watched as the man trudged up the stone steps. He returned almost immediately, carrying a litre bottle of water.

He put the bottle next to the bed and said, 'I've got to work now. See you later.'

As he walked back up the stairs, she shouted after him: 'Will you leave the light on, please? I'm scared of the dark.'

The man didn't reply. The light stayed on, and she heard the key turn as he locked the door.

Jessica grabbed the bottle and took a long drink of the cool, fresh water.

Questions filled her head.

Where the hell was this place? Who was this giant who had snatched her off the street? How was she ever going to escape his clutches?

She needed to think, to work out the best way to survive.

39

9.00pm, 12 September 1988
MCIU Offices, Mansfield, Nottinghamshire

Danny, Rob and Rachel were the only ones left in the office. The three had remained behind to discuss the attempted abduction the previous night.

Danny said, 'How did you and Jane get on in Manton?'

Rob said, 'We spoke to Terry Jackson and Doreen Smedley again, and have a reasonable description of the vehicle used, and where it will be damaged. The description of the offender isn't great. None of the other neighbours we spoke to today managed to get a look at the offender's face. What they have all made comment on is how physically large he was. Sounds like a giant of a man.'

'Have you checked the computer to see if we have any indecency offenders in the area who match that description?'

'That thought did occur to me. So I conducted a speculative description search on the PNC for indecency offences. It didn't show any matches.'

'Let me have the full descriptions of the vehicle and the suspect in the morning. I'm going to put out another press appeal tomorrow. You never know, we might get lucky with the damaged vehicle.'

'We could arrange to visit all local garages and see if any Land Rovers have been brought in for repair.'

'Good idea. Arrange that with Worksop CID tomorrow morning.'

Danny looked at Rachel and said, 'I know it was a long shot asking for any similar scenarios on the missing persons files you've been looking at, but did you find any?'

'I've found three reports that are similar, in as much as they are all young women who went missing as they walked home alone at night. They all apparently disappeared without trace.'

'Are they all local?'

'Two from Nottinghamshire and one from Lincolnshire, just over the border.'

'Okay. I want you to talk to the officers currently investigating those reports. See what inquiries have been done, if any. If it's anything like the response when Fiona Wright went missing, it won't be much. I need to make sure that we aren't missing something glaringly obvious. Let me know when you've spoken to them all, and I'll decide if there's anything else we can do to investigate those missing persons reports better.'

'Will do, boss.'

'That's enough for one day; let's get off home. See you tomorrow at seven o'clock.'

The two detectives left the office, leaving Danny alone. His thoughts turned to the murder inquiries of Margaret White and Florence King. He took out photographs of the two murdered women, from their relevant files, and placed them side by side on his desk.

Staring at the photographs, he suddenly realised how closely they resembled one another. Both women were in their late sixties, both had collar-length, permed white hair, both were slightly overweight and just over five feet tall.

Danny continued to stare at the images, wondering if their physical appearance was anything to do with the reason a killer had targeted them. He placed the photographs back into the folders and grabbed his jacket. It was already late, and he needed to be back in the office early tomorrow morning.

40

7.30pm, 10 July 1987
Sunnybank Cottage, White Gate Farm, Misterton, Nottinghamshire

Jessica placed the huge dinner plate down in front of the man and poured gravy over the two pork chops and mountain of fresh vegetables.

The man said, 'This looks great. Pork chops are my favourite, and I'm starving.'

'I knew you'd be hungry. I've done the fat crispy, just how you like it.'

He swallowed a mouthful of mashed potato and said, 'Aren't you having any?'

'I'm dishing mine up now; I just like to watch you eat, that's all.'

He smiled and said, 'Get yours and eat with me. Tell you what, there's bottles of cider in the pantry which would go a treat with this. Why don't you pour us a couple of glasses?'

She dished up her own dinner, one pork chop and a much smaller portion of vegetables, before fetching a bottle of cider and pouring two pint glasses.

The chain she was secured by gave her just enough scope to sit at the table opposite him. It was annoying to feel the manacle on her wrist every time she raised her fork, but she said nothing. She never said or did anything to antagonise her captor. Her strategy for survival was to play the long game and bide her time. It was no real hardship, doing what she had to do. She ate well and was comfortable. He never threatened her or became violent towards her. In fact, she thought he was quite sweet-natured; it was just his sheer size that was intimidating.

She picked at her own food and studied him eating. Once again, the scar on his top lip from the repaired cleft palate was obvious. He had shaved a couple of days ago, and the scar, normally concealed by stubble, was once again evident. She had noticed how often his fingers touched the disfiguring scar and it was obvious he was troubled by his appearance.

Not wanting to provoke an angry reaction, she had never mentioned it.

He finished the last of the cider, let out a huge belch and said, 'Oops, excuse me. I think we both need another glass.'

The alcohol in the strong cider had given her a warm glow and she readily poured more of the amber-coloured liquid into their glasses.

As she placed the drinks on the table, he said, 'Get me a thick slice of bread, three. I want to mop up this gorgeous gravy.'

She was always surprised whenever he referred to her as 'three'. He had never asked what her name was. She cut a thick slice of bread and handed it to him. His huge appetite never ceased to amaze her. It was no wonder he was the size of a small outhouse.

The strong cider was beginning to make her feel a little tipsy.

Feeling emboldened, she said, 'Can I ask a big favour?'

As he shovelled the bread smothered in the thick gravy into his mouth, he spluttered, 'What favour?'

'Can I have a hot bath?'

'What?'

'I'd like a hot bath. I wash in freezing cold water every day and I'd love a soak in a hot bath. That's not too much to ask, is it?'

The man stared at her, finished the last of the cider and said, 'Why don't we both have another glass of cider and then I'll run you a hot bath. There's no chain in the bathroom, so I'll have to stay with you.'

The thought of soaking in a hot bath was way above any concerns she had about him being in the room, so she smiled and said, 'I'll get another bottle.'

She refilled the two glasses with cider, which they drank a little slower. When he had a quarter of the amber liquid left in his pint pot, he said, 'I'll run the bath.'

He returned a brief time later, picked up his pint pot and drained it. He took a key from his trouser pocket and unlocked the manacle on her wrist.

He said, 'The bath's through here. Come on.'

She walked into the bathroom and slipped her fingers in the water; it was very hot.

He slipped the bolt on the door, sat down on the toilet and said, 'Get in then, before it gets cold.'

With her head feeling slightly fuzzy from the strong cider, she slowly began to undress.

She stepped into the bath and sat down, allowing her naked body to become accustomed to the hot water. The temperature of the water instantly amplified the effects of the alcohol and she suddenly felt extremely light-headed.

She lay back and allowed the water to envelop her body. It felt wonderful. She half-closed her eyes and let out a long sigh.

He asked, 'Does that feel good, three?'

She opened her eyes and saw him staring at her. His eyes never leaving her large breasts, just under the water.

The strong cider had made her lose any inhibitions she may have had. With her judgement impaired, she said, 'You can touch them, if you like.'

She could see the colour instantly flush the big man's face and he shook his head.

She said, 'Go on. I don't mind.'

At the back of her mind, she wondered about the possibility of exploiting this situation to affect an escape. It was a vague hope that was probably based on alcohol consumption and not strategy.

Before she could change her mind, he had knelt by the side of the bath and cupped one large hand under her right breast. She could feel the calloused skin of his hands as he gently stroked her breasts.

She felt nothing as his rough hand brushed across her nipple. She shifted a little in the bath and he withdrew his hand abruptly and sat back on the toilet, saying, 'I'm sorry. I didn't mean to hurt you.'

She sat up and looked at him. She could see the uncertainty in his eyes.

He looked away and said, 'You need to get out now. I need to go to bed. I've got an early start tomorrow.'

Emboldened by the alcohol, she stood up in the bath and turned her naked body to face him. 'I don't mind you looking at me. Don't be shy.'

He handed her a large towel and said, 'Get dry, it's bedtime.'

She dried her body and her hair, then wrapped the towel around herself, picked up her clothes and followed him out of the bathroom.'

They walked in silence to the basement door. He flicked on the light and followed her downstairs.

She lay naked on the bed and he slipped the first manacle on her ankle.

Feeling like she was making a real connection with her captor, which could help her eventually escape, she touched his hand and said, 'Why don't you stay here with me?'

'What do you mean?'

'Stay with me tonight. I don't want to be on my own again.'

He sat down on the bed next to her and again coloured up.

The alcohol coursing through her body increased her desperation to try anything to escape. She didn't recognise her own voice as she said, 'Take your clothes off, turn off the light and stay here with me. I know you want to.'

Without answering, he stood up and walked up the stairs. The light was turned off, but there was no sound of a lock turning. Instead, she heard footsteps coming back down the stairs and then a rustling sound as he took off his clothes.

He sat down on the bed and she touched his naked back.

She grabbed his wide shoulders and pulled him gently down onto the bed next to her. For the first time, they felt the warmth of each other's naked bodies, in the dark.

41

3.00pm, 13 September 1988
MCIU Offices, Mansfield, Nottinghamshire

Danny was walking out of the office; he only had thirty minutes to get to headquarters for his appointment with the press liaison officer. He wanted to get the details of the attempted abduction in Manton out to the media.

Rachel saw him and called out, 'Have you got a minute, boss?'

'Not really. I need to be at headquarters. What's up?'

'I've been working on the missing-from-home reports that I told you about. I wanted to have a chat about the police response so far.'

'Can you tell me about them on the way to headquarters?'

'Of course. Let me grab my jacket and the files.'

A few minutes later, Danny drove the CID car out of Mansfield police station. Rachel sat in the passenger seat. As he drove onto the A60 Nottingham Road, Danny said, 'These missing-from-home reports. Was the police response as poor as it was for Fiona Wright?'

'It's mixed. There's one case, that's also in Manton, that Worksop CID have done a lot of work on.'

'Details?'

'A young teenage girl, Susan Claymore. She went to the youth club on the estate one night and never returned home.'

'Christ. When was this?'

'May the tenth, 1986.'

'That's over two years ago. What did the CID do when she was reported?'

'They conducted a thorough investigation at the time. Susan Claymore had never been missing before and was last seen at the youth club with a young tearaway named Billy Ayers.'

'I take it he's been spoken to?'

'He denied seeing her at first, but then said he'd spent some time with her behind the youth club, doing what teenagers do. He told detectives she had left him to catch the last bus home.'

'Did the detectives believe his account?'

'Yes, boss. They traced and interviewed the bus driver, and he didn't recall Susan Claymore getting on the bus. It's like she just disappeared into thin air.'

'That must have put Billy Ayers securely in the frame for her disappearance?'

'It did briefly, but those two weren't the only ones snogging at the back of the youth club. Another pair of young lovers corroborated that Billy and Susan had gone their separate ways when he said they did.'

'We'll need to reinvestigate this one. When we get back from headquarters, we'll sit down and go over everything in detail. I think I'm going to need a meeting with the Worksop detective inspector.' Danny paused for a minute, deep in thought, then he said, 'Are there many others?'

'To be honest, boss, I've found quite a few, which all fit the pattern of a young woman alone on the street, at night, disappearing. The scale of it is frightening.'

'I see. Are there any among them that really set the alarm bells ringing?'

'There's one that really stands out. A young woman, Emma Bridge, who went missing from Bawtry in South Yorkshire, just over the border.'

'What are the details?'

'Emma had a part-time job, working behind the bar at the Crown pub in the town. She walked the short journey home every night after her shift. On the sixth of October 1986 she never arrived home and hasn't been seen since.'

'No contact at all?'

'Nothing, and it gets worse. Emma Bridge suffers from type-one diabetes and needed daily insulin injections. At the time she went missing, she had no insulin with her.'

'Without insulin, wouldn't she be at risk of serious illness or even death?'

Rachel nodded. 'Exactly.'

Danny drove the car along the winding driveway that led into police headquarters. As he parked the car, he said, 'Let me get this press release organised for the local television stations. Then we'll make a start on what needs doing on these missing-from-home inquiries. Hopefully, this release will get a response from the public. At least we can now give a good description of the suspect vehicle, if not the offender.'

42

6.25pm, 13 September 1988
Honeysuckle Cottage, River Street, Walkeringham, Nottinghamshire

Angie and Ben Reid were in the kitchen of their small cottage, eating their evening meal. At the side of the kitchen table was a small portable television. The couple had been watching the evening news as they ate.

They were still living out of boxes, having only moved into the cottage ten days ago. Unpacking everything and getting settled into their new home, while holding down busy jobs, was taking longer than they had expected. The move itself had been easy. They had moved into their dream cottage from a terrace house just two streets away in the village of Walkeringham.

The local news was now on the television and the lead

story was of a man suspected of attempting to abduct a woman from Worksop.

Angie said, 'That sounds like the bloke who brought Pippin back to us in the woods. He was massive.'

'Yeah, but he didn't have a Land Rover.'

'We didn't see a Land Rover, but he could have had one. I told you at the time I thought there was something weird about him.'

'Worksop's miles from here, though.'

'It's not that far. I'm going to call the police.'

'Finish your dinner first, then call.'

'No. I'm going to call them now. Grab me a pen; there's a number to call.'

He passed her a pen, and she jotted the contact number down on the back of an envelope before walking from the kitchen to the hallway. She picked up the phone and dialled the number. It was answered on the second ring. A woman said, 'DC Jefferies, Major Crime Investigation Unit. How can I help you?'

'I've just seen the police appeal about the bloke who tried to snatch that woman in Worksop.'

'Okay. Do you have information on either the suspect or the vehicle?'

'It's somebody we saw hanging around some woods near us, just over a week ago. He returned our lost dog to us, but he was acting very strangely and was a bit weird.'

'Why do you think this man is connected to the incident in Worksop?'

'You've described the man in Worksop as being big. Well, the man we saw in the woods was like a giant. My husband's quite tall, but he looked small next to this man.'

'Did he say anything to you?'

'No, he was carrying our retriever by the scruff of its neck. That's not easy because she's quite heavy. He just put the dog down in front of my husband, turned round and walked back up the track into the woods. I shouted "Thanks", but he didn't turn round and just disappeared into the woods.'

'Have you seen this man before or since?'

'No. We take Pippin somewhere else for a walk now. I've got to be honest, that man really unnerved me. I didn't like to think of him lurking in the woods, watching me, while I was walking my dog. That's why I remembered seeing him because he was so scary.' Suddenly doubting herself, she continued, 'But I don't suppose it's anything.'

'Where did you see this man?'

Angie placed her hand over the receiver and shouted, 'Ben, where did we see that bloke? What's the name of the woods?'

Ben swallowed a mouthful of steak pie and shouted back, 'Beckett Wood.'

'Thanks.'

She removed her hand from the receiver and said, 'It's a place called Beckett Wood.'

The detective's voice suddenly took on a new urgency. 'Can you give me your contact details, please? I'm going to arrange for somebody to come and talk to you tonight.'

'Of course. We live at Honeysuckle Cottage, River Street, Walkeringham. My name's Angie Reid, and my husband's name is Ben.'

'Will you both be at home all evening, Mrs Reid?'

'Yes.'

'Okay. Somebody will be out to see you within the hour. Thanks for your call.'

43

8.00am, 20 August 1987
Sunnybank Cottage, White Gate Farm, Misterton, Nottinghamshire

It was the third morning in a row that Jessica had been sick. It wasn't like the food poisoning she had experienced before, when she couldn't stop vomiting. This was more like a general feeling of nausea. She'd been physically sick each time she had tried to wash up the breakfast dishes after the man had left the cottage.

Each day was now a mundane routine. The man would wake her up just after five o'clock every morning, wait until she got dressed, then order her upstairs to the kitchen.

Once in the kitchen, he would place the single manacle on her right wrist that kept her restrained but allowed her to move around the kitchen, attached to the length of chain.

She never resisted or made a fuss. It was her way of surviving, of continuing to live with the strange man who had imprisoned her, to enslave her. There had been no repeat of the cider-fuelled sex she had experienced with her captor. He seemed totally disinterested in sex. He never spoke about that night, and she never raised the subject. She noticed that he had never suggested drinking alcohol with their evening meal again.

The sex that night had been over as soon as it started. No sooner had he entered her than he had climaxed. Afterwards, he lay on the small bed next to her, not saying a word. When she had tried to put her arms around him, he stood up, got dressed and walked slowly up the cellar steps, ignoring her pleas to come back.

She felt ridiculous that she had allowed it to happen, in the forlorn hope he might have fallen to sleep afterwards, enabling her to get the key from him to release the manacle that bound her.

The next morning, he behaved as though nothing had ever happened.

It had been the same routine ever since. Get up, prepare breakfast, tidy the kitchen, prepare lunch, do whatever tasks he wanted doing, laundry or anything else he requested.

Then she would prepare the evening meal, having it ready for when he finished work. Once she had tidied the kitchen, after the meal, he would unlock her from the single manacle and take her back down into the cellar. At least he only used one manacle to secure her to the bed now. It was so much easier to sleep with just the one manacle on her right ankle.

There was never any conversation. Just orders that he wanted fulfilling. Whenever she tried to talk to him, he just ignored her and continued eating.

At no time did he ever leave the keys for the manacles anywhere. They were always in his trouser pockets. There was no way she could get them and free herself. She still had no idea where she was being held. All she could see out of the kitchen window was countryside.

There were never any visitors to the remote cottage. Not even the postman called at this lonely place.

She was still being fed and watered, and he had never abused her physically. She had no idea how long she'd been captive, but she knew it was months, not weeks. There was no choice but to continue to play the long game. Eventually, there would be a chance, a moment, where she could get away. She had to be ready to seize that moment, whenever it arrived.

As she considered the length of time she'd been held captive at the cottage, she had a worrying thought. Her period was now well overdue. She couldn't be sure, but she thought she had missed two now.

A rising sense of panic swept through her brain. Surely, she wasn't pregnant from that single night, that one crazy, alcohol-fuelled fumble in the darkness.

She sat down heavily on one of the wooden chairs at the kitchen table.

Thoughts flooded her mind. How would she cope with the pregnancy and giving birth? How would pregnancy alter the dynamic between her and her captor? She knew he wouldn't be able to process the thought of her having a baby, and it terrified her.

She stood up and undressed. She looked down at her stomach and could already see it appeared larger. A little less flat than normal. She knew enough about pregnancy to know that it was impossible for her to see any changes yet. She chuckled at her own vivid imagination and slowly picked up her clothes.

Getting dressed again, she scolded herself for her worrisome nature. It was a ridiculous notion to think she was pregnant. She had made love, without taking precautions, with various men over the years, and never fallen pregnant. To imagine that she was now pregnant after those few minutes of drunken fumbling was just stupid.

No, her period would start soon enough. There was nothing to worry about.

44

8.00pm, 13 September 1988
Honeysuckle Cottage, River Street, Walkeringham, Nottinghamshire

After speaking to Fran Jefferies, Andy Wills had offered to visit the couple who had phoned in with information. Walkeringham village wasn't far from where he lived, so he could visit and speak to them on his way home.

The cottage was in darkness, save for one light on downstairs. He used the ornate knocker to rap loudly on the front door. A woman in her late twenties wearing a sweatshirt and jeans opened the door. Andy took out his identification and said, 'Detective Sergeant Wills from the Major Crime Unit. I'm looking for Mr and Mrs Reid.'

The woman opened the door a little wider and said, 'I'm Angie Reid. My husband's inside. You'd better come in.'

Andy stepped inside the hallway and followed the

woman into the tiny lounge. This was the room that had the light on. A man stood as Andy entered and said, 'Ben Reid. Do you think this could be important, then?'

Andy noticed a golden retriever dog asleep in a basket in the corner of the room and replied, 'We always follow up on any information we receive. It was a nasty incident in Worksop, so we're desperate to trace this individual.'

Angie said, 'Please take a seat. Can I get you a drink?'

Andy shook his head as he sat down. 'No, thanks. I'm fine.'

He waited until the young couple had sat down again and said, 'I understand that you told my colleague, on the phone, that this man you saw fitted the description we put out on the news. Is that right?'

It was Angie who answered. 'The description of the man you gave out was of him being very tall and big. Well, the man we saw was like a giant. I'm not joking. Ben's six feet tall and this bloke made him look small.'

Ben joined in. 'He was broad as well. Very intimidating. A proper man mountain.'

'What else do you remember about him?'

Ben said, 'He was wearing dirty overalls. They looked dirty as opposed to oily, if you know what I mean. I've got overalls that I wear when I'm working on my car, and they're covered in oil and grease. His looked covered in dirt.'

'Can you remember the colour?'

'They were dark – either a dark green or navy blue, I'm not sure.'

'Can you remember anything about how he looked?'

This time it was Angie who answered Andy's question. 'He had dark hair, which was quite short, and a few days' growth of stubble.'

'Anything else?'

'It was his eyes I remember most. They were so dark.

They were almost black. He stared straight at us and never said a word.'

'Any idea how old he might be?'

Angie said, 'Early thirties.' At the same time, Ben said, 'Late twenties.'

Andy smiled. 'So, between late twenties and early thirties, then.'

The young couple both nodded.

Andy continued, 'Do you think either of you would recognise him again?'

Ben was the first to answer. 'Don't get me wrong, this man would stand out in a crowd. I'm just not sure if I could say, hand on heart, that I'd be able to positively identify him.'

Angie remained silent, so Andy prompted her. 'What about you, Mrs Reid?'

'I feel the same way. I don't think I could make a formal identification.'

Andy was thoughtful for a moment, before saying, 'Mrs Reid, you seem to have got a better look at this man's face than your husband. Would you be prepared to sit down with a police artist and see if we can get a good likeness of the man you saw?'

'When?'

'I could arrange it for tomorrow. At a time to suit you.'

'I could be available tomorrow afternoon.'

'That's great. Would you be okay to travel to Retford police station, or would you feel more at ease if the artist came here?'

'I work in Retford, so I'm quite happy to pop into the police station. I finish work at two o'clock tomorrow afternoon.'

'Okay. I'll arrange for the artist to meet you there. Just walk in and give the desk sergeant your name. Everything will be organised. Now, exactly where did you see this man?'

Ben replied, 'Beckett Wood.'

'I know those woods quite well. Whereabouts in the woods?'

'We were at the bottom end. Our dog, Pippin, ran off as soon as we let her off the lead and wouldn't come back. Too many distractions in the woods, I suppose. Anyway, we were hollering and shouting for her to come back and slowly walking up the single track, deeper into the woods.'

'So, where were you when you first saw the man?'

'We had walked about fifty yards up the muddy track, the one that goes through the middle of the woods, when he emerged from the trees to our left. He was carrying Pippin in one hand.'

'How?'

In a disgusted tone, Angie said, 'He had her by the scruff of her neck, the cruel sod. He just walked over to us, dropped the dog at Ben's feet, turned round and walked back into the woods.'

Andy looked over at the dog, still asleep in her basket, and said, 'Pippin isn't a small dog. How did she react to being carried like that?'

Ben said, 'She was stressed and frightened. I put her back on the lead straight away and tried to calm her down. Angie shouted after the man, thanking him for bringing the dog back, but he just kept walking and didn't look back.'

'Did you see this man with a vehicle?'

'No.'

'Did you hear any vehicles in the woods that morning?'

'No. One of the reasons we used to take Pippin there for walks was because there were never any cars.'

'Have you seen this man since?'

Angie said, 'No. We've stopped taking Pippin for walks in those woods. We walk her around the park in Retford now.

I'll be honest with you, that man scared me. I didn't want to bump into him up there, if I was walking Pippin on my own.'

'Can you remember when you saw this man?'

'Just over a week ago. Eight days, to be precise.'

'How can you be so sure?'

'Because it was the morning after we moved in here. We moved on the fourth, so it would have been the morning of the fifth.'

'What time?'

'Early morning, around six o'clock. We always take her for a long walk before going to work.'

Andy said, 'I need to get a quick statement from each of you. Are you okay for time now?'

Angie said, 'We were only going to watch the TV, so nothing's spoiling. How long will it take?'

'No more than an hour.'

'That's fine.'

45

10.00am, 14 September 1988
MCIU Offices, Mansfield, Nottinghamshire

Andy Wills was the last of the supervisors to arrive for the meeting in Danny's office. Danny had called the meeting to discuss the latest developments and to consider how he could move the two inquiries forward.

He knew it was only a matter of time before something else happened that would require an investigation by the MCIU and, with Potter already breathing down his neck about the Margaret White murder and the abduction inquiry, progress needed to be made.

He leaned back in his chair and said, 'Now that we're all here, let's make a start. Rob, how are you getting on with the attempted abduction in Worksop?'

'We've conducted all the follow-up inquiries and nothing that's come up so far will take us any further. We're still no closer to identifying either the vehicle or the offender.'

It wasn't what Danny wanted to hear. He looked at Andy and said, 'I understand you saw somebody last night who called in with information following the press appeal. Anything useful?'

'Yes, boss. I think it could be very significant. I went to see a young couple who had seen a man in Beckett Wood who fitted the description of the offender from the Worksop job. More importantly, they saw him in Beckett Wood around six o'clock on the morning of the fifth.'

'The same day Fiona Wright was found on the railway track.'

'Exactly. Angela Reid is meeting with a police artist at Retford police station at two o'clock this afternoon. Hopefully, the artist will be able to give us a decent impression of the man she saw.'

'Did they see a vehicle that morning?'

'No, they didn't. But that doesn't mean a vehicle wasn't there.'

Danny was thoughtful for a moment, then he looked at Rob and said, 'Can you bring in the maps prepared by Jag and Phil?'

'Give me a minute.'

Rob left the office, returning a few minutes later. He spread the Ordnance Survey map on Danny's desk and said, 'Beckett Wood is in the centre.'

There was a large circle drawn on the map, which signified the thirty-five-minute drive time from where the dog had lost the trail in Beckett Wood.

Danny studied the map. He could see numerous farms and outbuildings, as well as three small villages, all within the confines of the roughly drawn circle.

'How long would it take us to visit every property within that circle?'

Rob puffed out his cheeks and said, 'That's a vast undertaking. Just visiting all the outlying farms would be huge; to incorporate the three small villages would be massive.'

'We need to take the initiative; we're running out of time. I don't want to wait until this lunatic tries to snatch another woman off the streets. Have the Special Operations Unit completed all the house-to-house inquiries for the Margaret White murder?'

Tina said, 'Yes, boss.'

'Good. Rob, I want you to see what staff the SOU can provide and then draw up an operational order to search that area.'

'All of it?'

'No. Let's prioritise the farms and outlying cottages first. We can then incorporate the surrounding villages, if we need to.'

'Okay, boss.'

'Andy, I want a copy of that artist's impression as soon as we have it. I want you to drive up to Retford and be there when Mrs Reid is with the artist.'

'Yes, sir.'

'Rachel, I know you've been working on other missing-from-home files, which could form part of what is emerging here. There does seem to be a pattern of women going missing, under similar circumstances, all within this geographical area. I want you to remain focussed on that until the search plan has been drawn up, then it's going to be all hands to the pump after that. I think we're all going to be involved in this search operation.'

There was a pause, and then Danny looked at Tina. 'What else needs doing on the Margaret White inquiry?'

'All the deceased's family and friends have now been seen, interviewed and statements obtained. As you now know, the house-to-house inquiries have been completed and we are waiting on new lines of inquiry to be generated from the results of the forensic tests.'

'Have you spoken to Tim Donnelly about chasing the Forensic Science Service?'

'I'm in regular contact with Tim, and we contact the FSS every day for an update.'

'Christ, they're so slow. What's the hold up now?'

'It's just volume of work. They're inundated with requests from police forces all over this area.'

'Okay. Keep chasing them. We need those results.'

'Will do.'

'Was there anything at all from the house-to-house inquiries?'

'Several sightings of various unattended vehicles being parked towards Mansfield Woodhouse were brought to light. These could be significant because, as you know, it's believed the offender left the scene on foot, heading across the fields towards Mansfield Woodhouse. We're following those up.'

'Okay. Let me have a full list of those vehicle sightings, please, and let me know as and when the owners are traced. Right, that's it. You all know what needs doing, and I don't need to tell you that we need to start making some progress, so let's get cracking.'

46

8.00pm, 28 February 1988
Sunnybank Cottage, White Gate Farm, Misterton, Nottinghamshire

Jessica walked slowly down the stone steps into the cellar, followed by her captor. She felt exhausted. She was now heavily pregnant and desperately trying to hide the fact from the man who held her prisoner.

He paid so little attention to her these days that it had been easy for her to hide her pregnancy and the weight she had gained. Only once had he made a comment, telling her that she was getting fat. She had laughed and said it was because she was content and had been drinking a bit too much full-fat milk.

Providing she could cook his meals and do the odd jobs he asked her to do, he wasn't interested in her at all.

A month earlier, she had complained of stomach pains and told him that she might need medical attention, as they were getting steadily worse. He had become flustered at first, saying it wasn't possible for her to see a doctor and that he had medicines at the cottage if she wasn't well. He had handed her a box of paracetamol and told her to take some. When she had refused and insisted on seeing a doctor, he became angry, shouting at her that she couldn't get medical attention. He had grabbed her and pulled her downstairs to the cellar, where she was manacled to the bed. He had thrown the box of tablets at her, instructing her to take some.

He had then stomped back up the cellar steps, leaving the light on, before slamming and locking the door. He behaved like a petulant child whenever he was confronted with a problem.

She had picked up the box of paracetamol and had thought about taking every tablet in the box. The idea had been short-lived, as when she opened the box she saw it only contained half a dozen tablets.

Thankfully, the stomach pains she had experienced subsided on that occasion and she'd been able to continue doing her chores.

She sat on the bed now and stared at her right ankle, secured to the bed by the steel manacle. The restraint felt tight on the swollen ankle and she moved her leg to try and make it a little more comfortable.

She remained seated, as she had a dull ache in her lower back.

As she moved her leg, she felt a flutter in her stomach. It was gentle at first, like all her stomach muscles were contracting slowly. The longer it went on, the more intense the feeling became until it was almost unbearable.

As quickly as it had come, the contraction passed.

She felt fluid between her legs and squirmed a little. She reached down and touched the fluid, terrified that it would be blood. She was relieved that when she withdrew her fingers she could see it was only water.

That feeling of relief vanished in an instant. It could only mean one thing: her labour had started. She was terrified.

As another contraction began, she knew she was alone and would have to deal with this by herself.

Her baby was coming now, and there was nothing she could do about it.

47

3.15pm, 14 September 1988
Retford Police Station, Nottinghamshire

'Can you make the nose a little fatter?'

The police artist, PC Archer, responded to Angie Reid's instructions and used an eraser to remove the pencil lines of the nose, before redrawing the facial feature.

'Is that better?'

'That's it.'

'Take a long look at the face. Is that how you remember this man?'

Angie deliberated for a few minutes and then said, 'It is, and it isn't.'

PC Archer remained silent, allowing her time to work out what was wrong for herself. He was an experienced police officer, as well as a talented artist, and he knew that sometimes silence was the best way to enable a witness to remember what they had seen.

Finally, she said, 'It's the eyes that are wrong. This is going to sound stupid, though.'

'In what way?'

'They aren't evil enough. There was something malevolent about the way he looked at us. I'm not sure how you're going to be able to sketch evil, though.'

Once again, the artist set to work. He erased the eyes he had previously sketched and then redrew them. This time, he gave them a slight angle, so they were lower in the centre of the face and higher towards the sides. He drew them narrower, and instantly the eyes took on an almost demonic look.

Angie's jaw dropped and she cried out, 'That's it!'

'Are you sure?'

'Yes, that's who I saw. It's giving me chills looking at it now.'

'I want to try and put some colour onto the face now. I'll use blank paper until you're satisfied that the colours of the man's hair, eyes and skin are correct. Tell me when you're happy, then I'll apply the colour to the drawing. Okay.'

After another thirty minutes, the artist's impression of the man in Beckett Wood was complete. The face had been the hard part. Earlier, the artist had completed an impression of the man as a standing figure, showing the dirty, dark green overalls.

The artist took a quick witness statement from her and then walked Angie Reid to the front door of the police station. He said, 'Thanks for taking the time to come in this afternoon, Mrs Reid. Sorry it took so long, but it's best to take our time and get it right. We only ever get one chance at this.'

'It's no problem. You've captured him perfectly. That's the man I saw in Beckett Wood.'

'Thanks. I'll make sure this sketch gets to the MCIU. They may well want to see you again later.'

PC Archer made his way upstairs to the CID office. Waiting for him was Andy Wills.

'How did it go?'

PC Archer took out the completed drawings and said, 'These are what we've produced. She's convinced the face is accurate.'

'What do you think?'

'I only ever draw what the witness asks me to. Have I ever seen such a pair of evil eyes on a person? I wouldn't like to comment.'

'What does that mean?'

'If I were drawing a face, I would never make the eyes this shape. To me, they look false, almost comic-book, cartoon false, but she insisted they were exactly right. If they are, I don't think you'll have any problem knowing you've got the right man. There can't be too many men out there who are that size and with such distinctive facial features.'

'Thanks for taking the time to do this today. You've done a fantastic job.'

'No problem, I enjoy it. I've taken a quick witness statement from Mrs Reid and I've completed the exhibit labels. The completed pictures will be Police Item numbers BA 1 and BA 2. I hope they help you catch him.'

48

3.00am, 1 March 1988
Sunnybank Cottage, White Gate Farm, Misterton, Nottinghamshire

The pain in her stomach had been horrific for hours. Every time a new wave of pain raged through her body, she bit down hard onto the bed sheets, trying to stifle her anguished cries. The last thing she wanted to do was attract the attention of the man upstairs.

She had known for weeks that this time was fast approaching, and she knew it would be an ordeal. In a few hours, the baby would be born, then it would be down to her to get her captor to accept it. That thought terrified her, as she had no idea how he would react to the infant, and to her.

Her entire body ached, but especially her back. Because her right leg was still manacled to the wrought-iron bed, she could only partially move to alleviate the pressure on her back. The pain had gradually increased throughout the night.

Suddenly, a new pain tore through her exhausted body. This pain started in her lower back and rapidly spread to the front of her abdomen. It felt like a burning, tearing sensation, and it was agony. She could contain herself no longer and screamed in agony. She kept on screaming, as this pain didn't relent like the other waves had. This pain increased, until she was half-screaming and half-sobbing.

As suddenly as it had started it stopped, but now she felt something different. Fluid was gushing from between her legs. She sat up and raised her knees as high as the chain would allow and dragged them into her chest.

She looked down and could see the head of her unborn child. To her horror, she could also see a lot of blood. Too much blood.

She looked up at the stone ceiling and let out an anguished cry. 'Help me!'

She looked down again and saw that the infant was now completely out of her, but was unmoving. She was panicking and shouted for help again.

The door to the cellar opened and the man came down the steps. He shouted, 'What the hell's going on down here?'

In desperation, she panted, 'I need your help. The baby's here and something's wrong. I need a doctor, now.'

The man approached the bed and saw all the blood that was still issuing from her, the unmoving baby between her legs, and he panicked. He had no idea what was happening, and even less idea of how to help. He reacted in the only way his simple brain would allow; he took himself away from the horror.

He turned and ran back up the stone steps and locked the cellar door.

She knew that her only hope of salvation had just disappeared, and she cried out, 'Nooooo!'

The cry left her breathless and dizzy. Her head slumped back, and she allowed her legs to straighten on the bed. She could still feel the blood pumping from her and she knew the end was close.

She reached down and grabbed her unmoving infant, clutching it to her chest. In her heart, she knew her child was dead. She closed her eyes, said a silent prayer and hoped she would see her baby soon.

49

5.45am, 1 March 1987
Beckett Wood, near Misterton, Nottinghamshire

A lone owl hooted as the man trudged through the trees to the clearing in Beckett Wood. He had wrapped his grisly burden in the bottom sheet, which had been on the blood-covered bed.

The weight of the two bodies, slung over his right shoulder, was easily borne by him. In his left hand, he carried the long-handled shovel he would need to complete his macabre task.

When he reached the open space surrounded by trees, he got his bearings and moved to an area away from where he had previously buried numbers one and two. He picked a location and allowed the bodies to slide from his shoulder onto the soft earth.

As he began to dig the shallow grave, he thought about the sight that had confronted him when he had returned to the cellar an hour ago. He had sat in the kitchen of the cottage and heard the dreadful scream of pain from number three. Not knowing what was happening, or what he could do to help, he had remained stock still and hadn't moved from the chair.

Then silence had filled the cottage once again.

He had remained unmoving for another hour before finally plucking up the determination to go back down those cellar steps.

He had stared at the sight before him in disbelief. A baby covered in blood lay on the chest of number three. Her arms were wrapped tightly around the dead infant. Her head had slumped forward so her chin was on her chest, and her eyes were half-closed. She was alabaster white, and cold to the touch. He had felt for a pulse in her neck. There hadn't been one.

The bed that mother and infant lay on was covered in blood, which had begun to dry at the edges. He had used the heavily bloodstained bottom sheet as a makeshift shroud for mother and baby, using twine to secure the bodies inside.

He had then carried the bodies from the cellar, outside to the Land Rover.

As he drove to Beckett Wood, he couldn't understand the emotions he was feeling. His eyes were streaming with tears, and he could hardly breathe. He had really enjoyed three's company at the cottage, and now she was gone. He felt the same sense of abandonment he'd felt when his mother had died.

By the time he reached the dark, lonely wood that would be mother and child's final resting place, he had regained control over his emotions.

He no longer felt sad at the deaths but a growing sense of worry over who was going to look after him now. Three had been perfect. She never argued or moaned. She always had a delicious hot meal ready for him when he returned to the cottage after a hard day's work in the fields.

His selfish, childlike nature had very quickly turned to wondering if he would ever find another number three.

He already knew he would try.

Having finished digging the shallow grave, he dragged the bed sheet towards the hole. He was glad he had secured the sheet with the twine so well, as he had no wish to catch another glimpse of the contents of that makeshift shroud. What he had already seen in the cellar was an image that had been burned into his subconscious. It was a vision of hell that he knew would be there for a long time.

He tipped the sad bundle into the grave and heard the thud as the two bodies landed at the bottom. Without looking down at the bloodstained sheet, he began shovelling the heavy soil back into the hole. Only when the bedsheet had been covered did he look down, as he continued to shovel more soil back into the crude grave.

He trod the soil down until it looked like a small mound in the woodland clearing, then made his way back through the trees. He was sweating slightly from his labours and was glad of the cold, early morning air, which caused his exhaled breath to make white clouds in front of him.

He threw the shovel into the back of the Land Rover and began the twenty-minute drive back to the cottage. He still had the cellar to clean before he could go to work. It was another Brussel sprout harvest day. Field number six was ready for picking and he daren't be late. He would need to be at the field ready to supervise the foreign labourers, as well as pick the vegetables himself, by six thirty at the latest. Glancing at his battered wristwatch, he saw the time and pressed the accelerator of the Land Rover.

He wouldn't have time to clean the cellar now. He would have to do it after he had finished for the day. That thought worsened his already foul mood. The last thing he needed to do, after a hard day's labour, was to mop up blood from the cellar's stone floor.

Any sadness he had previously felt at the horrendous fate which had befallen number three and her baby was already a distant memory. The only thoughts in his head now were about his own situation, and how the devastating chain of events would affect him.

He cursed under his breath at his continued misfortune.

50

12.30pm, 18 September 1988
Wheatfield Crescent, Mansfield Woodhouse, Nottinghamshire

Audrey Hollis got out of the taxi and waited for the driver to get her single suitcase from the boot. Without being asked, the cabbie carried the small, blue case from the car to the pensioner's front door. 'Would you like me to take it inside for you, love?'

'No, thanks. I can manage it from here.'

She took a five-pound note from her purse, gave it to the driver and said, 'Keep the change, duckie.'

The driver smiled and said, 'Thanks very much. See you soon.'

She felt tired after the coach journey from the Derbyshire Miners Holiday Camp at Skegness. It had been a lovely week; the weather had been glorious. All she wanted to do now was fetch a glass of water from the kitchen and then have a nap in her own bed. Leaving the small suitcase in the hall, she walked into the kitchen of the bungalow.

She immediately saw the smashed window and muttered, 'Oh no.'

With a sense of rising panic, she went into her bedroom and opened the bedside cabinet drawer. She reached inside, feeling for the precious envelope at the back. She was relieved when her fingers located the Manilla envelope. She quickly took it out and tipped the contents onto the bed. It contained half a dozen photographs of her late husband, his wedding ring and wristwatch, and a smaller envelope that contained over two thousand pounds.

Feeling grateful the thieves who had broken into her home hadn't found her most treasured belongings, she walked into the hallway and picked up the phone. She could hear no dial tone, and when she dialled three nines, nothing happened.

Starting to get annoyed, she walked to the neighbouring bungalow and knocked on the door.

Her neighbour, Bill Roberts, answered the door and said, 'Hello, Audrey! Good holiday, duck?'

'It was until I got home, Bill. Some little tow rag has broken in and my phone's dead. Would you mind if I use yours to call the police?'

'Of course not. Come in and I'll make you a cup of tea. You look white as a sheet.'

'Thanks. I'm okay, it's just been a bit of a shock.'

'The phone's on the table there. I'll put the kettle on.'

Audrey picked up the phone and dialled.

An officious-sounding voice said, 'Emergency. What service do you require?'

The elderly lady hesitated a second, before saying, 'I need to see the police. Someone's broken into my house while I've been away on holiday.'

'What's your name and address, caller?'

'Audrey Hollis, and I live at 46 Wheatfield Crescent, Mansfield Woodhouse.'

'An officer will be with you in the next ten minutes. Do you require anything else?'

'No, thanks.'

The phone immediately went dead. She replaced the receiver and stepped into the kitchen, where her neighbour was waiting with a cup of tea.

He said, 'I've put a couple of sugars in, Audrey. Hot, sweet tea is the best thing for shock.'

'Thanks, Bill, you're a star.'

51

12.45pm, 18 September 1988
Wheatfield Crescent, Mansfield Woodhouse,
Nottinghamshire

PC Chris Walker was working alone.

He brought the patrol car to a halt outside the address he had been given. From the car, he surveyed the exterior of the detached bungalow. He could see the handrail at the side of the path and another next to the front door. He knew immediately that the occupant would be elderly.

He grabbed his notepad and walked down the path, knocking loudly on the front door. He heard voices to his left and saw an elderly couple emerging from the neighbouring bungalow.

The woman shouted, 'Won't be a second, duckie. I had to call you from Bill's, as my phone won't work.'

Chris waited patiently for the woman to walk from the

neighbouring bungalow to her own. When she reached the front door, Chris said, 'Audrey Hollis?'

'That's me. Somebody's broken in while I've been away.'

'Have they taken much?'

'I haven't had a proper look yet, but all the important stuff is here. They didn't find that.'

As they stepped inside the neat bungalow, Chris asked, 'What's the important stuff?'

'I keep precious memories of my husband and a bit of cash in my bedside cabinet.'

'How much is a bit of cash, Mrs Hollis?'

The old lady leaned forward and whispered, 'Two thousand pounds. It's my emergency money.'

The experienced officer shook his head and said, 'How would you have felt if these thieves had found it and took it?'

'Awful. But I don't trust banks.'

'When I've finished taking your report today, I'll help you find a bank you can trust, okay? You need to put that cash in a safe place.'

'If you think that's best.'

'I do. Now, how did they get inside? The front door looks okay.'

'They got in through the kitchen window. They've made a right mess – just smashed it in. I'll show you.'

Chris followed her into the kitchen and saw the smashed transom window. He said, 'Did you say there was a problem with your phone?'

'It doesn't work.'

'I want you to wait here and don't touch anything. I want to have a quick look outside. Won't be a minute.'

Chris stepped outside and quickly located the telephone cable. He could see it had been neatly cut. He muttered under his breath, 'Good job you were away, love.'

He reached for his personal radio and said, 'PC Walker to control, over.'

'Go ahead, over.'

'Can you contact the MCIU and ask them to attend this burglary at 46 Wheatfield Crescent. The entry looks identical to the break in at Margaret White's bungalow and the telephone cable has been cut. Over.'

'Is the occupant okay?'

'She's fine. She had been away on holiday for a week. Over.'

'I'll contact the MCIU and see if anybody is available to join you there. Do you want scenes of crime travelling? Over.'

'Yes, please. Over.'

52

1.30pm, 18 September 1988
Wheatfield Crescent, Mansfield Woodhouse, Nottinghamshire

Danny and Tina were standing in the rear garden of the bungalow, looking out across the farmland. The two detectives could clearly see the boot prints that had been left near the fence. Danny said, 'Have you requested dog section to attend, for a track?'

'I've contacted the control room and the request has gone in. All the handlers had jobs already allocated. Hopefully, one will be able to resume soon.'

'This burglary has all the hallmarks of the method used by the killer of Margaret White and Florence King. I think Audrey Hollis has had a very lucky escape. The only thing puzzling me is why this has occurred now, so close to the Clipstone Drive offence. It was four years between Florence

King and Margaret White, and now this happens in less than four weeks.'

'The killer's circumstances have obviously changed. Perhaps he's moved back into the area for good, after being away.'

Danny could feel his frustration rising. 'If only we could get a definitive answer from the FSS, with evidence to show the two murders were carried out by the same offender, then I could start throwing resources into looking at that four-year gap.'

Sensing Danny's rising tension, Tina remained silent.

Danny turned away and stared at the smashed window.

After a minute's silence, he growled, 'Definitive answer or not, we need to start looking at reasons why this person waited four years to commit a second offence. If this burglary is the work of the same man, this could quite easily have been another murder. I want you to start with the prison service. We still have good contacts at HMP Whatton, where the sex offenders are housed. I want you to start there and then gradually widen your search. I want a list of all offenders who served four years and who were initially sent down within a three-month window after Florence King was killed.'

'That's going to be like searching for the proverbial needle in a haystack, boss.'

'What's the alternative? Wait for another old lady to be raped and suffocated in her own home? We need to do something. I want a discreet presence watching this woman's house for the next month or so. The offender could well return and try to finish the job. He's obviously carefully selecting these women. Did you notice how much Audrey Hollis looked like the other two victims?'

Before Tina could answer, Tim Donnelly stepped out the back door and said, 'The dog handler's here. Shall I send him through to you, boss?'

'Yes, please. Have you found anything inside?'

'Plenty of glove marks that look like the marks found at the Clipstone Drive scene. There is one thing I'd like to show you, near the point of entry.'

Danny said to Tina, 'Wait here for the dog handler. I'll see what he's found inside.'

Danny passed the dog handler at the back door and pointed him towards Tina, then he turned to Tim and said, 'What have you got?'

'It's a scuff mark on the frame of the transom window, where the offender has reached through to open the larger window. I thought it was mud at first, but then I realised it was grease, or something similar. I've taken a sample of it for testing. It's interesting because it looks like the residue that was found below the point of entry at Clipstone Drive.'

'That we initially thought was soil?'

'Yes.'

'Didn't you say there was grease of some description on that scrap of cloth you found at Clipstone Drive?'

'I said I thought it could be. That's something else we're waiting for the FSS for.'

'Sod this! Tomorrow morning, you and I are going to the Forensic Science Service at Birmingham. I'm sick of waiting.'

'It might not do any good, boss.'

'We're going anyway. I need some answers, and we're getting nowhere fast speaking on the phone. I need to see somebody there, face to face. Be ready at seven o'clock tomorrow morning. I'll pick you up from headquarters.'

The dog handler walked back into the bungalow, followed by his German shepherd and an unhappy-looking Tina Cartwright. A now very disgruntled Danny said, 'Is that it?'

The dog handler replied, 'Sorry, sir. The dog couldn't pick up the track. It's been too long since the offender was here. If there had been a track to find, this dog would have found it. Sabre is one of our best trackers.'

Danny turned away and cursed under his breath.

Quickly regaining his composure, he said, 'Stay here and work the scene, Tina. I'm going back to the office to find out exactly how many other burglary offences we've had, where this method of entry has been used.'

He started to walk away, then turned around and shouted back, 'Tim, I'll be at headquarters at seven o'clock tomorrow morning. Make sure you're ready, with all the paperwork for our submissions. We're going to get some answers tomorrow.'

53

10.25pm, 18 September 1988
Bridgegate, Retford, Nottinghamshire

Vanessa Tyler was deep in thought as she waited at the bus stop in Retford town centre. She had spent the night with her best friend from work, Amanda, drinking white wine and discussing the parlous state of their respective marriages.

Vanessa was now approaching her thirty-third birthday and had been married to her husband Geoff for eight years. She knew they were slowly drifting apart. Each year that passed amplified how different they had become. She was desperate to have a child, but Geoff was more of a child himself and wouldn't entertain the idea of starting a family.

He was also bone idle. The beautiful house they owned was now in a state of disrepair, because he was too lazy to do the simplest of maintenance tasks.

He had also recently been sacked from his job at the

warehouse, for poor timekeeping. It had been the last straw for Vanessa. She had phoned Amanda and arranged to meet at Carlo's in the town centre.

Emboldened by the copious amount of Pinot Grigio they had consumed, the two women had promised to leave their husbands and get a place together. They were both convinced they didn't need useless husbands in their lives.

Amanda had got a taxi home, but Vanessa had insisted on catching the late bus, as it was cheaper and there was a stop only a hundred yards from her front door.

She would tell her feckless husband she was leaving in the morning. Vanessa Tyler had finally seen the light. She knew she was still an attractive woman, and life was too short to be stuck in a relationship with a man she no longer had any feelings for. She could now clearly see that she had stopped loving Geoff years ago. It was time for her to move on and start enjoying life.

Her thoughts were interrupted by the loud hiss of air brakes, as the late bus pulled into the bus stop. She boarded the bus, along with the two other people who had been waiting at the stop.

Ten minutes later, she got off the bus on North Road, near to its junction with Randall Way. She was the only passenger to get off at this stop. She waited for the bus to pull away before crossing the road and walking slowly towards Randall Way.

The cold air, after the warmth of the bus, heightened the effects of the alcohol from the two bottles of wine she had shared with her friend, and she started to totter unsteadily on the three-inch heels she was wearing.

She held onto a wall to steady herself and giggled. The alcoholic glow of the wine felt so good, she might even tell that useless lump of lard she was leaving him tonight.

54

10.40pm, 18 September 1988
Randall Way, Hallcroft, Retford, Nottinghamshire

Sam Morgan, sitting in the Land Rover, had watched the woman with the high heels and short skirt as she walked through Retford town centre. He had been transfixed by her long legs, as she walked alone to the bus stop on Bridgegate. He had thought about making a move there and then, but a young couple had also turned up at the bus stop, scuppering any bad intentions he had.

When the bus arrived, he had followed it, maintaining a short distance between the blue-and-white single decker bus and his Land Rover.

He had driven slowly behind the bus until it pulled in at the stop on North Road. He had been delighted to see the woman with the heels get off the bus on her own.

She looked unsteady as she crossed the road and staggered her way towards the junction. He quickly scanned the dark road, front and back, and couldn't see anybody else around. The woman was obviously the worse for drink, and he hoped this would make his task a little easier.

He drove the Land Rover onto Randall Way, switched the engine off and waited for the woman to totter around the corner. Randall Way was a smart residential street, but it had the old, white street lighting that gave off a very poor light and left dark recesses along the road.

He had parked the Land Rover in one of those shadows, and when the woman staggered past he made his move.

He made one last check of the street, then leapt out of the Land Rover, grabbing the unwary woman from behind. He clamped a large hand across her mouth, stifling any screams, and dragged her to the back of the Land Rover. He was finding it difficult to hold onto the woman, who was now struggling violently, and open the rear door of his vehicle at the same time. Not wanting a repeat of five nights ago, in desperation he punched the woman hard on the back of her head.

He felt her instantly go limp in his arms, as she slumped into unconsciousness. Moving with a sense of greater urgency, he yanked open the rear door and threw the woman inside. He tied her wrists and ankles and placed a gag in her mouth.

She smelled delicious. The perfume she wore was strong and heady. It made his eyes water.

With the woman now secure, he closed the rear door and walked to the driver's door. There were no lights coming on in houses this time, and the street remained deathly quiet.

With a smile of satisfaction at how easy the capture of number five had been, he started the twenty-minute drive back to the cottage. With any luck, she would still be out for the count when they got there, and he wouldn't have any drama getting her into the cellar that was to be her new home.

55

11.30pm, 18 September 1988
Sunnybank Cottage, White Gate Farm, Misterton, Nottinghamshire

Vanessa shivered as she woke up in the dimly lit room. The air felt cold and damp. Her bare legs had goosebumps. As she sat up to have a look at her new surroundings, she was surprised and shocked to find that both her wrists and both her ankles were now restricted by steel manacles. They felt cold and sharp to the skin, and every movement she made rubbed the tender flesh in those areas a little more.

Moving slowly, she eventually sat upright and could now see that there were lengths of chain that ran from each of the manacles. These chains were, in turn, secured to the metal bed frame. Looking down at her feet, she saw that she was no longer wearing the shoes that were her pride and joy. She had paid over two hundred pounds for the three-inch designer heels.

Questions raced through her wine-befuddled brain. *What the hell was going on? Where was this place? Who had brought her here? Was her husband behind this?*

She felt the back of her head and could feel a lump. It stirred a memory of her walking past a battered Land Rover that was parked near her house. She remembered being grabbed from behind and trying to struggle, then nothing until this.

Panic started to rise within her, as she looked at her surroundings. She was in what was either a basement or a cellar. The only furniture in the room was the single wrought-iron bed she was sitting on and a dark-wood ottoman that was shoved against one of the side walls. There were no windows; the only light came from the single, dim bulb that hung from the centre of the ceiling. On the far side of the room, she could see a flight of stone steps that disappeared up into the darkness.

The thought that disturbed her the most was the notion that her husband could be behind this. She had spent the entire evening with her best friend Amanda, discussing strategies on what would be the best way to leave boring Geoff. What if he'd been plotting with his own friends to do the same? What if he'd come up with some hairbrained scheme of his own to make her disappear?

A chill ran through her that made her physically shudder, as she thought of the huge life insurance policies they had both signed up to recently. What if his plan had darker intentions that meant her being left to die in this place and him becoming a very wealthy man?

Surely, he couldn't do that to her, could he?

56

8.30am 19 September 1988
Forensic Science Service, Marston Green, Birmingham

The journey from Nottingham to Birmingham had been tiresome. The early morning traffic had been heavy, and Danny's mood hadn't been helped when there was a delay at headquarters, as Tim gathered all the paperwork that would be required for today's meeting with Fay Weaver, the lead scientist at the Forensic Science Service.

As they walked towards the main reception doors, Tim said, 'I don't think this trip will help us, boss. The FSS have too big a workload; there are no favours done to anyone. Everything's done on a strictly first-come, first-served basis.'

Danny growled, 'We'll see, won't we?'

Having signed in at reception, they were asked to wait in the foyer.

The lift doors opened and a woman wearing a white laboratory coat walked towards them. Tim stood up first, as he recognised Fay Weaver. Danny also stood to greet the forensic scientist. He studied her as she approached. She was in her late forties, with short, dark brown hair. Her brown eyes were somewhat obscured by dark-rimmed spectacles.

She extended her hand and smiled warmly. 'Detective Chief Inspector Flint, I presume.'

Danny shook her hand and said, 'Yes. It's good to finally meet you, Ms Weaver. Thanks for taking the time to meet with us this morning.'

'Call me Fay, please.'

She turned to Tim and said, 'Hello again, Tim. I hope you haven't had a wasted trip. Let's all go and talk in my office, shall we?'

Tim picked up his briefcase, which contained the exhibit documentation, and followed on behind as Danny and Fay walked briskly towards the lifts.

A few minutes later, Fay opened the door to her office on the second floor. 'Come in.' Once everyone was seated, she said, 'How can I help?'

Danny said, 'I know you've been in regular contact with Tim, but I wanted to hear for myself why there are such long delays in processing these vital forensic samples. I'm currently investigating two separate murders, where elderly women were raped and suffocated in their own homes. The samples were submitted on September the third, sixteen days ago. At the time of submission, Tim was informed by this service that you would have results in between nine and twelve days' time. What's causing the delay?'

'Can I see the request forms submitted?'

Tim handed over the file containing all the forensic submissions.

After studying the files, Fay Weaver said, 'I see you've

submitted further samples for analysis under that same reference number on September the eleventh and twelfth.'

Danny said, 'Is that a problem?'

'It can be. Sometimes cases are dealt with by the latest submission date and not the first. Scientists, myself included, like to complete the entire task before sending out results. If all these samples have been sent under the same reference number, that could be the reason for the delay. It's quite possible that the earlier submissions have been completed.'

'Is it possible for you to check? The sooner I can establish if there is a viable DNA profile from these exhibits, the better. I don't know if this maniac is going to strike again soon.'

'We'll go to the labs and talk to the scientist working on this reference number. This way, gentlemen.'

After a five-minute walk through the sprawling building, they arrived in a waiting room outside one of the larger laboratories.

Fay said, 'Wait here while I find the scientist working on your reference.'

She returned shortly afterwards and was followed into the room by a young man wearing a white laboratory coat and protective glasses.

Fay introduced the scientist. 'This is John Mercer. He's working through the submissions on your reference number.'

The man removed the protective glasses and said, 'How can I help?'

Danny said, 'I need to know if you have any updates on the submissions we made. I don't understand why it's taking so long. There could be lives at risk here.'

Mercer took the folder from Fay Weaver and read the submissions.

He said, 'I'm working on the last submissions on this reference number this morning. I can tell you there is a viable DNA profile from the earlier submissions, and I'll know later today if there's a viable profile obtained from the second and third submissions. If there is, all that will need to be done then is a comparison of the three profiles.'

'When you say "later today", when exactly?'

'If the second and third samples produce viable DNA profiles, I'll have completed the comparison work by two o'clock this afternoon.'

'That's great. One question: when did you complete the work on the first samples submitted?'

'September the twelfth. Why?'

Tim said, 'Does that include all the samples we sent? The soil swabs and the strip of cloth found near the point of entry?'

'Everything.'

Danny said, 'So the delay in getting those results was caused by the later submissions?'

Fay interjected. 'That's what it looks like. You can get back to work now, John. Thank you.'

Mercer donned his protective glasses and said, 'No problem. I'll have those results faxed to your scenes of crime department by three o'clock this afternoon.'

Danny said, 'Thank you.'

As they walked back to the main reception, Tim said, 'How can we avoid similar problems in the future?'

Fay said, 'There's only one way. You need to submit every sample on a different reference number. There are no short-cuts. Because of the demands on us as a service, we must work on a first-come, first-served basis.'

Danny said, 'Won't that cause you more bureaucracy?'

'Surely it's better to generate a little more paperwork than have delays on your results, wouldn't you say, chief inspector?'

Danny nodded. 'Definitely. Thanks for your time today.

I'll wait to see the results this afternoon and we now know how to avoid similar delays in future.'

'Glad we could help. I hope you get the results you're wanting this afternoon. Have a safe drive back to Nottingham.'

57

10.45am, 19 September 1988
MCIU Offices, Mansfield, Nottinghamshire

Fran Jefferies had seen Danny arrive back at the office. She had waited a few minutes, then limped across the office and knocked on Danny's door. She carried her notepad in one hand and leant heavily on her walking stick with the other. Her ankle felt extremely sore this morning. It was always the same when the air was cold and damp.

She opened the door and said, 'I thought you should see this, boss.'

'Sit down, Fran. What's up?'

'I've just taken a call from Retford control room. As you know, after the attempted abduction at Manton, I notified all the control rooms to let me know if there were any other similar attempts, or any reports of lone females who went missing during the hours of darkness. Retford took a call yesterday morning, of a woman who didn't come home after a night out with her friend.'

'Details?'

'The missing woman is Vanessa Tyler, thirty-three years of age, married, no kids, lives with her husband Geoff.'

'Has she gone missing before?'

'No.'

'Was it her husband, Geoff, who reported her missing?'

'No, it was her best friend from work, Amanda Smith. She reported her missing when she didn't come into work the next day.'

'Do you have the work address?'

'Yes, she works at Johnson Textiles, which is just outside Retford.'

'Have you checked to see if Mrs Tyler turned up for work today?'

'Yes, boss. I wondered if she may have met somebody and just spent the night elsewhere, but she hasn't shown up for work today either.'

'It's a bit strange that the best friend and not the husband reported her missing.'

'The woman making the report told the police that her friend was experiencing severe marital problems. She also said that she had called her friend's house and spoken to the husband. He told her that his wife hadn't come home the night before.'

'Do you think there could be a domestic violence issue?'

'The friend didn't go as far as that, but it's always possible.'

'And there's been nothing from the husband today?'

'Nothing.'

'Tell DS Moore and DC Pope to drive to Retford. I want them to interview both the best friend and the husband. It does sound a similar scenario to other women that have disappeared at night, but I'm struggling to understand why the husband hasn't come forward. There could be a bit more to this than meets the eye.'

'Will do, boss.'

'Thanks, Fran. How's the ankle today?'

She half-smiled and said, 'This damp weather makes it ache like a bastard. I'll be okay when I've been in the warm office for a while longer.'

58

11.30am, 19 September 1988
Johnson Textiles, Retford, Nottinghamshire

Amanda Smith had a worried expression on her face as she walked into the manager's office. All she had been told was that the police were there to see her. She was worried about Vanessa, who hadn't turned up for work again this morning.

The manager asked her to sit down and said, 'This is Detective Sergeant Moore and Detective Constable Pope. They are here to ask you some questions about Vanessa Tyler. I'll leave you all to it.'

As he reached the door, he turned and said, 'DS Moore, just let my secretary know when you're finished, please.'

'Of course, and thank you for the use of your office. We shouldn't be long.'

He said, 'No problem.' Then closed the door behind him.

Amanda looked nervously at the two detectives and said, 'Is Vanessa okay?'

Rachel said, 'I don't know. When did you last see her?'

'Two days ago, on the nineteenth. We'd had a lovely evening in town. I got a taxi home and she caught the bus. She left me at the taxi rank, so the last time I saw her she was walking through town towards the bus stops at Bridgegate.'

'Was the town centre busy that night?'

'It wasn't that busy, but there were still people milling around, making their way home. I wasn't worried about her because Bridgegate is always busy. Do you know if she caught the bus?'

'We're going to the bus company after we've spoken to you. Did you meet in town for an occasion, or is it something you do often?'

'We go out every now and then for some girly time, away from our useless husbands.'

Jane said, 'Talking of husbands, have you spoken to Geoff yet?'

'I spoke to him briefly yesterday. He doesn't like me much.'

'What did you two talk about?'

'I asked him if I could speak to Vanessa.'

'And?'

'He said, "I was about to ask you the same question; she didn't come home last night."'

'Has he spoken to you since then?'

'No.'

'Not even to ask where Vanessa is?'

'No.'

'Don't you find that a bit strange?'

'Strange is Geoff's middle name. He's a very odd character.'

'Was everything okay between them?'

There was a long pause. Then Amanda said, 'I did mention to the police when I reported her missing that Vanessa was going to leave him. The reason we met up that night was to discuss all the arrangements. She already knew I'd made the decision to leave my old man, and now she's decided to leave Geoff. We were discussing finances, and what we could afford if we moved in and lived together. It made more sense for us to do that, as we would both have more money. We've always got on okay, so it seemed the obvious thing to do.'

Rachel said, 'When was she going to tell Geoff?'

'The next morning. That's why I was so worried when she didn't come into work. And now I haven't been able to get any sort of answer from Geoff , I'm even more worried. You don't think he's done something bad to her, do you?'

'Thanks for being so candid with us, Amanda. We'll go and speak to Geoff now. Is there anything else you think we should know, before we speak to her husband?'

'I can't think of anything else. Will you let me know if she's okay?'

'Of course.'

59

12.30pm, 19 September 1988
Randall Way, Hallcroft, Retford, Nottinghamshire

The curtains were still drawn on the scruffy, semi-detached house with the overgrown garden. Rachel knocked again, and this time rang the doorbell as well. Pushing her ear next to the small pane of glass in the front door, she knocked again, louder this time, before listening for any movement in the house.

There was a scuffling noise coming from upstairs. Using her balled-up fist, she banged on the door again. This time, she lifted the letterbox and shouted, 'Mr Tyler! It's the police. Will you answer the door, please?'

Staring through the small pane of glass, she saw a pair of bare legs descend the stairs. She knocked again, then stepped back from the door as Geoff Tyler opened it. He was dressed in shorts and a scruffy vest and looked half-asleep.

Rachel held out her identification and said, 'I'm Detective

Sergeant Moore, this is DC Pope. May we come in? We need to ask you some questions about your wife.'

Geoff Tyler opened the door wider and said, 'You'll have to excuse the mess.'

The two detectives followed Tyler along the hallway and into the lounge.

He sat down heavily in an armchair and gestured for the detectives to sit on the settee. He immediately reached for a packet of cigarettes and lit one up. He took a long pull on the cigarette and asked a question, as he exhaled the smoke. 'You said you have news about my wife?'

Rachel said, 'We don't have any news. We want to ask you some questions.'

He nonchalantly flicked ash into the overflowing ash tray and said, 'What do you want to know?'

'When did you last see her?'

'Two nights ago. She went out on the town with that slapper who's her best mate at work.'

'What time did she get home?'

'She didn't.'

'Why haven't you reported your wife missing? Aren't you worried about her?'

There was a pause as Tyler took more pulls on the cigarette. Finally, he said, 'Look, it's no secret that me and Vanessa aren't getting on right now. I don't think she can stand the sight of me. Ever since I lost my job, all she ever does is moan at me. I just figured she'd met somebody else that night. Let's face it, that's what her and her tarty mate were going into town for. I just felt too ashamed to call the police and tell them my wife's left me.'

Jane Pope said, 'Was your wife seeing somebody else?'

'Not that I know of, but that doesn't mean she wasn't. I just know she's sick of me. I think she's planning on leaving me, and I don't really blame her.' He put his head in his hands and said quietly, 'I'd walk out on me, too. I'm useless.'

Rachel said, 'We know your wife caught the bus home that night. The bus driver remembers her getting off at the stop, at the top of this street. Are you saying she never made it home?'

Stubbing out the cigarette, Tyler leaned forward and said, 'That's weird. I waited up until gone midnight, thinking she would be coming home on that bus. If she caught the bus, why didn't she come home? The bus stop's less than a hundred yards away from here.'

'Is it normal for your wife to catch the bus home? Couldn't you have picked her up from town?'

'Neither of us drive. I've got a provisional licence, but I've never passed my test, so we don't own a car.'

Rachel stood up and said, 'Do you mind if we have a look around, Mr Tyler?'

Geoff Tyler lit up another cigarette and said, 'Be my guest.'

The two detectives searched the house and the gardens. Apart from her clothes and shoes in the wardrobes, there was no sign of Vanessa, and more important, no sign of a struggle. No rooms had been hastily cleaned and tidied up. In fact, the whole house looked tired, in need of redecoration, and reeked of stale cigarette smoke.

Rachel was satisfied that Tyler was telling the truth, and that Vanessa Tyler had disappeared somewhere between the bus stop and her own home. She walked back into the lounge and said, 'Can you think of anywhere your wife would go, if she wanted to get away for a few days?'

'You're better off asking her best friend, Amanda. She confides in her much more than me these days. If you mean family or friends, we don't have either any more. We are both only children, and our parents are dead. We have no family, and since I lost my job I don't appear to have any friends either. The only friend of Vanessa's I know is Amanda. I don't know if she had any other mates at work. She works at Johnsons Textiles across town. You could try asking there.' He paused and then said, 'I know it looks strange that I haven't reported my wife missing. I'm not stupid. I didn't call the police because I was too ashamed to think she'd probably left me for some other bloke. It was the final straw in what's been a shit six months.' He looked thoughtful and then continued, 'I didn't call the police, so how come you're here now, asking me all these questions? Is Vanessa in trouble?'

'We don't know, Mr Tyler. Are you going to be around if we need to speak to you again?'

'Where else am I going to be?'

'Okay. We may need to speak to you again later. Do you have a recent photograph of Vanessa?'

He took a photograph from a drawer in the sideboard, handed it to Rachel and said, 'This was taken about a year ago, but she hasn't changed.'

He walked with them to the front door and said, 'You should talk to Amanda. She'll know if there's another man on the scene. She couldn't just vanish into thin air. That doesn't make any sense.'

Rachel said, 'No, it doesn't. We'll be in touch.'

60

5.00pm, 19 September 1988
MCIU Offices, Mansfield, Nottinghamshire

Danny had asked his supervisors to attend a strategy meeting in his office to discuss the day's developments.

He said, 'We now have the results back from the Forensic Science Service on all our submissions in relation to the murders of Margaret White and Florence King. They make for interesting reading.'

Tina said, 'Did they manage to get DNA?'

'Viable DNA profiles were found on the samples from both murders. They are an exact match. We now know for certain that the man who killed Florence King four years ago also murdered Margaret White.'

He paused, allowing that information to register, then said, 'We have all wondered why there was such a long delay in between the murders. One of the results that came back from the Margaret White murder could give us an answer to that question. The strip of cloth that was found at the point of entry has been analysed. It was found to have traces of oil on it that matched the traces of oil found on the windowsill below the broken window.'

'How does that help?'

'Because this is crude oil, not refined. It's not petrol, diesel or grease. It's crude oil, pre-refinery.'

Andy Wills said, 'He works on the rigs?'

'It's not quite that narrow. He works in the oil industry. That could mean anything from working the rigs to being a merchant seaman on oil tankers, or working at one of the many refineries here in the UK.'

Andy said, 'We need to look at any occupation in that industry that could mean being away for that four-year period. Possibly working overseas on a long contract.'

A hush fell over the room as the gathered detectives realised the enormity of that inquiry.

Danny said, 'Tina, I want you to take three detectives and commit solely to this inquiry. It's obvious that Fran Jefferies should be one of those. I want you to establish every oil company that recruits from this country. I want to know who those oil companies have recruited over that four-year period and where they have worked. This is going to be a mammoth task, and normally I would throw more staff at it but I also need to make progress on these abductions. Do you think you'll be able to manage that inquiry?'

'I'll gather the team and we'll make a start. I'll keep you informed of the size of the inquiry when I know better what's entailed.'

'Let me know as soon as you've selected the other two detectives, and I'll keep them out of the planning for the abduction inquiry.'

'Will do, boss.'

He looked at Rachel and said, 'You've been looking at this latest missing-from-home report in Retford. What's your first impression?'

'At first, I thought the husband had to be involved. We initially spoke to Vanessa Tyler's best friend, who had reported her missing. She last saw her as she walked through Retford town centre, to catch the late bus from Bridgegate. We made inquiries at the bus depot and spoke to the driver of that late bus. He could remember the woman with the long legs and high heels. He recalled how she had got off the bus at the stop on North Road, near to its junction with Randall Way, in Hallcroft.'

'Did any other passengers get off at that stop?'

'No. The bus stop is less than a hundred yards away from Vanessa's house. He did remember her tottering across the road and thought she looked a bit tipsy.'

'Does he remember seeing anything else? Any other people or vehicles on the street?'

'Nothing.'

'Is his bus fitted with an onboard camera?'

'Unfortunately not. They aren't being phased in until the beginning of next year.'

'Okay, so she was last sighted a hundred yards from her home address. What did the husband have to say?'

'He was at home, waiting for her to arrive. He just assumed she'd gone off with another bloke in town.'

'Why would he assume that?'

'Their marriage is on its last legs, boss. From what we gathered from Vanessa's best friend, it seems that she was about to leave Geoff Tyler. Having spoken to Geoff, it's obvious he knew that was happening, too.'

'Why are you so convinced he's not involved in his wife's disappearance?'

'It was the way he spoke about the shame of having to call

the police to say that he thought his wife had left him. It was genuine emotion. He just seems desperately sad at the situation he finds himself in. It's like he's lost all self-respect.'

'I take it you've done all the relevant checks at the property?'

Feeling somewhat annoyed at the insinuation, Rachel snapped back, 'Of course. We carried out a thorough search of the marital home, inside and out. There are no signs of a struggle and no sign of any major clean-up being done. We interviewed all the neighbours, and none of them had heard or seen any violent behaviour or arguments between the couple. Geoff Tyler has no previous criminal convictions, and there's no record of Vanessa Tyler ever being treated at the hospital for any injuries.'

Danny had picked up on Rachel's annoyance and said, 'I wasn't trying to teach you how to suck eggs. I just need to know that everything's been done correctly.'

'Yes, sir.'

'So, if we're satisfied that the husband isn't involved, that means Vanessa Tyler went missing or was abducted somewhere between the bus stop and home.'

Tina Cartwright said, 'Which fits the pattern of the mispers we've been looking at, and the attempted abduction at Manton. Another female walking home alone, along a dark street, who just vanishes into thin air. This has got to be an abduction.'

'I agree.'

He was thoughtful for a moment, then turned to Rob and said, 'I know you've been speaking with the special operations unit. When can they let us have some staff to start the search inquiry we've planned? I know you've got everything else in place.'

'Just before this meeting started, I took a phone call from Chief Inspector Chambers. He's giving us two sections of

SOU. They will be available for one week, starting tomorrow morning. I've arranged for them to be briefed here at six o'clock. They'll be available to carry out the searches of the farms and outbuildings within a five-mile radius of Beckett Wood.'

'That's great news. I want a full briefing at six o'clock tomorrow morning. I want all our staff involved in this search operation, as well as special ops. Let's flood the area with cops and get as many of the farms and outbuildings searched as possible. If it is the maniac from Manton who has struck again in Retford, there's every likelihood that Vanessa Tyler is still alive. I want everybody back here at six o'clock, and the searches to begin no later than seven o'clock.'

61

6.00am, 20 September 1988
MCIU Offices, Mansfield, Nottinghamshire

The main MCIU office was packed with detectives and officers from the special operations unit. Rob carried out the briefing, which was short and to the point. Officers were split into teams containing two detectives and four SOU officers. Each six-man team was given a list of farms, cottages and outbuildings to search that were all within the five-mile radius.

They were all given a copy of the artist's impression of the suspect from Beckett Wood, as well as a full description of the suspect vehicle, the scruffy Land Rover.

The SOU vans were loaded with the equipment and supplies needed for a search. The normally smartly dressed MCIU detectives were wearing jeans, sturdy boots and waterproof tops, suitable for searching a rural environment.

At the end of the briefing, Rob said, 'You've all got your

lists of premises to search. I'm going to be at Retford police station monitoring progress. As and when you're satisfied that a location on your list has been cleared, contact me on the radio, so I can mark it off on the map. If you get to the stage where you've completed all the tasks on your list and it's still daylight, contact me and I'll provide you with further locations. Are there any questions?'

DC Lorimar asked, 'If we locate a suspect and feel there's enough to make an arrest, where do we take the suspect?'

'Any prisoners are to be taken to the cell block at Retford police station. If you locate the suspect vehicle, contact me and I'll arrange for a full lift to the forensic bay at headquarters. Anything else?'

The room remained silent, so Rob said, 'Okay, let's get cracking. I want you all in position to start searching your first property by seven o'clock. Good luck.'

Danny sought out Andy Wills. They had been tasked to work together, along with four officers from C Section of the SOU. He spotted him talking to the SOU men and walked over. 'Morning, Andy. Have you got our list?'

Andy said, 'We've got a place called White Gate Farm at Misterton first.'

'Do you know where that is?'

Andy spread out a copy of the Ordnance Survey map for the area and pointed to its location on the map, saying to the SOU men, 'Are you happy you know how to get there?'

PC Naylor said, 'It looks straightforward, Sarge, but we'll follow you, so we don't get separated. We've got plenty of food and hot drinks in the van to keep us all going. Do we know how big White Gate Farm is?'

'I believe it's an arable farm that covers quite a large area. The main farmhouse is an old stone building, quite grand in its own way. I know there are several tithe cottages on the farm, as well some that aren't marked on the map. There's also several outbuildings, Dutch barns and silos, etc. I think we'll be at White Gate Farm for quite a while.'

'Do we know who owns the farm?'

'It's owned by Thomas Morgan. As is usual with rural properties, there are several shotgun licences issued for the property, so be aware and think tactically.'

'I was going to ask about any registered weapons at the farm – you've just answered that question.'

Danny said, 'Let's get cracking, then. The sooner we get up to Misterton, the sooner we can get started.'

62

7.00am, 20 September 1988
White Gate Farm, Misterton, Nottinghamshire

Sam Morgan heard the diesel engine of the plain white van as it drove into the courtyard of the main farmhouse, twenty yards away. The van was following a plain red Ford Escort. Both vehicles came to a stop and four men wearing navy blue boiler suits got out of the van and began to stretch. Sam was in the barn, working on the fuel pump of a tractor that had broken down the previous day.

It was only when he saw the word 'Police' on the men's overalls that he became concerned. He continued to watch the new arrivals through the slightly open barn door and saw an older man, wearing jeans and a wax jacket, get out of the red car. Another man also got out of the car, and both men then walked to the front door of the farmhouse. He saw the older man knock and then get out an identification badge, after which he started talking to his uncle's wife.

It was obvious they were police officers, too.

Opening the barn door a little wider, he heard the older man say that they were at the farm to make a search of all the buildings.

He silently pushed the barn door closed and then walked to the rear of the building. He knew he had to get back to his cottage before they searched it.

It would take him ten minutes to run from the main farm back to his cottage across the fields. Making sure he wasn't seen, he slipped through the vehicle entrance and started to run. As he crossed each field, he counted them down in his head.

He knew why the police were there, and who they were looking for. He was satisfied that he would still have time to prepare and make sure everything was hidden before they arrived to search his cottage.

63

7.10am, 20 September 1988
White Gate Farm, Misterton, Nottinghamshire

Thomas Morgan invited Danny and Andy into the farmhouse, saying, 'My wife says you want to search the house. Can I ask what for?'

Danny said, 'We're investigating the abduction and false imprisonment of a woman who was found on the railway line at Soss Lane just over a fortnight ago. I understand Soss Lane isn't that far from your farm.'

'It's between a ten- and twenty-minute drive, depending on what part of the farm you're on. Is it just this farm you're searching?'

'No. Over the next week or so, we'll be carrying out searches, right across this area.'

'Are you looking for anybody in particular?'

Andy took out the artist's impression of the suspect from

the Manton abduction and said, 'We'd like to speak to this man. Do you have anybody working on the farm who looks like this artist's impression?'

The blood in Thomas Morgan's veins ran cold when he saw the image. It could easily be a picture of his nephew, Sam.

He feigned indifference and said, 'It's not a very realistic picture, is it? The bloke on there looks almost deformed.'

Danny asked, 'Apart from you and your wife, does anybody else live in the farmhouse?'

'My two daughters. They'll be getting up for school soon. Have you got to search their rooms as well?'

'It will be a very cursory look, Mr Morgan. We'll wait for them to get up, so we don't disturb them.'

'Thanks.'

'I see you've got a Range Rover outside. Are there any other vehicles on the farm?'

'There are three tractors, a variety of trailers and an old Escort van. They're all in the main barn.'

'Do you have a Land Rover Defender here as well?'

'No.'

'Do you have any labourers or seasonal workers living on the farm?'

'No.'

Thomas Morgan's wife, Sally, had walked back into the kitchen just in time to hear Danny's question and her husband's response. She said, 'Don't forget Sam. He lives on the farm.'

Thomas shot his wife a dagger's look and said, 'He doesn't live *here*, though, love.'

'Who's Sam?'

'Sam's my sister's boy, my nephew. He's got his own cottage on the other side of the farm.'

'Will he be at the cottage today?'

'He's always on the farm somewhere. Will you be searching his cottage as well?'

'We're going to search every building on the farm, every cottage, every outbuilding, every barn, the lot. I'll get the men to start on the barns and outbuildings around the farmhouse first. That will give you time to get your daughters up and ready for school.'

Sally Morgan said, 'If you're starting in the barns, you'll probably see Sam. He was in the main barn earlier, trying to repair a broken-down tractor. If he works at his normal speed, he'll no doubt be in there all day.'

Danny nodded and said, 'I'll get my men started, then come back and have a chat with you to see if all the buildings on your farm are marked on our map. We don't want to miss any.'

'No problem.'

As Danny and Andy left the farmhouse, Thomas Morgan rounded on his wife and snarled, 'Why did you have to mention Sam?'

Sally glared back and said, 'Why shouldn't I? He lives on the farm, so what's your bloody problem?'

'Go and get the girls up and ready for school. I don't want them getting upset by all this nonsense today.'

As Sally flounced out of the kitchen, Thomas sat down heavily on one of the wooden chairs. Thoughts raced through his head. *What has Sam done now? Was he responsible for abducting that woman?*

He prayed the police didn't find anything incriminating at Sunnybank Cottage, and that they somehow overlooked the resemblance Sam had for their artist's impression.

He didn't dare start to contemplate all the problems it would cause him, and his family, if Sam was involved.

His troubling thoughts were banished by a sharp rap on the kitchen door.

Danny stepped back inside carrying the map and said, ‘Can we have a look at the map now, Mr Morgan?’

‘Yeah, no problem. I’ll put the kettle on and make us a brew.’

64

7.25am, 20 September 1988
Sunnybank Cottage, White Gate Farm, Misterton, Nottinghamshire

Sam Morgan stomped down the stone steps into the cellar. He was immediately met with a torrent of foul abuse from the woman manacled to the wrought-iron bed.

He shouted above her tirade. 'Shut your noise!'

Intimidated by the sheer size of her captor and the aggression in his voice, the woman stopped shouting abuse, but yelled, 'Who are you? Why are you doing this to me?'

Sam didn't answer. Using the tea towel he had brought from the kitchen, he gagged the woman. He tied the makeshift gag tightly around her mouth, leaving her nostrils clear, so she could breathe. He checked the gag couldn't be moved, then each of the manacles to make sure none of them had worked loose and that she was still secure.

He was trying to remain calm and controlled, but he felt frightened and panicky. He leaned over the woman, grabbed a handful of her hair and pulled her face close to his. He could see the fear in her wide eyes, as he snarled, 'Stay quiet. If you make a sound, I'll bury you like the others. Understood?'

The woman nodded frantically, as tears started to well in her eyes.

Sam shoved her head back onto the mattress and made his way back up the steps. He closed and locked the door, then dragged the heavy Welsh dresser across the stone slabs until it entirely covered the cellar door.

By the time he had finished, there was no trace of the entrance to the cellar.

He sat down at the kitchen table and tried to stem the panic he could feel rising inside.

If the police didn't find the cellar, he would be okay. There was nothing to connect him to the missing women in the cottage. Everything was in the cellar. He reached into the back pocket of his dirty trousers and took out his wallet. He opened it, looking for the solicitor's card. He felt comforted when he saw the black card with the fancy gold lettering. If the worst came to the worst, Mr Carruthers would help him. He put the wallet back in his pocket. Everything would be alright.

He stood up and walked to the fridge, counting aloud as he paced across the room. He grabbed four rashers of bacon and again counted out loud as he placed them in the frying pan on the stove. He lit the gas and started to butter two thick slices of bread.

The smells and sounds of frying bacon soon filled the kitchen.

For the first time since he had seen the police arrive at the farmhouse, Sam Morgan started to relax a little.

65

8.30am, 20 September 1988
White Gate Farm, Misterton, Nottinghamshire

From the kitchen window, Thomas Morgan saw the officers in boiler suits climbing back into their Transit van. There was no sign of Sam anywhere. The search of the farmhouse itself had been as promised, a very cursory look in each of the rooms. The searches undertaken in the outbuildings and barns had been far more thorough.

He was relieved that his wife had left to take the girls to school. The last thing he needed was for her to drop any more poison out to the two detectives in charge of the search.

He saw the CID men walking towards the farmhouse, so he stepped outside to meet them. He said cheerily, 'All done, then?'

Danny replied, 'All finished here. Thanks for your cooperation. Hope we didn't trouble your daughters.'

'I don't think they even noticed you were here; they were too busy moaning about having to go to school early.'

Danny chuckled and said, 'That's kids for you.'

'Where you off to next? I suppose Broad Oaks farm is closest. Will you be searching there next? You won't get much cooperation there, I'm afraid. Frank Soames is a miserable old bastard.'

'Broad Oaks is on our list, but we've got to finish up here first. We need to search the cottage your nephew lives in before we leave.'

'Didn't you speak to Sam in the barn?'

Andy said, 'He wasn't there. The tractor's still in bits, so he may have gone to get a part. Hopefully, he'll be at his cottage.'

Hopefully, he isn't, thought Thomas.

'What will you do if he isn't there?'

'We'll wait. We need to search his cottage, so if he does come back here in the meantime, will you send him home, please?'

'Of course, no problem.'

Thomas Morgan was filled with trepidation as he watched the white van and the small red car drive away from the farm. He had a very bad feeling about all this.

66

8.35am, 20 September 1988
Sunnybank Cottage, White Gate Farm, Misterton, Nottinghamshire

Andy stopped the CID car outside Sunnybank Cottage and said, 'Bloody hell. You'd never know this place was here, it's that far off the beaten track. It must be a lonely existence, living right out here.'

Danny stared at the remote cottage and replied, 'I know what you mean. I bet it's bleak in the winter. Let's go and see if anybody's home.'

As the two detectives got out of the car, the white Transit van containing the four SOU men also pulled into the courtyard.

Danny walked over to the van and said, 'Grab a quick coffee while we see if anyone's home.'

PC Naylor said, 'Right you are, boss.'

As Danny and Andy walked towards the cottage, the front

door was opened by a giant of a man. Andy whispered, 'Look at the size of him. He's not a million miles from our artist's drawing, is he?'

Danny whispered back, 'No. He isn't. Which raises the question, why didn't his uncle mention that, when you showed him the picture earlier?'

The giant said, 'Can I help you?'

Danny said, 'We're police officers. We've just come from White Gate Farm. Thomas Morgan told me that I could find Sam Morgan here.'

'I'm Sam Morgan. What do you want?'

'We want to have a look around your cottage and the outbuildings.'

'What for?'

Danny could immediately tell that Sam Morgan wasn't the brightest man he'd ever met. He was a giant of a man who looked immensely powerful, but he spoke in a very matter-of-fact, almost childish way.

He said gently, 'Does anybody else live here with you, Sam?'

'Not any more. Mum died. It's just me now, and that's how I like it.'

'Can we come inside and talk to you?'

'I don't know. The police frighten me.'

'There's no need to be afraid of us, Sam. All we want to do is have a quick look around, then we'll leave you alone. Will that be okay?'

Reluctantly, Sam nodded. 'Alright. Are you all coming in?'

'No. Just the two of us for now. I'll tell the officers in the van to look in the outbuildings and the barn, if that's okay?'

'Okay.'

Andy walked back to the SOU van and said to Tom Naylor, 'We could be onto something here, gents. Have you seen the size of this bloke? Bin the coffees and go and search the outbuildings. We'll go and have a look inside the cottage.'

'Okay, Sarge. Watch your step. If you do find something and he kicks off, it's going to be a nightmare trying to restrain him.'

'Don't worry, Tom. Whatever we find in there, we won't push him until we need to.'

As Andy walked back towards the front door of the cottage, the SOU officers made their way to the main barn.

Once Andy had joined him inside the cottage, Danny said, 'Right, Sam. How many rooms does the cottage have?'

'Not many. I like to count them. There's this room, where I cook and eat, number one. Next door is the toilet and the bath, number two. Upstairs there are two bedrooms, mine is number three and my mum's, number four. That's it. There's also a toilet outside, but I never use it, because it's full of spiders and it stinks, so I don't count it. It doesn't have a number.'

'I get that, Sam. Let's start upstairs, shall we?'

The search of the two bedrooms didn't take long; it was quickly apparent that nobody else was staying at the cottage. As the two detectives followed Sam back down the stairs and into the kitchen, there was a loud knock on the front door.

Andy opened the door and saw Tom Naylor standing there. 'I need a word, Sarge.'

Andy stepped outside the cottage and walked a few paces away from the door. As soon as he was far enough away to be out of earshot of Sam Morgan, he said, 'What's up?'

Tom whispered, 'There's an old, battered Land Rover Defender with a smashed nearside brake light in the barn. It was hidden under a tarpaulin.'

'Good work. Get your colleagues and wait out here. If we need to nick this bloke and he turns nasty, it will take all of us to arrest him safely.'

Tom sprinted off and returned seconds later with the other SOU men.

Andy said, 'Wait here.' Then he walked back inside the cottage.

Danny asked, 'Everything okay?'

Andy looked at Sam Morgan and said, 'Is that your Land Rover in the barn?'

'Yeah, but it doesn't start, the engine's knackered. I haven't driven it in years.'

'Where are the keys?'

'There, on the table.'

Andy grabbed the keys and said, 'Come with me. Let's see if this motor starts, shall we?'

Sam became agitated. 'I'm telling you, it won't start. I never go anywhere in it. The engine's blown up.'

He followed Andy out of the front door of the cottage but stopped when he saw the four SOU officers all standing in the courtyard. He started to turn to go back inside the cottage, but Danny blocked his path and said quietly, 'Let's all wait out here, Sam. If the Land Rover doesn't start, there's no problem, is there? And if it does start, we'll just need to have a longer chat, okay?'

Still slightly agitated but placated a little by Danny's calm, quiet voice, Sam nodded. Andy walked into the barn and saw the Land Rover Defender in the corner. On the floor next to the vehicle, he could see the old tarpaulin that had covered it before it was removed by Tom Naylor and his colleagues.

Andy sat inside the vehicle, slipped the key into the ignition and turned it. The engine fired into life first time. Andy glanced down and saw that the fuel tank was three-quarters full.

He switched off the engine and walked out of the barn. As he emerged, he could see Tom Naylor and his colleagues all desperately trying to hang onto the man mountain. Andy immediately ran over to help, but by the time he got to the melee, Tom had managed to place his handcuffs onto Sam Morgan's thick wrists.

Once he was handcuffed, he stopped struggling and started to whimper. Danny shouted, 'Calm down, Sam! Nobody's going to hurt you. We need to take you to the police station, so you can answer some questions, that's all. I'll make sure you're looked after when you get there. Okay?'

Sam looked down at the floor and nodded.

Danny recited the words of the caution and said, 'Sam Morgan, you're under arrest on suspicion of the attempted abduction of Doreen Smedley at Worksop, on the eleventh of September.'

Sam didn't reply to the caution, and Danny said, 'We'll talk to you properly when you're at the police station, but I need to ask you one thing before we take you there.'

Sam didn't raise his head. 'I'm frightened.'

'Don't be frightened; nobody's going to hurt you. I just need to know if you've got anybody else here with you. Either hidden in the cottage or in one of the outbuildings.'

He lowered his eyes and shook his head.

Danny looked at Tom Naylor and said, 'I want two of you to take him to Retford police station. Don't question him en route. Get him booked into custody and make sure the custody sergeant knows that I think we'll probably require the services of an appropriate adult to look after his welfare. I think he may have some special needs. Keep him quiet and try not to antagonise him any more than he already is. I don't want him kicking off in the cell block and causing any injuries when you get there.'

'Understood, boss. I'll go with Matt and book him in myself. There won't be any dramas. By the time we get to Retford, I'll be his best mate.'

'Thanks, Tom. Be careful.'

Danny and Tom walked over to Sam Morgan, who was now sitting in the back of the SOU van, being watched by Tom's three colleagues. Tom climbed into the van, sat next to the man mountain and said cheerily, 'Don't worry, Sam. We're just going for a little ride. I'll sort you out with a nice cuppa when we get to the police station, okay?'

Danny said, 'Sam, do you want me to tell your uncle what's happening?'

Sam Morgan remained stock still and stared at the floor of the van. He didn't acknowledge Danny's question and continued slowly counting out loud: 'Thirty-three, thirty-four, thirty-five...'

Danny said, 'Straight to Retford, Tom. Remember what I said about an appropriate adult.'

Tom closed the side door of the van and said, 'Let's get going, Matt.'

As the white van pulled out of the courtyard, Andy said, 'Do you think it's wise to have just one man in the back of the van with him? If that giant starts playing up, it could get very messy.'

'I think it would frighten him, and possibly wind him up quicker, if he was surrounded by burly cops. Tom and Matt are both experienced. They know what they're doing.'

He paused before continuing, 'I want a scenes of crime team out here, and I want a full lift organised for the Land Rover. I want that vehicle under cover and in the forensic bay at headquarters sooner rather than later.'

'I'm on it, boss.'

Danny looked towards the remaining SOU officers and said, 'Before we do anything else, I want you two to give all these outbuildings a thorough search. Let's make sure we're not missing something obvious here.'

As the two officers walked towards the barn and the outbuildings, Danny walked back into the small cottage. He stood in the kitchen and looked carefully around. There was no sign of there being anybody else in the property. There was one plate, one mug, and one knife out on the kitchen table. The only clothes to be seen were a pair of scruffy overalls on the floor, next to the ancient washing machine.

He walked into the bathroom. At the side of the dirty sink was one disposable razor, one tube of shaving foam, one toothbrush, one tube of toothpaste and one bar of soap. Hanging from the sink was one grimy, dirt-stained hand towel, which looked as though it had been in the bathroom for ever.

As he walked back into the kitchen he sat down on a rickety wooden chair next to the table and looked around the room. Outside, the morning sun was low in the sky and the sunlight shone directly under the front door.

The light highlighted something on the flagstones that he hadn't noticed before.

The door suddenly opened, flooding the kitchen with sunlight. Andy walked in saying, 'Everything's in hand, boss. Scenes of crime are travelling, and the vehicle examiners are on their way with a low loader.'

'Close the door and come here.'

'Boss?'

'Close the door and come here. Look back towards the door. What do you see?'

'Drag marks on the flagstones.'

Danny was already on his feet and staring at the heavy pinewood Welsh dresser. 'Give me a hand to shift this bloody monstrosity.'

Using all their combined strength, the two detectives slowly dragged the solid wood dresser back along the same drag marks to what would have been its original position, exposing the hidden door.

Danny tried the handle. It was locked. He said, 'We need

to get this door opened. Start looking for the key. It won't be far away.'

After five minutes, Andy opened the cutlery drawer next to the oven and saw an old mortice key. He slipped it into the door lock, gave it a half turn and unlocked the door.

Slowly, he began to open it, revealing a flight of stone steps that led down into a black void.

67

10.00am, 20 September 1988
Sunnybank Cottage, White Gate Farm, Misterton, Nottinghamshire

Andy pushed the door wide open and stared down into the darkness. Danny was standing right behind him. 'Can you see a light switch?'

Andy felt along the cold stone wall until his hand brushed against a light switch. He flicked the switch down and the space below was illuminated with a dim light. The two detectives could now clearly see the stone steps that led into a cellar.

With a rising sense of trepidation, they made their way slowly downwards. Andy saw the bed first, then the woman, manacled and gagged, and shouted, 'Boss!'

They dashed across the room. Danny could smell the acrid stench of urine and see the fear in the young woman's eyes as they approached. He grabbed Andy, stopped him before he reached the bed, and said to the woman, 'Don't be frightened, we're police officers.'

He took out his identification card and held it, so the woman could see it.

'My name's Detective Chief Inspector Flint and this is Detective Sergeant Wills. We've arrested the man upstairs. I'm going to remove that gag now. Please don't be frightened.'

He stepped forward and started to untie the tea towel that was bound tightly around the woman's head. As he did so, he looked at Andy and said, 'Get some drinking water from upstairs.'

Finally, Danny managed to loosen the tight knot and remove the makeshift gag. He said, 'What's your name?'

The woman coughed and tried to clear her dry throat before spluttering, 'Vanessa.'

Andy returned with the water and helped the woman to sit up and take a drink. She was able to move her arms enough to take the glass and swallow the much-needed liquid.

Danny looked at one of the steel manacles that kept her chained to the bed. 'Do you know where he kept the keys for these bloody things?'

Vanessa shook her head and said, 'I've never seen the keys. I was grabbed near my home in Retford and, when I woke up, I was already chained to this bed.'

Danny said to Andy, 'Contact Rob at Retford police station. Tell him to talk to Tom Naylor in the custody suite. I want any keys found in the property of Sam Morgan bringing back here as soon as possible. When you've done that, search the kitchen to see if the keys are upstairs anywhere. My guess is he would keep these keys on his person somewhere, but we need to look here, too.'

'I'm on it, boss.'

He looked back at Vanessa and said, 'We'll get these off you as soon as we can. Are you okay to talk now? Can I get you anything else?'

'I've been here ages; I've already wet myself a couple of times, and I'm desperate to spend a penny again now.'

Danny looked around the room and saw the bucket in the corner of the room. He grabbed it and said, 'It's not ideal, but it will do until we can get these manacles off you. I'll put it here, so you can reach it. I'll go back upstairs, and you can call me when you've finished doing what you need to do.'

'Thanks, Detective.'

Danny smiled and said, 'Call me Danny, okay?'

He placed the bucket next to the bed, turned and walked up the stone steps. He closed the door at the top of the steps and waited on the other side.

After a few minutes, Vanessa shouted, 'It's okay to come back down now, thanks.'

Having walked back down the steps, Danny moved the used bucket back to the corner of the room and sat cross-legged on the floor. He didn't want to sit on the bed, as he knew there could be vital forensic evidence on the sheet.

He asked, 'What's your full name, Vanessa?'

'Vanessa Tyler. How did you know I was here?'

'We didn't. We knew you were missing, and we were looking for you, but we had no idea you were here.'

'Did my husband report me missing?'

'No. Your best friend, Amanda.'

'Thank God for that.'

'Can you remember anything about how you got here?'

'I'd been out in town with Amanda. We'd had a few drinks and I caught the bus home. I was bit tipsy and wasn't paying attention. The next thing I know somebody had grabbed me. I tried to fight back, but he was too big and strong. Anyway, he punched me or hit me with something, and must have knocked me out because when I woke up I was chained to this bed.'

'We'll talk to you properly later, when we've got you out of here and you've been checked over by a doctor, but I need to know if this man has touched you in any way?'

'Sexually?'

'Yes.'

'Not at all. I've only seen him twice since he put me down here.'

'What happened?'

'The first time he came down with a mug of water and a sandwich. I'd been down here ages by then, and I was starving hungry and thirsty as hell, so I ate and drank the lot. Then he shouted at me for wetting the bed sheet and scolded me for not using the bucket. When I tried to explain that I hadn't seen the bucket, he got mad and moved it out of my reach. He told me I would have to lie on the wet sheets as a punishment.'

'What about the second time?'

'That was about an hour before you came down here. He looked panicked and told me not to make a sound or he'd bury me like the others. Then he tied that fucking gag around my head so tightly I thought I was going to suffocate. I could barely breathe.'

'He said he'd "bury you like the others"?'

'They were his exact words. It terrified me. I thought he was going to kill me. I just never made a sound. I could hear things being moved around upstairs, but I was too scared to try and make a noise down here. I honestly thought I was going to die down here.'

Danny could see the tears starting to form in Vanessa's eyes, and that she was becoming visibly upset.

'Try and stay calm; we'll have you out of here soon. If we can't find the keys, I'll arrange for somebody to come and cut these things off you. It won't be long now, I promise. I'll be back in a minute.'

'Please don't be long. I'm frightened down here.'

68

10.15am, 20 September 1988
Retford Police Station, Retford, Nottinghamshire

As Tom Naylor and Matt Jarvis walked into the custody area at Retford police station, escorting the handcuffed giant Sam Morgan, they could see the eyes of the custody sergeant widen at the sheer size of the prisoner.

Sgt Steve Matthews was old school; he had been a sergeant for over twenty years and was resigned to the fact he would never be promoted to inspector. He looked at the huge prisoner standing in front of his desk and heard that he was muttering something to himself.

Steve Matthews looked at Tom Naylor and Matt Jarvis quizzically. 'What's he saying?'

Tom said, 'He's counting, Sarge. Reciting numbers. He's been doing it non-stop since we set off in the van to bring him here. He gets to a hundred, then starts again.'

The sergeant stared at Sam Morgan, who remained head down and looking at the floor.

'Do you know his name?'

'Sam Morgan.'

'Did he give you any trouble?'

'Not a bit. He's been fine in the van.'

'Okay. Let's leave the cuffs on him until we get him in the cell, just to be on the safe side. Have you searched him yet?'

'We made a cursory search for weapons, but we haven't searched him properly yet.'

'Let's get him booked in first, then we'll search him in the holding cell. Are you the arresting officer?'

'No, Sarge, that was Detective Chief Inspector Flint from the MCIU.'

'Reason for the arrest?'

'He's been arrested on suspicion of the attempted abduction of Doreen Smedley at Worksop, on the eleventh of September this year.'

'Were you present at the arrest?'

'Yes, Sarge. Those are my handcuffs.'

'Where was he detained?'

'At his home address, which is a cottage on White Gate Farm, Retford. I'm sorry, I don't remember the name of the cottage.'

'No problem, "White Gate Farm" will do. I take it searches are being carried out and that the chief inspector will want to interview the prisoner at some stage?'

Tom nodded. 'That's correct.'

For the first time, the sergeant addressed Sam Morgan directly. 'Sam, look at me.' He waited until the giant raised his head and made eye contact. 'Sam, you've heard what this officer has said to me. Do you have anything to say about the circumstances of your arrest?'

He slowly shook his head.

Steve Matthews obtained all Sam Morgan's personal details before saying, 'Sam, I'm authorising your detention at this police station, so that officers can obtain evidence by carrying out searches at your home address and by questioning you later. Do you understand what's happening?'

Once again, Sam Morgan nodded but said nothing.

The telephone began to ring behind the sergeant. He turned and snatched it off the receiver. After a short conversation, he put the phone down and turned back to face Tom Naylor. 'That was DI Buxton upstairs. There have been developments at White Gate Farm. You need to take Sam to the holding cell, search him thoroughly, and then bring him and anything you find back here.'

Tom and Matt walked Sam to the holding cell. Tom said quietly, 'Don't panic, Sam. I need to have a look through your pockets now, to make sure you haven't got anything in them that you shouldn't have, or that's valuable and needs to be looked after, okay?'

Sam did not respond, so Tom started to go through his pockets. From his right trouser pocket, he removed a dirty handkerchief and two small keys on a chrome ring. From his left trouser pocket, he removed a wallet. There was one five-pound note, several bits of loose paper and a fancy black card with gold lettering.

Tom completed the search and found nothing else.

They walked Sam back to the custody sergeant. Tom said, 'This is all he's got on him, Sarge.'

The sergeant listed the prisoner's property and then said, 'Sam, you're entitled to free legal advice while ever you're here at the police station. Do you want me to contact a solicitor?'

It was as if somebody had switched on a light. Sam Morgan became suddenly very animated, and said, 'Yes. Solicitor. In my wallet.'

Steve Matthews picked up the wallet and found the black card with the gold lettering. 'Do you want me to contact this solicitor – Frank Carruthers?'

'Yes. He'll help me.'

'Okay, Sam. I'll give him a call and sort that out for you. These officers are going to take you to a cell now. Are you going to behave yourself, if I ask them to take the handcuffs off you?'

Sam nodded. 'I don't want any trouble. I'll behave.'

The sergeant looked at Tom and said, 'Take him to Cell One. I can keep an eye on him in there.'

Tom and Matt walked with Sam to the cell, opened the door and walked in. Tom said, 'Sit down on the bench, Sam. I'm going to take these handcuffs off you now. Any trouble and I'll put them straight back on. Understand?'

'No trouble.'

Tom unlocked the cuffs and removed them. Sam immediately lay down, turned over and faced the wall. He drew his huge legs up to his chest, as his giant frame barely fit on the wooden bench.

Tom said, 'Can I get you a cup of tea or anything?'

There was no reply from the giant.

The SOU officers locked the cell door and returned to the custody area. Rob Buxton was waiting for them. He handed them the keys that Tom had found during the search of Morgan and said, 'You need to get these keys back to Morgan's home address as quick as you can. DCI Flint has found a woman locked up in the cellar of the cottage. She's currently secured to a bed with steel manacles that they can't get off. Hopefully, these keys will unlock them.'

'Bloody hell. Okay, boss, we're on our way.'

Tom turned and spoke to the custody sergeant. 'There was one other thing Chief Inspector Flint wanted. He thought that Morgan should have an appropriate adult supporting him for any interviews. I know that's ultimately your decision, but that was the boss's take on it.'

Sgt Matthews said, 'I don't think it would hurt. It's always a little disconcerting when you see a person of Morgan's physical size who also appears educationally challenged. I'll get that arranged.'

'Thanks, Sarge. I hope he doesn't give you any trouble down here. I've taken the cuffs off him now, so be careful if you need to go into the cell.'

69

11.30am, 20 September 1988
Sunnybank Cottage, White Gate Farm, Misterton, Nottinghamshire

Danny and Andy were standing outside Sunnybank Cottage, talking to Tim Donnelly, the scenes of crime supervisor.

Almost three-quarters of an hour had passed since Vanessa Tyler had been released from her steel shackles and taken to Bassetlaw General Hospital by ambulance.

The keys found in the pockets of Sam Morgan had unlocked the manacles. More damning evidence against the man mountain currently in the cells at Retford police station.

Danny had immediately contacted Rachel Moore and informed her to travel to the hospital and arrange for a subsequent medical examination by a police surgeon. Danny knew this would be an unpleasant ordeal for the victim, but it was necessary to establish, evidentially, if there had been any sexual assault committed against the imprisoned woman. The clothing Vanessa was wearing would also need to be seized as evidence, and clean, dry replacement clothing found.

The priority was to get the woman medically examined to ensure she wasn't suffering any health issues after her three days of captivity. Rachel would ensure that the subsequent police procedures would be carried out in a sympathetic and caring manner. An interview and witness statement could come later.

Danny looked at Tim and said, 'How are your people getting on in the cellar?'

'It's a veritable gold mine of forensic opportunity down there, boss.'

'Go on.'

'There's a large ottoman pushed against one of the side walls that's stuffed full of stained bedsheets. We're in the process of bagging all that bedding individually. It's going to need to be dried out properly before we can examine it forensically.'

'Good. Anything else?'

'We've found minute traces of blood splashed on the wall that the bedhead was against. I think it will be worthwhile to do a full Luminol procedure down there, once we've completed the initial examination and obtained all the photographs we need.'

Danny had seen how the Luminol procedure worked on previous cases and was shocked. He said, 'Shouldn't you do the Luminol first?'

Tim shook his head 'It will have to be done last. Once we've applied Luminol in that confined space, we won't be able to work down there for a few days. In a confined space such as that, with very little ventilation, the fumes created would be too toxic.'

'Won't all your activity damage or destroy any evidence that may be there?'

'It might, but I don't think so. It must be done in that order, boss. I'm sorry.'

'I understand; no problem. Let's hope, when you do it, it still shows plenty.'

'I've also got a team ready and waiting to make a full forensic examination of the Land Rover at headquarters. How long since the vehicle examiners left?'

Andy Wills said, 'They left about fifteen minutes ago, so they should be about another thirty or so minutes before they get to the forensic bay.'

'Thanks, Andy. I'll go and let them know.'

Tim walked back to the scenes of crime vehicle to use the radio to contact headquarters.

Danny said, 'Andy, you're local to this area. Roughly, how long would it take to drive from here to where Fiona Wright was found on the railway tracks?'

'To Soss Lane from here would take around twenty to twenty-five minutes in a car. Don't forget that the dog handler lost the track in the middle of Beckett Wood, and that's no more than fifteen minutes from here.'

Danny stroked his chin and said, 'If it was Morgan that our witnesses saw in Beckett Wood that morning, which now seems more and more likely to be the case ... what the hell was he doing there at that time of day?'

'There could be any number of reasons.'

'Something that Vanessa said to me in the cellar has got me worried.'

'What?'

'When Morgan gagged her and ordered her to be quiet, he followed it up with a verbal threat. He told her that if she didn't remain silent he would bury her like the others. It could have been just a threat to menace the woman into staying quiet, but if you couple that remark with Fiona Wright's comment about her being "number four", it becomes more sinister.'

Andy remained silent, as he could see that Danny was deep in thought, weighing up all his options.

Finally, Danny said, 'What if Sam Morgan was in Beckett Wood that morning to dispose of Fiona Wright's body? And what if, somehow, she was still alive and managed to escape his clutches? I think Beckett Wood could be Sam Morgan's dumping ground.'

'You think there could be other victims in those woods?'

'I want to find out once and for all. Draw in the SOU personnel from the other search teams. We've found Vanessa Tyler, so there's no need to continue with the searches of other farms. There's no need for DI Buxton to remain at Retford police station, now the search is over. I want him and everybody else I've mentioned to rendezvous at the entrance to Beckett Wood. I want a cadaver dog from the dog section to also be available for the search. I'll go and talk to Tim and see if he has any staff available who can also travel to the wood.'

'I'll get onto the control room and start getting things organised, boss.'

'Thanks, Andy. I'll need you to stay here and control this scene.'

'No problem.'

Andy turned and walked back to the CID car to contact the control room, leaving Danny alone with his thoughts.

Something deep inside his subconscious was already telling him that Beckett Wood held a deadly secret. His wife's comment suddenly rushed into his brain: *Trust your instincts.*

70

2.00pm, 20 September 1988
Beckett Wood, near Misterton, Nottinghamshire

The small column of police officers walked along the dirt track that bisected Beckett Wood. At the front were PC Davis and PC Stark from the dog section. PC Davis had his springer spaniel, Tikka, on a lead. PC Stark had attended with his colleague, so he could point out where his dog had lost the track he had followed when Fiona Wright had been found.

Danny Flint and Rob Buxton walked a few yards behind them, and they were followed by a dozen or so officers from the special operations unit, led by Sergeant Graham Turner.

The SOU officers were carrying tools and equipment they might need to carry out a search of the woodland. They were also carrying digging implements.

Bringing up the rear of the column were three scenes of

crime personnel. They had been the last to arrive after being called out from home by the control room. They would be supervised by Tim Donnelly just as soon as the Luminol procedure had been completed in the cellar of Sunnybank Cottage.

At the front of the column, PC Davis suddenly stopped and said, 'This is where I lost the original track, boss.'

Danny said, 'Thanks.'

He called up Sgt Turner and said, 'I need your men to form a line each side of the track and make their way into the woods. I'm interested in any areas of disturbed earth or signs of recent digging.'

'Yes, sir.'

Sgt Turner organised his men. He spaced them out two metres apart on either side of the path. He didn't have enough staff to complete a sweep of the woodland in one go, so knowing he would need to form further lines to finish the search, he placed a marker at the furthest point.

When they were in position, he shouted, 'Right, lads. Put your tools and any other items you're carrying on the track behind you. You know what you're looking for. Take your time and stay in line. There are no prizes for being first. I want a thorough search doing. Let's go!'

After fifteen minutes, Danny heard a shout from the woods. 'Over here, Sarge!'

A few minutes later, a breathless Sgt Turner emerged from the woods and said, 'You'd better come and see this, boss.'

Danny and Rob followed the experienced sergeant back into the woods, being careful to follow exactly in his footsteps. After a few minutes, they saw the line of SOU officers still standing in line. At the far end of the line, there was a clearing in the woods about the same size as a tennis court. It was obvious that the trees in that area had been felled for some reason and never replaced with new planting. There were still stumps of oak, sycamore and ash trees protruding from the ground, like ancient stone monoliths.

There were at least three areas of disturbed soil that Danny could see at various points around the clearing.

Sgt Turner said, 'What do you think, boss?'

'I want you to get the dog handlers up here. Let's see if PC Davis and his dog get any indications.'

'Yes, sir.'

There was a brief delay and then Danny heard the dog handlers approaching with Sgt Turner.

Danny looked at PC Davis and said, 'I want you to work your dog on the mound of disturbed earth that's nearest to us. Just that one first. If there's any kind of indication, come back here and let me know, okay?'

As PC Davis put the working lead on his small, excitable dog the change in the animal was immediate and evident. As soon as the different leash went on, the dog knew it was now expected to work.

PC Stark, standing behind Danny, said, 'I love watching these springers work. They're such amazing dogs.'

Danny said nothing, but stared intently at the liver-and-white-coloured dog as it traversed back and forth over the disturbed earth.

Suddenly, the dog stopped and started to scratch at the soil with its front paws. Then it stopped and lay down on the disturbed earth and began barking at its handler.

PC Stark said, 'That's the sign for an indication. The dog's onto something. It could be an animal, but there's something dead beneath that disturbed ground.'

PC Davis produced a small plastic toy from his pocket as a reward for his dog. The gleeful dog began to chew on the toy, as the working leash was replaced with the ordinary one.

The dog handler walked back to Danny and said, 'That's a clear indication, sir. You'll need to dig that area.'

'Thanks.'

Danny turned to Graham Turner and said, 'The dog has given a positive indication. I'll need you to detail four of your men to start digging that first patch of disturbed earth.'

'We'll need to fetch the tools from the path.'

'Quick as you can, Graham. If there is something down there, it's going to be a long job getting them out, and we'll be running out of light soon. Get scenes of crime up here as well. I want the dig photographed and video recorded, if possible.'

The sergeant started barking instructions at his men, and within ten minutes the dig had started. The spades were pushed carefully into the soil, then the earth removed onto a separate pile. When the hole was approaching three feet in depth, one of the SOU men suddenly stopped and said, 'There's something here.'

Sgt Turner, standing at the side of the hole, shouted, 'Stop digging!'

Danny and Rob walked over to the sergeant. Danny peered into the hole and could see the remains of what was obviously a human foot. There was flesh still on the bones, but it had plainly been under the earth for a lengthy period.

He looked at Rob and said, 'Well. Now we know. Let's start getting things organised. I'll need all the vehicles bringing up onto the track. We'll need emergency lighting and generators up here for when the light goes.'

He glanced at his watch. 'I reckon we've only got about another four hours. I've no idea what the weather forecast is for this evening and tonight, so we'll need tents organising. I want a Home Office pathologist here as soon as possible to supervise the excavation of the body.'

Rob replied, 'What about all the other areas of disturbed earth?'

'That's what I was just thinking, Rob. How many other bodies are we going to find here?'

71

4.00pm, 20 September 1988
Beckett Wood, near Misterton, Nottinghamshire

Danny was pacing up and down impatiently. Once again, he glanced at his watch and said to Rob, 'How much bloody longer is it going to take Seamus Carter to get here?'

'He was still in the city when he was contacted; he shouldn't be much longer. At least the lighting and everything else is organised.'

'I know, but I've got to consider we have a suspect in custody as well and the detention clock is ticking.'

'On that point, boss – I think it would be a good idea if we have a preliminary interview with Morgan. We should at least question him about the attempted abduction for which he's been arrested.'

'That's a good idea. Arrange for DI Cartwright and DC Lorimar to travel to Retford and have a quick interview with the suspect. That way we can make sure that legal advice, appropriate adults, etc. are all organised and everything's in place for when we want to interview him about what we've found here. '

'I thought you wanted Tina to supervise the inquiries into the oil companies?'

'Right now, this has got to take priority. The other three detectives can continue with those inquiries; they don't need a DI to hold their hands. I need Tina up here working on this.' Danny was thoughtful a moment, then continued, 'I think it would be a good idea to get a police surgeon to examine Sam Morgan first. I don't want any accusations being made later that he was unfit to interview. There's something not quite right with that man. Depending on what else we find here, we will also need to consider going to the magistrates for a warrant of further detention.'

'Okay, I'll get things organised, boss.'

As Rob walked to the CID car, Danny sought out PC Davis, who was sitting in the dog section van. He said, 'I've got a question for you. Would your dog still be able to work other areas of that clearing, even though a cadaver is already exposed to the air?'

PC Davis said, 'The dog works on ground scent, not airborne scent, so theoretically she should. Why?'

'While we have some daylight left, I want you to work your dog over the other areas of disturbed earth in that clearing. Can you do that?'

'Yes, sir. I'll get Tikka from the back of the van and we'll give it a go.'

Danny followed the handler and his dog back to the clearing, where he found Sgt Turner having a coffee with his men.

The burly sergeant said, 'Any sign of that pathologist yet, boss?'

Danny said, 'He won't be much longer. PC Davis is going to cast his dog over the other areas of disturbed earth while we're waiting to see if she makes any further indications.'

'We were just saying the same, sir. We were wondering how many other bodies may be buried here.'

'Time, and a little springer spaniel, will tell us soon enough, Graham.'

Sgt Turner looked at his men and said, 'Finish your drinks, gents. There may be more work to do shortly.'

PC Davis slipped on the working leash and cast the dog over another area of disturbed earth. The dog worked excitedly, dashing from side to side, with its nose to the ground.

Nothing.

The experienced handler shook his head and moved to the next area. Once again, the dog started working. This time, there was the same pawing at the ground, followed by the dog laying down and barking at the handler.

PC Davis rewarded the dog with its toy and shouted, 'This area's a possible, boss.'

Sgt Turner walked over and drove a spade into the top of the soil.

The dog worked four more areas that were all negative before moving onto the one area of disturbed soil left. It was on the far side of the clearing. Almost as soon as the dog started to work the area, it began pawing at the ground before barking furiously at its handler.

PC Davis said, 'Wow! I've never had such a strong indication. This area will need digging, boss.'

Once again, Sgt Turner marked the area with a spade, turned to his men and said, 'Right, gents. I want four of you at each indicated site. Start digging and be careful. I don't want anybody driving a spade through something they shouldn't. Take your time.'

72

5.00pm, 20 September 1988
Retford Police Station, Retford, Nottinghamshire

The police surgeon emerged from the examination room and said, 'Sam Morgan does have educational and social issues, but they are not related to any mental illness. His standard of education is very poor, but he understands why he's here and what is happening to him. He's fit for interview.'

Tina Cartwright replied, 'Thanks, doctor. We've already arranged for an appropriate adult to be present at all interviews, and he does want legal advice. His solicitor is here and has been given disclosure.'

The doctor completed the detail of her examination of Sam Morgan on his custody record and left the cell block with a cheery 'Good luck' as she left.

Glen Lorimar watched the doctor leave, then said, 'How can anybody be that happy in their work?'

Tina replied, 'Beats me. Let's get this interview started and see what Mr Morgan has to say.'

Twenty minutes later, the two detectives were sitting opposite Sam Morgan in the cramped interview room. He was flanked by his solicitor, the chain-smoking Frank Carruthers on one side, and by his appropriate adult, Stephanie Dawson, on the other.

Glen Lorimar introduced everyone present. He reminded Morgan that he was still under caution and then said, 'Sam, you were arrested earlier today on suspicion of the attempted abduction of a woman on the Manton estate in Worksop on the eleventh of September. Do you understand why you've been arrested?'

Sam Morgan leaned forward, placed his elbows on the table and nodded.

'Sam, you must answer the questions. We need to hear what you've got to say. Okay?'

'Sorry. Yes, I know why I've been arrested.'

'Where were you on the night of the eleventh of September?'

'I went for a drive.'

'Where did you go?'

'All over. I can't remember where, exactly.'

'What did you go for a drive in?'

'My Land Rover.'

'Is that the same Land Rover the police found at your cottage, when it was searched earlier?'

'Yes. I've only got one.'

'I've been told that vehicle at your cottage has some damage to the rear lights. How did that happen?'

Sam looked down at the table and began tapping his index finger on his thumb. Without looking up again, he mumbled, 'Can't remember.'

'I didn't quite catch that, Sam. Can you speak up a little?'

'Can't remember.'

'You must remember how it happened. Does anybody else drive it?'

'No. Just me. And I can't remember.'

'We have a witness who states he used a baseball bat to smash the rear light on a Land Rover after the driver had tried to abduct one of his neighbours. Is that how the damage was caused?'

Sam remained silent.

Glen matched the silence and waited.

Eventually, there was an almost imperceptible nod of the head.

Glen said, 'Are you nodding again, Sam?'

When Sam Morgan looked up, there were tears in his eyes. 'Yes, that's how it happened. I thought that man was going to smash my windscreen. He scared me.'

'What happened just before he did that to your vehicle?'

'I didn't mean to hurt her. I just wanted her to look after me, like my mum used to.'

'Didn't mean to hurt who?'

'The woman from the shop. She looked kind. I thought she would look after me, if I took her back to the cottage.'

Glen was a little taken aback at what he had just been told, but he recovered quickly and said, 'Have you taken other women back to your cottage to look after you?'

Morgan nodded again, then said hurriedly, 'Yes.'

'How many?'

'Five.'

'And where are those women now, Sam?'

Once again, he started tapping his index finger against his thumb and said quietly, 'Can't remember.'

Frank Carruthers took a deep pull on his latest cigarette and said, 'I would like to talk to my client before this line of questioning continues.'

Tina made eye contact with Glen, indicating that she wanted to speak.

She said, 'Let's take a break there, Sam. I'm sure your solicitor will want to talk to you first, then we'll get you a cup of tea.'

'Okay.'

She then looked at Frank Carruthers. 'In light of what's just been said, I can see why you need another consultation with your client.'

The solicitor stubbed out his cigarette and immediately lit another, before saying, 'I think I should. I think we'll need to have a chat as well. I think there's information I haven't been made aware of yet, don't you, detective?'

Tina said, 'Let us know when you've finished your consultation, and we'll have that talk.'

She turned to Stephanie Dawson and said, 'Do you want to come with us, Mrs Dawson, while Sam talks to his solicitor? I don't think we'll be interviewing him again for a while, so you can either wait here at the police station or go home and wait for our call.'

The middle-aged woman said, 'If it's all the same to you, I'll nip home and get my kids' tea ready. I'll make sure I'm near the phone at home. I'm only a five-minute drive away.'

'Perfect. We'll call you as soon as we're ready for the next interview.'

The detectives left Sam Morgan alone with Frank Carruthers in the interview room and walked back to the custody office.

While Glen completed the custody record, Tina found a telephone and contacted the control room.

After a brief pause, she said to the control room inspector, 'I need to get this message to DCI Flint: I want you to inform him that Sam Morgan has admitted the attempted abduction at Manton, and has indicated that he's abducted five other women previously. We've closed the interview down, until we know what's happening at Beckett Wood. I'll be in the CID office at Retford police station, so ask him to contact me on a landline as soon as possible. Thanks.'

She ended the call and walked back into the custody area just in time to see Frank Carruthers walking back towards the desk. For once, he didn't have a cigarette in his fingers.

He said, 'Can we talk, inspector?'

'I'm sorry, Mr Carruthers. I don't exactly know what's happening yet. What I can tell you is that we are currently searching woodland where we suspect there may be several graves.'

'I see. And you suspect my client referred to the occupants of those graves in that interview?'

'When I have more facts, I'll provide you with full disclosure. That's the reason I closed down the interview when I did.'

'A good call in my opinion, detective. I'm sure my client will continue to talk to you, despite my best efforts. It's his open, trusting nature, I'm afraid. There is another matter I'd like to discuss with the senior investigating officer in this inquiry. What I have to say is for their ears only, at this stage. No offence intended.'

'None taken. The senior investigating officer is Detective Chief Inspector Flint of the MCIU. He's currently at the search site. I'll get a message to him that you have information, and I'm sure he'll be keen to listen to what you have to say.'

'Thank you. It might go some way to explaining, if not excusing, my client's actions. I take it you *do* intend to carry out further interviews with Sam. Any idea when that might be?'

'I think it will be some time yet. There's no point interviewing him again until we know exactly what we're dealing with.'

'Quite so. The custody sergeant has all my numbers. Call me when you're ready, detective.'

Frank Carruthers turned and walked away, lighting yet another cigarette as he made his way towards the exit.

73

9.00pm, 20 September 1988
Beckett Wood, near Misterton, Nottinghamshire

The only sound was the constant hum of generators providing power for the three sets of white arc lights that cast eerie shadows around the clearing in the middle of Beckett Wood.

It was now over five hours since the cadaver dog had made the last indication. Supervised by the Home Office pathologist, Seamus Carter, the men from the special operations unit had worked tirelessly to unearth the human remains the springer spaniel had found.

The pathologist approached Danny and said, 'A quick update for you, Danny. The undertakers will be here in the next ten minutes. We're ready to remove the four bodies.'

Danny knew that only three burial sites had been located, so there was an element of surprise in his voice when he replied, 'Four bodies?'

'Three bodies appear to be those of adult females on first inspection. The fourth body is that of an infant, possibly new-born. The child was buried in the same shallow grave as one of the women.'

'Bloody hell. Just when I thought this situation couldn't get any grimmer.'

'It's hard to fathom what's happened, but it's possible the woman and the baby died during childbirth, and they were just buried together for convenience. I'll know more when I do the post-mortems tonight.'

Danny shook his head, struggling to come to terms with the horror that had happened in this tranquil place.

'Where are you taking the bodies? Bassetlaw Hospital?'

'Bassetlaw isn't suitable. It's far too small. No, I'm taking them to the City Hospital, where the facilities are so much better. It's going to be a long process; it would be far more efficient to have everything to hand.'

'When you say a long process, how long?'

'If we start the post-mortem examinations at ten-thirty tonight, it will take me well into the early hours of tomorrow morning before I've completed them all.'

'Okay. Let me know when the undertakers arrive. Have scenes of crime got everything they need?'

'They finished forty minutes ago. I'll get them to photograph the actual removal for continuity. Will I see you at the City Hospital, Danny?'

'I'll be there at ten-thirty. I'm going to leave Rob here with you, to manage the scene. I've been asked by the control room to attend Retford police station before I drive to the city. Apparently, Sam Morgan's solicitor has information that he will only give to me, and I need to make sure everything is in place ready for more interviews with Sam Morgan.'

Seamus nodded, then walked back across the clearing to

the first excavation site. As he left, Rob approached Danny. Walking alongside him was Andy Wills.

Danny said, 'What are you doing here, Andy?'

Andy said, 'I've been trying to contact you from Morgan's cottage, but that area must be a radio blackspot in places. The control room hasn't been able to receive my signals.'

'Is everything okay at the cottage?'

'Yes, boss. Scenes of crime have finished, and the cottage is now secured as a crime scene.'

'Did the Luminol procedure reveal anything?'

'I didn't see the process, as I was made to wait outside, but apparently there were numerous bloodstains revealed on the cellar floor and walls. The technicians told me that somebody had tried to clean up, using some sort of disinfectant. Despite this attempt to destroy evidence, there were still traces of blood evident in various places. It's all been photographed.'

'Have scenes of crime taken all the exhibits?'

'Yes, boss. All that stained bedding has been taken to headquarters for drying before it's submitted for forensic examination. I was trying to contact you to see what you wanted me to do now. When I couldn't get through on the radio, I thought I'd come here instead. I got the two SOU lads to bring me in their van.'

'We're almost ready to remove the bodies and convey them to the City Hospital. Rob's going to stay here until they're removed, so there's nothing left to do here. I'm going to Retford nick shortly, to speak with Tina and Glen about the interview they had with Morgan, and to brief them fully about what's been found here. I also need to speak with Rachel, to see if she's got an account from Vanessa Tyler yet.'

Danny stared at the piles of recently dug earth that punctuated the clearing. He was silent for a few moments before saying quietly, 'There is something I want you to do, Andy.

Go back to White Gate Farm and speak to Thomas Morgan. Find out why the fuck he lied about his nephew.'

Andy glanced at his watch.

Danny noticed the glance and said tersely, 'I know it's late, but I want you to tell him what we've found at the cottage, about the woman being held in the cellar. I want to know his justification, if he has any, for deliberately lying to us.'

'Do I tell him about the bodies here?'

'No. If you say anything about that, I think he'll clam up completely. From all the evidence we have so far, it looks like Sam Morgan has acted alone, but I want to keep an open mind about his uncle. I'm not happy about his evasive behaviour earlier; he would have let us walk off that farm without even speaking to his nephew. Concentrate your questions about his nephew. I want to know what he's like. Who his friends are, if he has any? Has he ever seen women at the cottage? Has he ever had a girlfriend? We don't know anything about Sam Morgan yet, and it's time that changed. You know what I want, Andy. Take Rob's car. He can get a lift back with special ops.'

74

9.30pm, 20 September 1988
White Gate Farm, Misterton, Nottinghamshire

The dogs around the farm barked fiercely as Andy Wills knocked on the front door of the farmhouse at White Gate Farm. The door was opened by Sally Morgan, who recognised the detective from earlier in the day.

She said, 'Hello again, detective. Did you want to see my husband?'

'Yes, please. I have an update for him.'

'You'd better come inside; it will shut the dogs up.'

As he walked into the spacious hallway, Thomas Morgan was descending the stairs. 'What's all this, Sal?'

'The detective has some news for us.'

Morgan glared at his wife. 'I'll deal with this.'

Sally shot him a furious look and went to walk up the stairs.

Andy noticed the friction between the two and said, 'Actually, I need to talk to both of you.'

Thomas Morgan scowled and said, 'Come through to the kitchen.'

Andy followed the husband and wife. 'There's been a development at Sunnybank Cottage. We've found something suspicious, and I need to talk to you both about your nephew, Sam.'

Thomas said, 'What about Sam?'

'Sam's at the police station for questioning, but we don't know anything about him. I want you two to tell me ... what he's like?'

'There's nothing to tell. Sam keeps himself to himself. He always has done.'

'Don't you ever visit the cottage?'

'No need. Why would I go to the cottage?'

'I don't know. To see if he was okay, maybe?'

'Sam's a grown man. He doesn't need me to make sure he's alright.'

Andy made eye contact with Sally Morgan and asked, 'Did he ever come here to the farmhouse?'

There was sharp edge to her voice when she replied, 'Not if I could help it.'

Again, a look of real venom flashed from Thomas to his wife, but before he could say anything, Andy said, 'Can you explain that comment, Mrs Morgan?'

'Yes, I'll explain. I never trusted him around our daughters. It's as simple as that.'

Thomas bellowed, 'That boy would never harm a hair on our girls' heads and you know it!'

Sally rounded on her husband and said, 'I *don't* know it, and neither do you. You know what happened before.'

'Hush, woman.'

'Don't you hush me. The detective needs to know what Sam's like.'

Andy said, 'What happened before?'

Sally answered first. 'There was some trouble with a Romanian picker. Sam had sex with her, and she told us that he had raped her.'

Thomas stood up and raged, 'That's enough! That's not what happened at all.'

Andy said, 'Why don't you sit back down and tell me exactly what happened, Mr Morgan?'

Thomas Morgan took a couple of deep breaths as he sat back down. Through gritted teeth, he said, 'That woman was trouble. She was approaching her mid-forties and liked the company of men, if you know what I mean. She caused fights between the male pickers, as she turned her favours from one to another. She was a tart.'

'What's that got to do with what Sam did?'

'Sam didn't do anything. He was a boy of fifteen at the time, but you've seen him. He's like a man mountain now; at fifteen, he was like a fully grown man. That whore got Sam on his own in one of the barns. She took off all her own clothes and stripped him naked. Tormented him until he became aroused and then made accusations when he wouldn't stop what she'd started. It was all her doing.'

'Were the police involved?'

'No.'

'Why not?'

'She didn't want to make a complaint.'

'But if Sam was only fifteen, and it happened the way you've just told me, she also committed a serious offence.'

'I just wanted her off the farm. I paid her what she was owed, and she left.'

Sally muttered, 'She was paid a lot more than she was owed.'

Thomas glared at his wife and said angrily, 'You don't know what you're talking about! Shut it!'

Andy said to Sally, 'Has Sam ever acted inappropriately around your daughters?'

Before she could answer, Thomas said, 'No. He has not.'

Sally shook her head and said, 'No, he hasn't. But I still don't trust him. I never know what's going on in his head.'

Thomas said, 'He can't help being a bit slow. That's just how he is.'

Andy said, 'What do you mean, slow?'

'My sister refused to send Sam to mainstream school. As a child, he had a very pronounced harelip scar. It was far more prominent then than it is now. He doesn't shave regularly, so it's almost always hidden by stubble. He was a big child, raw-boned and clumsy. My sister feared he would become the target of playground bullies, so she home-schooled him. He was a slow learner anyway, but because he never went to school and mixed with other kids he never developed any personal skills. He's painfully shy and doesn't know how to act around strangers or talk to people.'

'Has he ever had a girlfriend?'

Thomas made a snorting sound and shook his head. 'He has no interest in women, detective.'

'Have you ever seen him with a woman at the cottage?'

'Like I said before, I never go to the cottage.'

'What about you, Mrs Morgan?'

Sally shook her head and remained silent.

Andy said, 'Does Sam have any friends?'

Thomas said, 'No. As I've already told you, Sam's a loner. He keeps himself to himself.'

Andy paused before saying to Thomas, 'You seem very protective towards your nephew.'

'I suppose I am. I made a promise to my sister when she

died that I would look after him and make sure he always had a home here.'

Sally muttered, 'That bloody stupid promise. I'm sick of hearing about it.'

Thomas growled, 'Shut it, woman.'

Andy said, 'I don't want to cause an argument, but there's obviously a massive dispute between you two about Sam.'

Thomas said, 'My wife wanted him to go. Plain and simple. She didn't want him around the place, for reasons best known only to her. Sam's harmless. He wouldn't hurt a fly, and he certainly wouldn't hurt our girls.'

Andy remained silent for a few seconds. Then he said, 'Neither of you have asked me what we've found at the cottage that's made us suspicious about Sam.'

Thomas said, 'I didn't want to ask. I thought you'd tell us, when you were ready.'

'We found a woman bound and gagged in the cellar of the cottage.'

Sally gasped and Thomas spluttered. 'You've found what?'

'A woman was being held captive in the cellar.'

Thomas shook his head. 'Is this some kind of sick joke? Sam would never do anything like that.'

Sally said quietly, 'Was she still alive?'

'Yes, she's alive.'

She glared at her husband with a look that was a mixture of disbelief and horror, and said angrily, 'Thank God for that.'

Thomas was in a state of shock himself and muttered, 'What's going to happen to Sam now?'

'He's been arrested, and will be questioned about this and other matters.'

'Will he be charged?'

'It's too early to say, but there's a lot of evidence that implicates him.'

'Does he have a solicitor, to look after him?'

'I don't know. If he requests legal advice, a solicitor will be provided before we interview him.' Silence filled the farmhouse kitchen until Andy said, 'Thank you both, for being straight with me. Is there anything else you think I should know about Sam before I leave?'

Thomas said, 'Nothing I can think of.'

Sally just stared at the floor and never said a word.

Andy stood up and said, 'We'll want to talk to you both again.'

Thomas walked the detective to the door and said, 'No problem. We'll both be here.'

As he watched the detective walk back to his car, Thomas Morgan felt physically sick. If Sam had asked for a solicitor, the real trouble for him and his family was only just beginning.

75

3.00am, 21 September 1988
City Hospital Mortuary, Nottingham, Nottinghamshire

The examination room was busy.

The pathologist Seamus Carter and his student, Brigitte O'Hara, had been assisted by three scenes of crime officers as they carried out individual examinations on the bodies recovered from Beckett Wood. Danny and Rob were both present, observing the pathologist in his grisly task. DC Phil Baxter had carried out the exacting role of exhibits officer.

The four bodies had been laid out on separate stainless steel examination tables.

Seamus Carter had completed the final examination, that of the dead infant found with the third body. He looked exhausted as he approached Danny. 'All done, Danny.'

'What are your initial findings?'

'Mixed.'

'Go on.'

'I've only found injuries consistent with violent death on one of the bodies. As we still have no identifications, I will call this female Body One. She has a massive head injury to the rear of her head. The shape of the skull fracture looks like it was caused by a heavy instrument, cylindrical in shape.'

Rob said, 'Like a crowbar?'

'No, wider. More like a heavy metal pipe of some description. Body One also has a fractured cheekbone and eye socket, so two sites of physical violence.'

Danny asked, 'Murder?'

'Certainly, the head wound alone would have caused a massive haemorrhage. She could easily have bled out from that injury.'

'Okay. What about the next one?'

'On Body Two, I can find no physical injury that would have caused death. There is evidence of damage to the heart. It's possible she died of heart failure, but it's also possible there was an underlying health condition that has contributed to her death. Without her medical records, I have no starting point where to look.'

'Such as?'

'There are numerous examples I can think of. One of the more common ones would be something like type-one diabetes.'

'If that was the case, and Body Two was a diabetic deliberately deprived of insulin, could that constitute murder?'

Seamus let out a sigh and said curtly, 'That's not for me to speculate. My job is to tell you how these people died, not to tell you whether it's murder or not.'

There was an edge to the burly pathologist's voice that wasn't usually present. He paused, rubbed the bridge of his nose, and then continued. 'I'm sorry, Danny. I know you already know that, and that you were only speculating. Please ignore my terse comment. It's been a long day.'

'No problem, Seamus. You're right, it has been a very long day, and it was a bloody stupid question. What can you tell me about Body Three?'

'This poor woman died during childbirth. There is evidence that she suffered what's called a placental abruption. This would have caused the unborn infant to die rapidly, and the mother to suffer a severe haemorrhage. Even with immediate medical assistance this condition is often fatal for both mother and child. Without medical intervention, death for both would have been very swift.'

Rob said to Danny, 'If this woman was deliberately denied medical assistance as she gave birth, we could be looking at two separate murders.'

Danny said to Seamus, 'Is there any way of knowing if this infant ever lived independently of its mother?'

'I've carried out all the tests I can. Because of the level of decomposition, I can't say one way or the other. I can't say for certain that Body Four ever drew a single breath and had a separate existence.'

Danny looked at Rob and said, 'Without that evidence, we couldn't support a murder charge for the unborn child.'

He turned back to Seamus and said, 'What about identification of the three women?'

'Brigitte has managed to get partial fingerprints from all three adult victims. The level of decomposition has made it a very difficult task. As soon as the examination room empties, I'll get the portable X-ray machine in here. I'll obtain X-rays of their jaws, so dental records can be checked.'

'Thanks. Is there anything else that could be helpful for identification? Any operation scars, old fractures or tattoos?'

'Sorry, I haven't found anything else.'

'How soon can you let me have your report?'

'I'll have the reports to you by tomorrow evening. I'll make sure the X-rays of the teeth are with your exhibits officer before we leave.'

'Thanks, Seamus. You need to go home and get some rest. You look beat.'

The big pathologist nodded. 'If I close my eyes, I think I'll sleep for a week.'

Danny said, 'Have that week off after you've done my report, okay?'

Seamus smiled and nodded, but said nothing.

Danny said to Rob, 'I want you to make sure everybody's at Retford police station for a full briefing at eight o'clock this morning.'

'Will do. I'll get the control room inspector to start putting calls in to people at home.'

'How's Tina getting on with the warrant of further detention?'

'Everything's completed. Morgan's initial twenty-four hours runs out at ten-fifteen this morning. Tina will be in court at nine o'clock to see the magistrates. With everything we've discovered in Beckett Wood and Sunnybank Cottage, getting the extra twelve hours to question Morgan will be a formality.'

'It might be a formality, but it will still only give us until ten-fifteen tonight before we have to charge Morgan. We need to plan and carry out the interviews and do our utmost to identify these three women. I want everyone not involved in the interviews to concentrate on identification. Have you had any update from Rachel at Bassetlaw Hospital?'

'The last I heard, Vanessa Tyler had finished with the medics and Rachel was sitting down with her, obtaining a full witness statement.'

'That's some good news. At least we'll know how Morgan abducted her and what happened to her at the cottage.'

'Why don't you go home, boss? You'll need to be sharp later today. I can help Phil Baxter get all the exhibits back to Mansfield nick. There's no need for us both to stay.'

'I'm not going to argue, mate. I'll see you at Retford, eight o'clock sharp.'

'I'll be there, boss.'

76

7.00am, 21 September 1988
Retford Police Station, Retford, Nottinghamshire

Danny walked into the main briefing room at Retford police station. He had spoken to the station superintendent and arranged for the MCIU to be allowed to use the large room as a base for their ongoing investigation. It was the only room large enough to accommodate all the detectives involved in the Beckett Wood investigation.

Even though he was an hour early for the planned briefing time, he wasn't surprised to see Tina Cartwright, Rob Buxton, Rachel Moore and Andy Wills, his supervisors, already in the room. They were huddled in a tight group, deep in conversation.

Danny said, 'Morning, everyone. It's going to be another long day; I hope you all managed to get some rest.' He looked at Rob and said, 'Have you been home at all?'

'I got a couple of hours. I'm fine.'

Rachel said, 'I came in early, as I wanted to talk to you before the briefing. I obtained a detailed statement from Vanessa Tyler at the hospital, then as I was leaving, I was approached by the staff nurse who was overseeing the intensive care unit last night. She told me that Fiona Wright had regained consciousness and that she would be ready to be interviewed by us in a day or so. They wanted to monitor her progress for another forty-eight hours before placing her under too much stress.'

'That's great news, Rachel. Did the nurse indicate if Mrs Wright had made a full recovery?'

'She told me that all the early indications were good, and that they expected her to make a complete recovery. There didn't appear to be any sign of long-term cognisant damage, but that it was still a little early to be certain.'

'I want you to stay with that. Stay in contact with the hospital today. I want to know the moment we can talk to her. We need to obtain as full an account as we can get from her, as soon as the doctors allow. What did Vanessa Tyler have to say?'

'Some of her recollections of the actual abduction were quite hazy. She had been drinking and could only remember parts of what happened. She remembered getting off the bus at the stop nearest to her home and walking along the empty street. She recalled seeing a dirty, scruffy Land Rover, then being grabbed from behind. She started to struggle and was struck on the head.'

'Did she see her attacker?'

'No, she was grabbed from behind. She does remember thinking how strong he was, but that's all.'

'What else does she recall?'

'She remembers waking up in the cellar and realising that

she had been chained to the bed. Her head was sore, and she was extremely thirsty. She was still wearing the same clothes as she had been wearing for her night out. She was relieved that she was still wearing her bra and knickers, and that she didn't think she had been touched sexually.'

'Has that been confirmed by her medical examination?'

'Yes, it has. There's no evidence of any sexual assault.'

'When did she see her attacker?'

'She saw him twice. The first time, he came down and gave her food and water, but shouted at her for wetting the bedclothes. He scolded her for not using the bucket next to the bed. The second time, he came running down the cellar steps in a state of panic. He told her to be quiet, and then gagged her so she couldn't make a sound.'

'Would she be able to identify him?'

'Definitely.'

'She made a comment to me when I found her in the cellar. Did she repeat that?'

'Yes. She told me that as he tied the gag around her head, the man said that if she made a sound, he would bury her like the others.'

'Did she say what she thought he meant by that comment?'

'Vanessa told me his comment had terrified her, because of the way he said it. She thought she was going to be killed by this man, and that she would die in that cellar.'

Danny looked at Tina and said, 'I know I asked you to concentrate on the inquiry into the oil companies, but I want you and Glen to continue with the interviews today. Are you okay with that?'

'No problem. The three detectives I've left working that inquiry are all fully briefed on what we're looking for and trying to achieve. It's only going to be preliminary inquiries for the first few days, gathering information to assess the size of the task.'

'That's good.'

'Me and Glen got on okay with Sam yesterday. His solicitor is quietly efficient, without wanting to interrupt all the time. I've arranged for the same appropriate adult to be present today. She did an excellent job yesterday and Sam seemed to trust her.'

'Have you told the appropriate adult about the findings in Beckett Wood? I don't want her to be surprised when you start talking about multiple bodies being recovered, including that of an infant. I don't want that awful conversation to come as a surprise to her.'

'I'll tell her when she arrives at the station this morning. I appreciate that the appropriate adult scheme is staffed by unskilled volunteers; it would be unfair not to pre-warn her. I just need to be careful how I word it. I don't want her to have any preconceived ideas about Sam's possible involvement.'

'Exactly right. She still needs to act as his appropriate adult and look after his welfare. Have you and Glen discussed a strategy yet?'

'We spent all yesterday discussing our options. I'm glad I've got the full statement from Vanessa Tyler now. My intention was to start with her abduction and deal with that first. If he does make full admissions as to his involvement in that offence, it will mean we are able to charge him with the two abduction offences, if we run out of time on the detention clock before we can identify the bodies. At least then we'll be able to remand him in custody and interview him later about the dead women.'

'It's one option. Ideally, I would like to interview him about the bodies found in Beckett Wood before we charge him.'

'Maybe the best way in would be to use the comment he made to Vanessa Tyler about burying her like the others?'

'That could work. You'll have to see how he responds to your questioning today. He could be totally different, and not want to speak to you at all.'

'We'll soon see. I've arranged for his solicitor and the appropriate adult to be here at nine o'clock for disclosure. I hope the mention of dead bodies doesn't make the solicitor change his attitude or advice to Sam Morgan.'

Danny shrugged his shoulders. 'If it does, it does. You'll have to work with what you've got.'

He turned to his other supervisors and said, 'I want you to divide the detectives into three teams. I want you to concentrate on one victim each, and get them identified. Start by using the missing person list prepared during the early stages of the investigation. We now have physical descriptions, partial fingerprints and dental records to compare against. I think it's highly likely that the three women we found will be on that list somewhere. Your only task today is to positively identify each of the victims as soon as possible. Once you've achieved that, Tina and Glen will be able to question Sam Morgan properly about their abductions, and how they died. Get started as soon as people arrive; there's no time to waste. We haven't got much time.'

As Rob, Rachel and Andy moved away and started to discuss which of the victims they would be trying to identify, Tina spoke quietly to Danny. 'Sam Morgan's solicitor, Frank Carruthers, wants to talk to you in private about his client.'

'Yes, I was informed about that by the control room yesterday. I was hoping to speak to him when I got to Retford last night, but he'd gone. Do you know what he wants to speak to me about? Does he want to make a complaint?'

'No, it's nothing like that. It was all very strange. He said he has something he needs to talk to you about, that might go some way to – he said, "explaining, if not excusing, my client's actions". '

'What the hell does that mean?'

Tina shrugged. 'Beats me, boss. I told you it was strange.'

'Okay, let me know when Mr Carruthers arrives, and I'll talk to him.'

77

9.45am, 21 September 1988
Retford Police Station, Retford, Nottinghamshire

Danny walked into the custody area and spoke to the custody sergeant. 'I believe there's a solicitor down here who wants to speak to me?'

The sergeant looked up from his paperwork and replied, 'It's Frank Carruthers, who's representing Morgan. I've put him in Interview Room Two.'

Danny walked down the corridor and into the interview room. Frank Carruthers was sitting facing the door. The elderly solicitor's briefcase was already open on the desk.

Danny said, 'Mr Carruthers, my name's Detective Chief Inspector Flint. I'm the officer in charge of the investigation into your client. I understand you wanted to speak to me in private?'

'I have something I need to show you that relates to Sam Morgan. It may or may not be pertinent to your inquiry.'

Danny was intrigued and sat down opposite the grey-haired solicitor dressed in the black three-piece suit. With his dour expression and sombre clothes, the man had the appearance of a funeral director.

'And what exactly is this something?'

'I am in possession of a letter from Sam Morgan's mother, Louisa. She came to see me in my office and drafted the letter shortly before her death. The instruction she gave me was both detailed and specific. The letter should only be opened, and the contents shown to the police, if Sam Morgan was ever evicted from Sunnybank Cottage on White Gate Farm, or if he was arrested for something that was likely to lead to him being imprisoned. From the disclosure I've just received, I think the latter criteria could be a distinct possibility. A long term of imprisonment is highly likely, if he's charged and subsequently found guilty of these offences at court.'

The solicitor leaned forward and took out a Manilla envelope that had been sealed with a red wax seal. There were two signatures either side of the seal.

Danny inspected the envelope and noted the signatures. One was Louisa Morgan and the other Frank Carruthers.

He made eye contact with the solicitor and asked, 'I take it you're aware of the contents of the letter?'

'Yes, I am. I drafted the letter at Louisa's dictation. Like I said to your colleague, the document in no way exonerates my client from the offences for which he stands accused, but it could provide you with answers as to why he is the way he is, and therefore could offer some mitigation.'

'As intrigued as I am by all this, Mr Carruthers, I don't want to open this letter right now. I understand you've now had full disclosure about the matters about which we wish to question your client. As you can appreciate, they are extremely serious matters, and I don't want any further distractions at this time. Unless you're going to tell me there's something in this document that totally exonerates your client from these offences, I'd rather deal with it at the conclusion of this inquiry.'

The solicitor picked up the envelope, returned it to his briefcase and said, 'As you wish, Chief Inspector. The letter does hold quite startling revelations, which will require your attention, but nothing in the contents relates to the matters you wish to question Sam Morgan over, so it will keep.'

'I promise you I will give it my full attention at the conclusion of this inquiry, Mr Carruthers. How long will you need to consult with your client?'

'Forty minutes tops. There's quite a lot to go through, but Sam doesn't hold his concentration well, so I'll need to go through things quite quickly. I warn you now, my advice will be for him to decline to answer all your interviewer's questions. Having said that, I doubt very much that he will follow that advice. Forty minutes should be plenty of time.'

'Thank you. Have you spoken to Stephanie Dawson, the appropriate adult, yet?'

'We said hello in the waiting area upstairs. She's a very competent woman. I'm happy that she'll look after Sam's welfare needs to the best of her ability.'

Danny stood up to leave and said, 'I will look at the letter and take the appropriate action when the time's right. I'll let the interviewing team know that it shouldn't be too long before you're ready for them to resume their interviews with your client.'

'Would you mind asking the sergeant to get Sam Morgan out from his cell, so I can have a consultation with him?'

'No problem.'

78

10.30am, 21 September 1988
Retford Police Station, Retford, Nottinghamshire

The atmosphere in the small office adjacent to the main briefing room was tense. Danny was deep in discussion with Tina and Glen about the imminent interview with Sam Morgan.

Danny said, 'It can't be much longer. The solicitor reckoned forty minutes would be long enough.'

Tina replied, 'All this waiting around is ridiculous. Talk about the wheels of justice grinding slowly.'

Glen grunted. 'That's PACE for you.'

Danny said, 'There are a lot of good points from the Police and Criminal Evidence Act, but the delaying tactics it allows some solicitors isn't one of them.'

There was a loud knock on the door and an excited Rachel Moore came into the room, followed by Rob Buxton.

Rachel said, 'We've just identified Body Two. She was a

young woman named Emma Bridge who went missing on the sixth of October 1986.'

Danny said, 'That's great work. I've heard that name before.'

'She was on our list of possibles from the missing persons files.'

'How did you make the identification?'

'From dental records. When we drew up the list of likely missing persons reports that fitted a similar pattern to Fiona Wright's disappearance, we made sure that the missing persons' dentists were also on the report. Emma Bridge was on that list of similar pattern offences, so it's been a quick and easy process to get in touch with the dentist Emma Bridge used and make the comparison.'

'How sure are you that it's her?'

'The dentist is certain that the X-ray taken of Body Two's jaw matches the X-rays they have on record for Emma Bridge. It's definitely her, boss.'

'What do we know about Emma Bridge, from the original missing persons report?'

'She was a type-one diabetic who needed insulin injections every day to prevent her lapsing into a coma.'

'Which would tie in with what Seamus Carter said at the post-mortem. He hypothesised that there may have been an underlying health condition which had contributed to her death.'

'If she was held in that cellar without insulin, it would only have been a matter of time before she fell into a coma and died.'

'Exactly. What were the circumstances of her going missing?'

'Emma worked at the Crown pub in Bawtry. She was last seen by the landlord as she left after her shift to make the short walk to her home a few streets away. She never arrived. Her parents reported her missing the same night.'

'Rachel, I need you to visit her parents straight away. They need to know what's happened to their daughter.'

'Will do, sir.'

'Leave everything you've found out about Emma Bridge here with me and the interview team. Good work, Rachel.'

Rob said, 'It gets better, boss.'

'Go on.'

'We've also got a positive identification on Body One in the same way. The decision to put the dentist details on the file has been key. It's saved us hours of work.'

'So, who is Body One?'

'A teenager named Susan Claymore. She went missing on the tenth of May 1986 after a night out at the local youth club on the Manton estate in Worksop.'

'Manton again.'

'Yeah. From what we can gather on the inquiries done on the original missing persons file, the circumstances were very similar to the attempted abduction of Doreen Smedley.'

'I remember this case. You highlighted this one as also being a possible when you were looking at similar abductions to the Manton offence. Remind me, who was the last person to see her?'

'A young lad named Billy Ayers. He was the main suspect at the time. From what I've read, it appears that he was a bit of a Jack the lad and a troublemaker. When he was interviewed, Billy admitted to having a fumble and a snog with Susan after the youth club, and before they went their separate ways. He always maintained that she left him to go and catch the last bus home. According to the time he said they split up, the timeline didn't fit because she would have been too late to catch the last bus. That's the main reason he was a suspect.'

'And maybe they were kids that just got carried away. I don't suppose either of them were looking at their watches. Maybe she ended up missing the last bus and had to walk home.'

'If that was the case, she could have walked straight into the clutches of Sam Morgan.'

'It's possible. He's already admitted to the attempted abduction of Doreen Smedley, so he knows the Manton estate. What else do we know about Susan Claymore?'

'By all accounts, Susan was a young, naïve teenager who was very much reliant on her parents. They doted on their daughter and did everything for her. She had never been missing before and had never even spent a night away from home.'

Danny was thoughtful. 'To be snatched off the street and put in that cellar would be terrifying for anyone, but for a young teenager it must have been horrific.'

Rob nodded. 'It doesn't bear thinking about. Did you notice how close in time the two abductions were? Only five months between them.'

'I saw that. It's something Tina and Glen are going to have to try and establish when they interview Morgan. I want you to go and see the parents of Susan Claymore straight away, Rob. It's vital they are informed of the situation before this information becomes public knowledge. Leave me everything you've got on Susan. Good job, mate.'

'Will do, boss.'

'Any news on Body Three?'

'Andy told me they've drawn a blank on the dental records. They are running fingerprint checks now on the list of likely missing persons. That's going to take a bit longer. You know what intricate, painstaking work fingerprint comparison is, and the prints from the post-mortem aren't the best.'

'I want every available member of staff they've got in the fingerprint bureau working on this as a top priority. We need to identify Body Three as soon as possible.'

Rob and Rachel left the office to go and give the devastating news to the two families, leaving Danny with Tina and Glen.

He was quiet for a few minutes, then he said, 'In this next interview, I want you to concentrate your questions to Sam Morgan on the abduction of Vanessa Tyler. I want you to get him used to talking to you again. Take it easy on him, allow him to feel more confident before you apply any pressure. Try and establish exactly why he wanted her in the cellar. What were his plans for her? Finish the interview by asking an open question. Something like, how many other women have you had staying in your cellar?'

Glen nodded. 'I like that plan, boss. There's every likelihood he won't want to talk to us at first, but if we take it slow and ease him in gently, I think he'll want to talk.'

'His solicitor was of a similar opinion. He thinks that whatever he advises his client to do, eventually he will start talking to you.'

'Let's hope so, boss.'

There was another knock on the door. DC Baxter opened the door and said, 'The custody sergeant has just been on the phone. Sam Morgan is ready to be interviewed now.'

Danny stood up and said, 'Finally. Thanks, Phil.'

He turned to Tina and Glen and said, 'Get cracking. You know what I want from this interview. With any luck he'll talk to you, and by the time you get back we may have identified Body Three. Good luck.'

79

10.55am, 21 September 1988
Retford Police Station, Retford, Nottinghamshire

The interview with Sam Morgan had been running for almost ten minutes before he decided to answer a question. He had maintained a silent response to every question asked, not even offering a 'no comment' answer.

Glen had allowed a long silence in between each question, and he could see Morgan starting to squirm in his chair, so instead of asking another question about Vanessa Tyler, he changed tack and said cheerily, 'It must be so nice living in that cottage on the farm, Sam.'

A beaming smile flashed across the giant's face and he immediately said, 'It's great. I love it.'

With a resigned air, Frank Carruthers took his pen from his pocket and made a note of his client's reply. He knew the floodgates would now open, and that his client would talk.

He had lasted five minutes longer than Carruthers had anticipated in maintaining the silence he had advised.

Glen continued the general questions about the cottage and the type of work he was expected to do, and then he said, 'Don't you ever get lonely at the cottage?'

Morgan replied, 'Sometimes. Since my mum left me, it gets very quiet.'

'What happened to your mum?'

'She got sick and died.'

'I'm sorry to hear that, Sam. I bet you miss her.'

'Oh yeah. She used to do everything for me. There was always breakfast and dinner to eat when Mum was here.'

'How have you coped since she left?'

'It's been okay. I just did what she told me to do before she died.'

'What was that?'

'I went and got a good woman to look after me.'

'You mean you have a girlfriend?'

The huge man sitting opposite coloured up a little and said, 'No. Don't like girlfriends. I just got a good woman to look after me, that's all.'

'I don't understand, Sam. Look after you in what way?'

'To cook my meals and clean up around the place, like Mum used to do.'

'Is that what Vanessa Tyler was in your cellar for, to look after you?'

Sam Morgan nodded.

'Remember I told you yesterday that we needed to hear your replies, Sam. You must speak your answer.'

'Sorry. Yeah. That's what I brought her back to the cottage for.'

'Where did you bring her from?'

'Retford. I saw her in the town centre. She had really long legs, and I thought she looked nice.'

'What do you mean, "nice"? Did you find her attractive?'

'Not sure what "attractive" means. I thought she looked happy and friendly.'

'Okay, so what happened?'

'I watched her get on a bus, so I followed it. When she got off the bus she was on her own, so I decided to take her back to the cottage, so she could look after me.'

'And how did you do that?'

'I made sure no one else was around, and I just grabbed her.'

'Wasn't she scared?'

'Yeah, she struggled, but I had my hand over her mouth so she couldn't scream. I didn't really want to, but I hit her once, so she would be quiet, then I put her in my motor and drove away.'

'Do you mean your Land Rover?'

'Yeah.'

'And what did you want her to do at the cottage?'

'Just to cook meals and clean up for me, that's all.'

'Nothing else? Didn't you want her to be a proper girlfriend, who you could kiss and cuddle with?'

'No. I don't like that. It's not good. Trouble comes from that.'

'How many times have you done this, Sam? How many women have you had staying in your cellar at the cottage?'

'She was number five.'

80

11.30am, 21 September 1988
Retford Police Station, Retford, Nottinghamshire

Tina and Glen were beaming as they walked back into the main briefing room. Danny was standing next to Andy and saw them come in.

'I take it the interview went well?'

Tina replied, 'He was refusing to speak at first, but then Glen got him talking about the cottage and the farm, and he opened right up.'

'What did he say about Vanessa Tyler?'

'He made full admissions. He saw her in Retford town centre, followed her until she got on a bus, then when she got off the bus alone, he snatched her off the street.'

'Did you find out anything about his motivation?'

'It's all a bit weird. All he wanted was a housekeeper. He took Vanessa Tyler because she looked happy and friendly. He wanted her to cook meals for him and clean the cottage.'

'Nothing else?'

'If you mean sexual needs, apparently not. He's not interested in having a girlfriend, as it causes' – she paused briefly – '"trouble".'

Danny shook his head. 'I don't get it. What on earth would give him the idea that it was okay to grab a random stranger off the street just to look after him?'

Glen said, 'I think Sam Morgan sees the world in very simplistic terms. There are no grey areas for him. It's either black or white, hot or cold. His dying mother told him that he had to find a good woman to look after him after she had gone. It seems to me that Sam took her words literally. He's gone out and tried to find just that: a good woman to look after him.'

'You could be right, Glen. From what Andy was just telling me, I don't think we're going to get a breakthrough on the identification of body three anytime soon, so I want you to start planning for the next interview while Morgan's still in the mood to talk. I want you to put the bodies we've found in Beckett Wood to him. Have you any thoughts on the best way to introduce it?'

Glen replied, 'I was thinking about this last night. I reckon the best way would be to question him about the sighting we have, when he grabbed the dog and returned it to its owners. If I can get him thinking he's done a good thing by returning the lost dog, it will get him in the mood to answer my questions. It will also show that he was in Beckett Wood at the time when Fiona Wright was found on the railway tracks. It's a short step then to asking him why he was in Beckett Wood.'

'That sounds good to me. Any other thoughts, Tina?'

Tina replied, 'I think that's the smart move. Morgan does seem to respond better when he's asked about things that aren't related to specific people, or when he's talking about things that are familiar to him. The good news is that once he starts talking, he finds it hard to stop. I think what Glen has suggested would work well.'

'Grab a quick coffee and decide the order of questioning. Who led the last interview?'

Glen said, 'I did.'

'Keep that the same. You lead again this time, Glen. As soon as you're ready, get straight back in there. I want chapter and verse this time. If we can't question him about body three and the infant until after he's been charged with other offences, then so be it.'

'I can still ask him about the woman and the child, even if we haven't identified them yet. Sam doesn't deal in names. He only ever referred to Vanessa Tyler as number five. He counts under his breath constantly. It's almost as if verbally reciting numbers settles him down. I don't think he'll have known any of these women by name. He's not interested in them enough to want to know their names. Do you remember Fiona Wright's comment when she was found?'

Danny nodded. '"I'm number four."'

'Exactly.'

'Okay. Put everything to him in this interview, and let's see where it takes us. Good luck.'

81

11.30am, 21 September 1988
Retford Police Station, Retford, Nottinghamshire

Sam Morgan was laying down on the hard bed in his cell, staring up at the ceiling. He didn't like this small space. He was used to the outdoors, seeing the sky above his head.

He sat up and drew his big legs up until he was resting his chin on his knees. He was worried. He knew the detectives talking to him would soon want to know about the secrets he had buried in Beckett Wood. Mr Carruthers had told him what the police had found.

Tears began to well in his eyes as he thought about the women he had buried there. They tumbled down his cheeks when he thought of the baby buried next to its mother.

His head was filled with questions.

How can I explain what I've done?

How can I tell the detectives that I hadn't meant for any of it to happen?

That I was too frightened to tell anyone?

When no answers to his questions were forthcoming, he bit his bottom lip until he stopped crying, then he used the sleeves of his shirt to wipe the tears from his face.

He thought about his mother. He had done what she had told him to do, if he was ever in trouble with the police. He had asked for Mr Carruthers to help him, but the old man didn't seem to want to help. He just told him to say nothing. He couldn't do that; his mother wouldn't want that. She had always told him that he had to tell the truth, no matter what, and that lying was wrong. He wished she was here with him now; she would know exactly what to do.

He stared at the painted bricks on the cell wall and did what he always did when he felt scared and alone. He began to count out loud: 'One, two, three, four...'

82

12.15pm, 21 September 1988
Retford Police Station, Retford, Nottinghamshire

Glen took a deep breath and introduced everyone present in the room, then made a note of the time and the date. Then he reminded Sam he was still under caution and said, 'Tell me about the dog you found in Beckett Wood, Sam.'

Sam looked up, stared at the detective and didn't say a word.

Rather than ask another question immediately, the experienced interviewer remained silent and held eye contact with Morgan.

After a long pause, Sam said, 'What about it? I took it back to the owners.'

Glen smiled. 'That's what I thought. I bet they were really pleased to get their dog back. They thought they had lost her for good. Did they give you anything for finding her?'

'What do you mean?'

'A reward. Did they give you anything for finding their dog?'

'No. The woman just said, "Thank you", that was it.'

'How come they had lost their dog in the woods?'

'I don't know. I just found it roaming around in there, barking its head off.'

'It was early in the morning, wasn't it, Sam?'

'Yeah, very early.'

'The people who owned the dog told me they always walked their dog early, before work, and that's why they were in the woods. Why were you in the woods, Sam?'

There was another long pause before Sam spluttered, 'I had some work to do.'

'What was that?'

'I can't remember.'

Again, Glen held the silence, waiting for more from the giant sitting opposite.

Eventually, Sam said, 'It doesn't matter anymore. You already know what I was doing.'

'I want you to tell me exactly what you were doing. I have my own ideas, but I need to hear it from you. Why were you in Beckett Wood that morning?'

'Number four.'

'Can you explain what you mean, Sam?'

'I had to put number four with the others.'

'Tell me about number four.'

'She made me upset and angry, so I lashed out at her. I didn't want her at the cottage anymore; she was horrible. I thought she would be like number three, but she was a cow. I had a hammer in my hand, and I hit her head with it. I didn't mean to, but I thought I'd killed her.'

'Where was she when you hit her?'

'We were in the cottage. She wouldn't stop nagging me,

and I just snapped. I know I shouldn't have hit her at all, and I never meant to hit her so hard. But I had the hammer in my hand, and before I knew what had happened she was on the floor.'

'What did you do with her?'

'I stripped all her clothes from her so I could burn them. Then I wrapped her in a blanket and took her to the woods, to bury her with the others.'

'Beckett Wood?'

'Yes.'

'How did you get her there?'

'I put her in the back of my Land Rover and drove there.'

'What happened at Beckett Wood?'

'When I arrived at the special place, I got out and there was this dog running towards me, barking like mad. I could hear people in the distance, shouting for the dog. I didn't want them to see the Land Rover and what was in it, so I grabbed the dog and took it back to them.'

'Did it take you long to take the dog back?'

'It took me five or ten minutes to find the people, that's all. When I got back to my Land Rover, the back door was open and number four had gone.'

'What did you do?'

'I searched everywhere, but couldn't find her. After a while I gave up, left the woods and drove back to the cottage. I had to be at work on the farm on time or my uncle would have got angry and shouted at me.'

'Didn't it bother you, what had happened to the woman?'

'I told you I didn't mean to hit her that hard. It just happened. I did go back to Beckett Wood that night to try and find her, but the woods were swarming with coppers, so I left straight away.'

'Thanks for telling me what happened, Sam. What I don't

understand is, how did this woman come to be in your cellar?'

'The same as number five. I brought her to the cottage because I wanted her to look after me.'

'Where did you find her?'

'It's a long time ago.'

'Try and remember, Sam, it's important.'

'I think I found number four in Blyth.'

'Can you remember where you saw her?'

'All I remember is seeing her near a shop in Blyth. She looked in a hurry and wasn't paying attention, so it was easy for me to grab her and bring her back to the cottage.'

'Why did you choose her?'

'Because she looked a bit like number three. Number three was the best. She really looked after me. I wanted four to be like three, but she was a nasty cow who was always horrible to me.'

'Tell me about number three.'

'Don't want to.'

Glen allowed a long pause, then said gently, 'What happened to number three, Sam?'

'She was the best. She cooked for me, ate meals with me and cleaned the house, but then she had a baby and died. They both died.'

'How long was number three with you?'

'A long time, nearly a year.'

'Can you remember where you found her?'

'She was from Gainsborough. I saw her walking alone, by the river, at night, and I thought she looked perfect. She *was* perfect.'

'Was she pregnant when you saw her?'

'No. She had a bath one night after dinner and did that special thing to me.'

'What do you mean, Sam?'

'That special thing men and women do.'

'Do you mean you had sex?'

Sam looked down at the table and nodded.

Glen said, 'You need to answer, Sam.'

He looked up and became agitated. 'Yes, but we only did it once. It wasn't right. We shouldn't have done it. Look what's happened now, because we did. I should never have given her the cider to drink. I knew it was wrong.'

'Was the baby she had yours, Sam?'

'It had to be. She was with me for ages. I didn't know what was happening when the baby came. I was scared and didn't know what to do.'

Tina said, 'Did you stay with her when the baby was born?'

'No. I couldn't stand it. What happened was horrible. There was so much blood. I ran outside to the barn, so I couldn't hear her shouting and crying.'

'Why didn't you get an ambulance, or a doctor to help her?'

Sam began to sob. 'I didn't know what to do. I just wanted it to stop.'

'So, you never called for help, even though you saw a lot of blood?'

'No. How could I do that? She shouldn't have been there.'

Sam's huge shoulders were now shuddering as he sobbed.

Stephanie Dawson leaned forward and said, 'Are you okay, Sam? Do you need to take a break?'

He nodded and began to wipe his face.

Glen said, 'One last question, and then we'll take a break. Is that okay, Sam?'

He stopped sobbing and said, 'Okay.'

'I know it's not going to be easy, but I need you to tell me what happened after the baby was born.'

There was a long pause before Sam said, 'They were both

dead, so I took them to Beckett Wood and buried them with the others.'

'Thanks, Sam. We'll take a break now and get you a drink, then we'll have another chat about the others, okay?'

'Okay.'

Glen turned to Tina and said quietly, 'I'll take him back to his cell and organise a drink for him. You need to let the boss know that body three was abducted about a year ago from Gainsborough, and that Andy needs to get in touch with Lincolnshire Police.'

'Okay. Just a twenty-minute break. We need to keep this momentum going. I'll give the boss a call and tell him what Morgan's said so far.'

83

1.00pm, 21 September 1988
Retford Police Station, Retford, Nottinghamshire

Glen Lorimar took a moment after he had reminded Sam Morgan that he was still under caution before saying, 'Are you okay, Sam? Ready to answer a few more questions.'

The big man gripped the plastic mug containing strong, sweet tea in both of his shovel-like hands and nodded, before saying hurriedly, 'Sorry. Yes, I'm ready.'

'Okay. Before we had a break, we talked about the woman you referred to as number three. Who came before number three?'

'One and two.'

'Tell me what you can about number one, Sam.'

'Can't remember much. It was too long ago.'

'What was she like?'

'I remember she was a big girl, and that she was bone idle.'

'Where did you first see her?'

'At Worksop. She was walking through the same estate where I tried to grab the woman from the shop.'

'That shop was on the Manton estate at Worksop. Is that where you mean?'

'I don't know the name, but it was the same place. The roads on that estate are dark, the streetlights are rubbish, so it was a good place for me.'

'You said she was walking. Was she on her own?'

'Yeah. I waited until there was nobody about and she walked into a really dark part, then I grabbed her.'

'Any idea how long ago this was, Sam?'

Morgan rocked back on the chair, his weight straining the back legs as he pondered the question. He was silently mouthing numbers. Then he sat forward and said, 'It's got to be just over two years ago. There have been two full harvests since I took number one.'

'What was she like, apart from being a big girl?'

'She was young. Too young, really. She hadn't got a clue about anything. I thought she was older when I first saw her because of the way she was dressed. She had a very short skirt on and wore lots of makeup.'

'Did you ever know her name?'

'No. I wasn't bothered about her name. She wasn't with me long.'

'How long?'

'I put up with her laziness for a couple of months. We never got on. She refused to cook or do anything around the cottage. I used to leave everything out ready for her to cook a meal and it would still be raw when I got home. She was a lazy cow.'

'What happened to her?'

'She did something nasty to me.'

Glen remained silent, knowing there was more to come from the big man.

Morgan leaned forward and his eyes locked onto Glen's. 'She tried to kill me.' He paused before continuing. 'I had left her with a small kitchen knife, so she could peel the vegetables. As usual, she hadn't done it, so I got upset and put her back down the cellar. As I went to put the first chain on her leg, she lashed out at me. She had hidden the knife I gave her and used it to stab my arm. Look.'

He rolled up the sleeve of his shirt, exposing his right forearm. 'You can see the scar where the blade went in.'

Glen looked at the vivid red scar that was about three-quarters of an inch long and said, 'She stabbed you?'

'Yeah. I don't know why she did it. She just went nuts.'

'What did you do?'

'I yanked my arm back and the knife came with it, before it fell out of my arm onto the floor. I lost my temper, lashed out and punched her in the face.'

'Then what happened?'

'The back of her head hit the iron bedframe as she fell backwards, then she went quiet.'

'What did you do?'

'I secured her to the bed so she couldn't run away, then I went upstairs to sort my arm out. It hurt like mad and was bleeding a lot.'

'When you had sorted out your arm, did you go and check on the girl?'

'No. I couldn't be bothered. There was no talking to that one. She was useless.'

'When did you next see her?'

'After a couple of days, I took her down some food and water.'

'Was she okay?'

'No, she was dead.'

'Dead?'

'Yeah. It was a right mess, and took me ages to clean up. There was blood under the bed and on the walls. It was horrible. The cellar reeked. It took a long time, using strong disinfectant, to get rid of that stench.'

'Where is she now, Sam?'

'Beckett Wood, same as the others. I buried her that night.'

'After what happened to number one, did you have any second thoughts about getting another woman to help you?'

'I did for a little while. Then I started to get lonely again and wanted somebody to look after me, so I went looking again.'

'You went looking for number two?'

'Yeah. I looked for somebody a bit older this time.'

'Where did you find number two?'

'I had been driving round and round, and it was getting late. It was gone eleven o'clock when I drove into Bawtry. I like Bawtry. It's a nice village.'

'What happened in Bawtry?'

'I saw a woman walking on her own. It was a bitter cold night. She had her head down with the collar of her coat right up and a scarf wrapped around her face and neck. She looked older than number one, and she wasn't looking around her. She was just walking quickly with her hands in her pockets.'

'What did you do?'

'I parked the Land Rover up ahead of her and opened the passenger door a little. I got out of the driver's side and hid by the side of the jeep. She slowed down to look at the open door as she walked by. I sneaked round from the other side of the motor and grabbed her from behind. I kicked the passenger door shut and carried her to the back of the Land

Rover. I remember using the scarf she had wrapped round her face to keep her quiet, then I tied her up and drove away.'

'Did you hit her?'

'No, I didn't have to. She was only small.'

'What was she like when you got her back to the cottage?'

Sam Morgan let out a huge sigh and looked up at the ceiling. 'I couldn't believe it. She was useless. Much worse than number one. I thought if I got a woman who was a little older, they would have a bit more about them, but when I got her back to the cottage I could see that she wasn't that much older than number one.'

'Was that a problem?'

'Yes. She didn't want to do anything. She never even got off the bed.'

'What do you mean?'

'I would take the chains off her and she wouldn't move. She constantly complained about being sick and needing medicine. She was dirty as well. She constantly wet the bed. I changed it the first time, but she kept doing it, so I did what mother always did to me when I wet the bed.'

'What was that?'

'I let her lie in it. I didn't change the sheets or blankets.'

'Did you ever ask what was wrong with her, when she complained of feeling sick?'

'No. There was nothing wrong with her. She drank plenty of water, but didn't eat much.'

'What about getting her a doctor?'

'No chance. I couldn't do that, could I?'

'So, what happened?'

'I remember this bit well because I'd been picking Brussel sprouts all day and my hands were sore. I had something to eat and drink, then went down to check on her before I bathed my hands. She hadn't moved a muscle. The smell in the cellar was awful. As well as wetting the bed, she had crapped in it. I went to shake her, but when I turned her over I could see that she was dead.'

'What had happened?'

Morgan shrugged his huge shoulders. 'No idea. One minute she was okay, and the next she was dead.'

'What did you do?'

'Same as before. I wrapped her up in the dirty bedsheets and took her to Beckett Wood to be with number one.'

'Do you think you should have taken her to the hospital, or fetched her a doctor, Sam?'

'How could I bring a doctor to the cottage? I'd have been in big trouble, wouldn't I?'

'You could have taken her to a hospital and left her outside, if you thought she was sick.'

'I didn't know she was sick. I thought she was just a lazy, moaning cow who didn't want to do anything.'

'Have you told us about all the women you've had in your cellar?'

'Yes. There were only five.'

'Did you have anybody helping you, when you went out at night to take these women?'

He shook his head. 'No, I was always on my own. It was just me.'

'Did anybody else know what you had hidden away in your cellar?'

'No, the cellar was my secret.'

'Do you regret any of this, Sam?'

The giant remained silent for a long time, before saying, 'I really missed number three. She was the best. I'm sorry she died.'

'And the others?'

Sam Morgan sat back in the chair, folded his arms across his chest, closed his eyes and began to softly count, 'One, two, three, four…'

84

3.00pm, 21 September 1988
Retford Police Station, Retford, Nottinghamshire

Tina Cartwright knocked once on the door of the small room being used by Danny as a temporary office and walked in, followed by Glen Lorimar.

Danny looked up and said, 'How did it go?'

Tina said, 'Full admissions to the abductions of Susan Claymore and Emma Bridge.'

'Did he tell you how both women died?'

'Susan Claymore bled to death after he punched her and she struck her head on the wrought-iron bed frame. He lost his temper after she had allegedly stabbed his arm with a kitchen knife. He gave us chapter and verse about burying her in Beckett Woods.'

'And Emma Bridge?'

'From what he's described, it sounds like she fell into a diabetic coma and died after he refused her any medical attention. When she died, he buried her in Beckett Woods as well.'

'Do you think he realised how sick she was?'

'I don't think he had any idea, but he told us he refused to get her any medical attention because he knew she shouldn't have been there, and that he would be in big trouble.'

'Murder by omission, then?'

'I think so. There's no doubt that with the right medical attention Emma Bridge would have survived.'

'Are we ready to charge Morgan?'

Before she could answer there was a knock on the door and Andy Wills walked in. 'Sorry to interrupt, but we've just got an identification for body three.'

Danny said, 'Go on.'

'I sent the circumstances of the abduction outlined by Morgan over to Lincolnshire police, along with a general description of the deceased and a copy of her fingerprints and dental records. I spoke to a detective from Lincoln earlier, who told me that there was a young woman answering the description of our deceased, who was abducted in Gainsborough just over a year ago. He remembered it because he thought it was strange that it had been the woman's boss at the factory where she worked who had made the missing person report, after she failed to show up at work. The clincher for him to call me was the river. The detective remembered that the woman's boss had told him that the woman always walked home the same way from the factory, along the river.'

Andy paused before continuing, 'The missing woman's name was Jessica Massey. She had previous convictions for shoplifting as a teenager.'

'If she has a record, we can compare the fingerprints.'

'I've had the fingerprint bureau working on a comparison

since we got them. They have just positively identified body three as being Jessica Massey.'

'That's great work, Andy.'

Danny looked at Tina and said, 'Start preparing charges for Morgan. I'm going to contact Tim Donnelly and see what progress there is forensically.'

85

10.00am, 22 September 1988
Nottinghamshire Police Headquarters

Danny was feeling tired as he climbed the stairs to the first floor at police headquarters. The last couple of weeks had been draining; long hours at work and very little sleep were now beginning to take their toll. He knocked once on Detective Chief Superintendent Potter's door and waited.

A reedy voice from within shouted, 'Enter!'

Danny walked in. Potter said, 'Good morning, Chief Inspector, take a seat. I understand you've had a bit of a result last night?'

Danny sat down in the chair opposite Potter's huge desk and said wearily, 'Yes, sir. Last night we charged a farm labourer, named Sam Morgan, with the murders of the three women whose remains we found in Beckett Wood. He was also charged with five abduction offences, a section eighteen wounding, a further count of attempted abduction and assault, as well as five counts of unlawful imprisonment.'

'Very impressive, but I understood that you found the remains of four bodies at Beckett Wood.'

'The fourth body was that of an infant, who we believe died at the same time as Jessica Massey, as she gave birth. Unfortunately, there's no way of proving that the infant ever had its own separate existence from the mother. Unless we can prove the child took an independent breath, we cannot charge Morgan with his murder.'

'The infant was a boy?'

'Yes, sir.'

There was a look of concern on Potter's face as he stared at Danny. 'Are you okay, Chief Inspector? I'm guessing this must have been a very harrowing inquiry for you and your team.'

'I'm just glad it's over, sir.'

'Indeed. I think you need to get some rest; you look exhausted.'

'Yes, sir.'

'Do we have the evidence to make all these charges stick at crown court?'

'Sam Morgan made full confessions of his actions, and we have a wealth of forensic evidence found in the cellar at the cottage, and in the Land Rover seized from the farm, to back up those confessions.'

'Excellent.'

Danny leaned forward in his chair. 'One thing that has been highlighted by this case is the fact that sometimes the police have been guilty of not investigating missing person reports with the right level of professionalism required. I think it would be a pertinent time to put something out on Weekly Orders, reminding all officers of their expected actions when taking the initial report of a missing person. This maniac could easily have continued to escape detection, purely because officers receiving initial reports of a missing person failed to carry out a thorough investigation.'

'Do you want to name names, Chief Inspector?'

'I've already spoken to a few individuals, but I think a more generic reminder for the force would be far more useful than a witch hunt for a few guilty of poor practice, sir.'

'Perhaps you could draft me something that would cover your concerns. I'll then ensure that it features in the next set of Weekly Orders. Now, how are inquiries progressing on the Margaret White murder?'

'We have had a small forensic breakthrough that could answer why there was such a long gap between the murders of Florence King and Margaret White. We now know that traces of crude oil were found at both scenes, which means the killer could work in the oil industry.'

'How are you using that information?'

'I have a dedicated team of four detectives, led by DI Cartwright, making inquiries with oil companies. They are trying to find someone from this area who was employed on a long-term contract between the two murders.'

'Sounds like a huge undertaking. Will a team of four be enough?'

'It is going to be a huge inquiry, so I'm going to increase the number of detectives working on it to eight.'

'Good idea. Are you still looking at more conventional leads?'

'Yes sir. Obviously, there will still be a lot of work to complete the inquiries into the murders committed by Sam Morgan. We need to get everything ready for any possible crown court trial, but I now intend to give my undivided attention to speeding up these oil company inquiries. I wholeheartedly believe this is the way we're going to find the killer of Margaret White and Florence King.'

'Good. Please pass on my regards to your team. I'll let the chief constable know of your team's efforts. Good work, Chief Inspector. Now go home and get some rest.'

86

9.30am, 23 September 1988
MCIU Offices, Mansfield, Nottinghamshire

Danny felt good to be back at his own desk, in his own office. That good feeling didn't last long, though; he let out an audible sigh as he surveyed the pile of reports requiring his attention.

He picked up the first report, but before he could start reading the telephone on his desk started to ring. He snatched up the phone. 'DCI Flint, Major Crime Unit.'

The front desk sergeant said, 'Sorry to disturb you, sir. There's a solicitor here to see you, Frank Carruthers. He says it's urgent, and that you'd know what it was about.'

Danny cursed under his breath. In the euphoria of the moments leading up to the charging of Sam Morgan, it had totally slipped his mind that he needed to read the contents of the letter held by the solicitor. If, as the solicitor had intimated, the contents of that letter offered some sort of mitigation for Sam Morgan, then it was vital it was made available to the accused man's defence team. Any failure by the police to do that could lead to an allegation of withholding evidence from the defence, which could in turn jeopardise the entire trial.

Danny said, 'Inform Mr Carruthers I'm on my way. Can you offer him a drink and find us somewhere to talk in private, please?'

'No problem, boss. I'll put him in interview room one, and sort him out with a brew.'

Danny walked into the main briefing room and saw Andy Wills sitting at his desk. 'Andy, are you free for half an hour?'

'I'm not doing anything that won't keep. What's up?'

'Follow me. Sam Morgan's solicitor is downstairs. He has a letter written by Morgan's mother before she died. He wanted me to see it prior to the interviews we had with his client. I refused at the time because he said that it didn't offer any direct evidence in the case. He did, however, intimate that it could offer some reasons, and maybe even some mitigation, for the subsequent conduct of Sam Morgan.'

'If that's the case, it could cause us an issue with disclosure rules, boss.'

'That's what I thought. Let's see what it says first.'

Frank Carruthers was sitting patiently in the interview room when Danny and Andy walked in. Danny offered his hand and said, 'Thanks for coming in, Mr Carruthers. You've saved me a trip up to Retford.'

The aging solicitor stood up and shook Danny's hand firmly. With a wry smile on his face, he said, 'Have I? I did wonder if our previous conversation had slipped your mind, Chief Inspector.'

Danny sat down and said, 'This is Detective Sergeant Wills. Have you brought the letter with you, Mr Carruthers?'

Carruthers said, 'Good to meet you, sergeant.' He bent

down to retrieve his briefcase and took the envelope from the briefcase. He said, 'Are you ready to read it now?'

Danny took the envelope, broke the wax seal and removed the hand-written document.

Danny scanned the contents, reading it twice before handing it to Andy to read.

He looked at the solicitor and said, 'These are very serious allegations.'

'I know they are. They are also the words of a woman who knew she was dying and wanted to protect her only child. I'm afraid they are just mere allegations, though. Now that Louisa Morgan is no longer with us, to be tested under cross examination about these allegations, I don't know how you could ever prove what she has alleged.'

'There are methods we can use now that could help us.'

'Such as?'

Andy placed the document on the table and said, 'Have you heard of DNA profiling?'

'I have read a few articles about it and how it can be used by the police. Would it help with this allegation?'

'It's perfect in this situation. It was a technique originally pioneered to prove paternity. The police have only recently started to see its full potential for investigating certain crimes.'

Carruthers looked back at Danny and said, 'So, you will investigate these claims?'

'Like I said, these are serious allegations, and we will investigate them fully. I don't really see how it offers Sam Morgan any mitigation for his subsequent crimes, though?'

'Maybe an explanation, but I agree, probably not any mitigation. The crown court isn't really interested in explanations, is it?'

'I take it you haven't discussed this letter with anybody else?'

'It was written under legal privilege, but now that the criteria stipulated by my client, Louisa Morgan, has been fulfilled, I needed you to read it and investigate her claims.'

'We will be looking into the issues raised, and I'll get back to you. If there's any truth to the allegations, we will need to get a witness statement from you in due course.'

'Thank you, Chief Inspector. I'll wait to hear from you.'

87

8.00am, 27 October 1988
White Gate Farm, Misterton, Nottinghamshire

Danny drove the CID car into the courtyard at White Gate Farm. Sitting alongside him was Andy Wills. A further CID car, being driven by Rob Buxton, followed them into the farmyard. The two cars came to a halt, skidding gently on the loose gravel. Glen Lorimar, riding in Rob's car, was the first to get out.

The three other detectives followed him along the path until all four stood outside the front door. Andy had been there recently on official business. That business was now about to pay off.

Danny said, 'Ready?' He knocked loudly on the door.

The door was opened by Thomas Morgan's wife, Sally, who said, 'Can I help you?'

Danny said, 'I don't know if you remember me. I'm DCI

Flint, and these are detectives from the Major Crime Unit. Is your husband home?'

'No. You've missed him. He went out early; he's working up at Sunnybank Cottage. Why do you need to see him?'

'I need to talk to your husband first, then I'll make sure you're informed why we need to have a chat with him.'

'Is it serious?'

'Let me speak with your husband, then he can tell you what it's all about. Sorry, I can't be any clearer than that.'

'Well, like I said, he's not here. He's working at the cottage all day.'

The four detectives got in their cars and drove out of the courtyard.

Ten minutes later, and the two cars were approaching Sunnybank Cottage.

Andy Wills let out a low whistle and said, 'Bloody hell, boss.'

A bright yellow JCB bulldozer was being driven into the side wall of Sunnybank Cottage, knocking one side of the stone structure down with a loud crash and a cloud of dust.

The four detectives got out of the two cars and approached the bulldozer. It was Thomas Morgan at the controls. Danny shouted above the noise of the diesel engine. 'Turn it off!'

Thomas Morgan saw the detectives and immediately turned off the engine, climbing down from the cab.

He walked over and said, 'What do you lot want?'

Danny looked at the partially demolished cottage and said, 'That's a bit drastic, isn't it?'

'I don't want any reminders of that freak around the farm. We've already had strangers hanging around the cottage. Rubbernecking bastards. I'm just going to wipe it from the farm. It will be like it never existed when I've finished.'

Danny thought to himself, *I bet that's not all you wished never existed.*

There was a pause before Morgan continued. 'Is there a problem with me demolishing the cottage? I own it. I can do what I bloody like with it.'

Recognising the rising anger in the farmer's voice, Danny said quietly, 'There's no problem with the cottage; you can do what you like with it. I'm here to talk to you about Sam, and who he really is.'

'What are you talking about? Who he is? You know who he is. He's my weirdo nephew.'

'We both know he isn't your nephew, Mr Morgan.'

'This is bloody ridiculous. You're talking in riddles, man.'

'Do you remember when Detective Sergeant Wills here took a blood sample from you recently?'

Morgan looked at Andy Wills and said, 'Yes. You said you needed it to compare against blood found at the cottage and in the Land Rover.'

Danny continued, 'That blood sample was also used to carry out a DNA test which has been compared with Sam Morgan's DNA. Those tests prove, conclusively, that Sam Morgan isn't your nephew. He's your son.'

'That's bullshit. How could he be my son?'

'Because you raped your own sister when she was only fourteen years of age. Thomas Morgan, I'm arresting you for offences of rape and incest.'

As Andy Wills placed him in handcuffs, the farmer became enraged and began shouting, 'You're making a huge mistake, copper! I'll have your job for this, you bastard!'

Danny said, 'Get him in the car.'

EPILOGUE

9.00am, 19 March 1989
Scatsta Airport, Shetland, Scotland

The man got out of the helicopter and lifted his heavy bags from the cargo bay underneath. He stooped as he walked below the still-whirring rotor blades across the tarmac to the waiting area. It would be another six hours before his connecting flight to Aberdeen was due to arrive.

The five and a bit months working offshore had seemed an eternity. His downtime in between shifts working as a rigger had been horrendous. His mind had been filled with thoughts of unfinished business. He had been frustrated before he had left for the rigs, and now he was keen to get back to Nottinghamshire and complete his task.

He walked into the small waiting area. There was nobody else on the flight from Piper Delta One, so he had the waiting room to himself. At the far end, he could see the woman behind the counter of the café area. She was busily stacking mugs and plates on the shelves, as though she were expecting a huge crowd to arrive any minute.

He picked a chair next to a radiator and dropped the heavy bags on the floor. He removed the crash helmet and the red-and-white survival suit that was statutory wear for all helicopter flights, and hung them on the rack that was provided. He then removed a thick jumper from one of his bags, slipping it over the top of his sweatshirt. Although the room was heated, it still felt cold after the heat of the survival suit.

He undid his rigger boots, took them off and slipped into a pair of Reebok trainers, placing the dirty boots into a plastic bag before stuffing them inside one of his rucksacks.

He removed his wallet from the same rucksack and walked to the counter.

Delighted to have her first customer of the day, the woman said, 'Good morning. Hope the flight wasn't too choppy. What can I get you?'

'Have you any hot food on?'

'Aye, pet. I can do you a sausage or bacon bun, if that's any good?'

'Two sausage buns and a large mug of coffee would be great, thanks.'

'I'll bring them over when they're ready. Do you take sugar in your coffee?'

'Nah. Just a splash of milk. I wouldn't mind some brown sauce on the sausage buns, if you've got any.'

'That will be two pounds fifty, please.'

The man handed over a five-pound note and waited for his change.

The woman handed him his change and said, 'Nae bother, you go and grab a seat.'

The man sat back down, next to his bags, and glanced at

his watch. Another six hours in this desolate spot was going to drag.

With nothing else to do, his thoughts quickly turned back to his murderous intentions. The boredom of the rig had polarised those thoughts and he knew that once he arrived home the feelings he got from being in that house, feeling that woman's presence, would soon begin to weigh heavily on his mind.

He knew it would only be a matter of time before he felt the compelling urge to kill again.

WE HOPE YOU ENJOYED THIS BOOK

If you could spend a moment to write an honest review on Amazon, no matter how short, we would be extremely grateful. They really do help readers discover new authors.

ALSO BY TREVOR NEGUS

EVIL IN MIND

(Book 1 in the DCI Flint series)

DEAD AND GONE

(Book 2 in the DCI Flint series)

A COLD GRAVE

(Book 3 in the DCI Flint series)

TAKEN TO DIE

(Book 4 in the DCI Flint series)

KILL FOR YOU

(Book 5 in the DCI Flint series)

ONE DEADLY LIE

(Book 6 in the DCI Flint series)

A SWEET REVENGE

(Book 7 in the DCI Flint series)

THE DEVIL'S BREATH

(Book 8 in the DCI Flint series)

I AM NUMBER FOUR

(Book 9 in the DCI Flint series)

Printed in Great Britain
by Amazon

17566148R00221